THE LAST KISS

ANNA BLOOM

For Andrea, without whom this journey would be so much duller.
Let's white sage this sh!t and get the good times rolling.

Don't be afraid your life will end; be afraid that it will never begin.

— Grace Hansen

1

THE END

MY LOVE STARTS at the end.

They say when one door closes, another opens in its place.

Maybe fate has a lot to do with it.

Maybe it's serendipity.

Maybe love is the biggest joke the universe has ever made.

If it comes though, for you, don't ever try to fight it. Learn from my story and never let go.

When something so perfect comes within your grasp, hold it tight. Immerse yourself until you don't know where the past, present, and future begin and end.

Love.

Laugh.

Live.

"I told you."

His fingers brush at my hair, delicately tracing down my cheek. "And I told you, ma petite fleur."

This is unfair. He's breaking all the promises, every damn one, taking a pickaxe to them and splintering them to pieces.

Smash.

A tear rolls from the corner of my eye and he catches it; popping it, caught on the tip of his finger, into his mouth. Stormy night eyes shining. "Another taste of you."

Unfair.

Smash.

I want to cry harder, want to give it some, but my chest hurts. Every breath is like running a marathon, yet I'm only sitting on the creaky sheet of a hospital bed. I hike in another gasped breath, as a large palm smooths my hair and lips press into the top of my head. A lifeline I want to cling onto even though I know my time is up.

When I can breathe, I shift slightly, looking up to meet his gaze. "You promised me." I guilt him with a deploring stare. *Please leave,* my eyes say, though my tongue is having a problem expressing the words. Stupid tongue.

That look of beautiful solemnity comes over his face. It's my favourite look, dark and brooding, all things that make my heart flutter. Stupid heart. Literally.

"Ma petit Julianna, I never promised." He leans a little closer, breath brushing my skin, making me ache for days full of sunshine, laughter and tangled cotton sheets.

My heart races again, pounding loud in my ears, I clutch at my chest, my touch weak, barely holding myself together. That beautiful solemnity darkens into heartbreak. It splinters what's left of me straight in two.

"Henri, please." I gasp his name, remembering another broken rule between us.

No names.

No strings.

Yet here we sit. Well, I lie on the bed. He stands, looking like a man on fire.

Rules are there for a reason; I must remember that for my next life.

Oh God. My breath comes even faster.

The next life... it's almost here and I still don't know if I even believe. How can I go not knowing?

Stop everything. I want a do over.

This can't be it.

Strong fingers entwine with mine. "Ma petite fleur, look at me."

I do, unable to keep my eyes from his. The shining pools staring back at me almost make me lose my mind. "I'll never leave. Be damned any promise I ever made."

A smile ghosts my mouth. "Cheater."

He shrugs, pure Gaelic charm. "Hey, I never said I wasn't." The brightening of his face calms my heart, exhaustion tugs me down.

I don't want to close my eyes.

What if I close them and nothing happens ever again?

What if that's it? Forever and ever.

"Don't be scared," he whispers.

Scared.

"I am," I whisper back.

Turning my face with gentle fingers, he stamps a soft kiss on my lips. Even at the end of my days it's still the most beautiful taste. Warm and succinct, just the perfect pressure, the perfect time; not too long, not too short.

"I'm so glad I got to kiss you."

"Well..." His lips curve. "That's not all we've done."

"Lay with me." My fingers feebly tap the bed.

"You know where that ends." He frowns at the size of the hospital bed. He's six foot four and built for rugby and doing things to me that turn me inside out and upside down.

"Squeeze on."

Henri glances at the door. For an awful moment I think he's going to leave me. That he's going to do as I asked. But then he toes his shoes and kicks them off, loafers on a hospital floor next to my unused fluffy slippers.

He settles down, curving a protective embrace around my failing chest. "I'm sorry," he mutters.

"Don't be."

Dampness lands on my shoulder and I feel him sob gently, his large frame rocking me like a babe in arms.

Undo me.

But then I am undone.

There's nothing left to untangle.

"I wish I could be your Juliette again. Wish we could go back, do it all over." I almost shout it. I don't want to go to the other side of never without him knowing just what it's meant, what he's meant. Being his Juliette was magical, it made the last few months something more than I ever would have thought they could have been. Being his *Julianna*...has changed my life.

Henri turns, a tear still dangling on the edge of his dark lashes like the last droplet on months of insanity.

"You'll always be my Juliette, my Julianna, my everything." He's humoured me so much, put up with my rules, the way I've needed things to be. I know he's left everything to be here with me right here at the end. God, it really must be a love thing after all.

I push my face into his chest, the cotton of his shirt,

desperately trying to inhale that spice that seems to cling to him. "I'm so glad I met you."

Using the tip of his finger he makes me look up. "Even though you fought me the whole way, ma petite fleur?" One of his dark brows arches. His teasing look. God, I love that look too.

I love all his looks.

Can't believe that I won't get to see any of them again. Can't believe that my stupid heart is going to fail, and no replacement can be found. Right when I want to...

Want to...

"Tell me what you'll miss the most?" I ask the buttons on his shirt.

Henri tightens his arms, and I could just melt right now. Become a puddle of chocolate ice cream against his sugar spun wafer. "You in black lace."

Ah, the lace.

His hands on my thighs, riding silk and lace across skin that didn't know it could be adored the way he did it.

"Just the lace?"

"Burnt pancakes. Coffee at midnight. Eurostar. Always wanting to find you and never knowing where I would see you again. Sand. Candy floss. Amber perfume on your skin."

Right now, in this very moment at the end of everything I am adored.

"I love you," I say.

"And I love you."

I look up, blinking against everything that could have been. "Henri, you have to keep this promise."

"What promise?"

"The one you're going to make now."

His face slips back to that beautiful shadow where the storm in his eyes brings rain and sun.

"Hold me until I sleep and then leave."

Henri shakes his head, lips pressing into a firm line. "No."

"I want you to. Remember me with lace and amber. Candy floss and laughter. Not a corpse who lies in your arms."

"Ma pe—" another shake of his head, "Julianna, they still might find a match."

Aw, he's so damn cute. Stupid big hulk of a man.

"Hold me until I sleep." I snuggle down, ignoring the beep of the machine as it shouts in dismay at my moving the tubes in my arm and airways.

Tears roll from his lashes and absorb into my skin.

My time is nearly up.

Every breath.

Every stuttered beat of my heart takes me one moment closer to the end. I'm so tired now. So drained. Energy is like treacle, moving too slow through my veins. Slug. Slug. Slug.

God, if you are there...

Thank you for bringing me the greatest gift I ever could have hoped for.

I close my eyes. Henri's hand brushes through my hair and I focus on the sensation: soothing, reassuring.

He plants a kiss on my mouth. My last kiss.

The last kiss.

On the cusp of nothing, I hold everything as my lips whisper their last word, exhaustion tying me into a final bow I know I can't undo.

"Henri."

2

BLIND SIDE

I BLINK RAPIDLY, like sand has kicked up on a warm summer day and stung my eyes. "I'm sorry." I shake my head, attempting to disperse the imaginary grains. "I don't really understand."

Dr Francis furrows his face into his most concerned frown. I'm sure they make them practice that look in med school. *Stand and look concerned in the mirror for ten minutes a day. Final test will be if you can pass the giggle test on week twelve.*

I'm not giggling.

My chest is tight.

Too damn tight.

There are dark smudges across my vision.

A buzzing in my ears which I'm not sure is coming from inside me or from the light flickering above my head.

"Julianna." His voice softens, and he reaches forward to cover my hand with his. There are probably a million different rules against him doing it, but I'm grateful all the same. "Is there no one you could have with you? I'm worried you won't be able to remember everything."

Unable to stop my face scrunching, I stare at him, through him, barely seeing him. The words he's just said, the sentence he has passed, are slowly clicking themselves into place inside my brain.

It's. Over.

"My sister..." I trail off, empty, barren, but then pick myself up and shake it off. "There isn't much to remember is there?" Half-heartedly, I huff a small laugh, more for his benefit than mine.

"Well, we need to talk things through," he pauses, his hand patting mine, "how you want this to go. You've got decisions to make: how much medication you want to take, what further procedures you'd like that could," he tilts his head here—*could... but might not*, the tilt of his head tells me— "help."

"So exactly how long are you saying?" Usually, I run from facts with my arms flailing in the air, but I think this is a fact I should know.

Another pause, another tilt of the head, full of unspoken things. Clearing his throat, Dr Francis pulls himself up straight. "Six months," he shrugs, because shrugging always helps, "a year at the most."

God. My heart. It's actually just going to disintegrate in my chest while I'm still sat in his office. We don't need to worry about the next possible twelve months.

"In a year, I will be dead." There's no point icing the cake with fancy frills and flowers. My cake is a plain Victoria sponge and it's about to become crumbs.

He nods. Simple. "That is the prognosis."

Prognosis. What a word.

"And there is nothing, simply nothing that you can do?" I ask. *How can this be? We live in the twenty-first century. People can do all sorts these days.*

"There are. That's what we're discussing." He speaks slowly, like he's talking to a small child, or a woman who's about to die. "The first thing to do is to create a medication regime to make things comfortable. We can talk about operating on the valves again."

Oh, those cranky valves. I rub at my chest, a throwaway bidding that they might just do what the fuck they are meant to do—pump blood around my body. I mean, it's not that hard is it?

"And...?" Give me more. Give me more.

"And we can get you on the waiting list for another heart."

"Another heart? What happens? Do you go to the supermarket and pick one up off the shelf?"

Dr Francis smiles wanly at my attempt at saving the moment from becoming the single most depressing of my life.

"No, we put you in the database. I'm afraid it's a list, like most things."

"A list of people waiting for hearts?" I mean, I guess that makes sense, right? I can't be the only poor bitch with a dodgy ticker.

"And it comes down to things like blood type, tissue type," he carries on, spewing more words in my direction my brain can't cope with. "Later, not right now, we would have you on medication so should a match come up, your body would be receptive to the new organ. The body is an amazing machine, but unfortunately it means it will spend the rest of your living days trying to reject an organ that doesn't belong to you."

"And... And..." It's almost heinous to think about it. "The heart is kept alive until it is put into my body?"

He nods, that sympathetic frown back on his face.

"Julianna, all of this can be discussed. I will refer you to Mr Simmonds at the transplant team. He's amazing and I know if anyone can help you, he will."

"But you can't anymore," I faintly whisper.

"Julianna. You are in the second stages of heart failure. At the end of the second."

"And how many stages are we talking?"

"Four. You know this. We discussed it way back at the beginning when the issues were found."

I nod, up and down. Up and down. "Four stages, right."

"The third and fourth stage run together, and no one knows how long each stage will last."

I don't move. I'm carved from stone.

"What will it feel like?"

Dr Francis meets my eye. "You want to know what the symptoms of total heart failure will be like?"

I nod. Up and down. Up and down.

"It will be much like you've been feeling for the last two years."

Well, that's not too bad. My smile grows.

"But worse," he adds before I get a chance to really scrunch my cheeks. "Eventually, your body will become weaker and weaker. If your heart, which is the pump for the entire nervous system, the entire body, can't move enough blood, exhaustion will become the norm. Your other organs will fail as they are starved of the oxygen they need from the blood that your heart can no longer pump."

See, no icing on this cake. Plain stale sponge of reality.

Twenty-nine years old and my body is going to stop working before I hit thirty.

If that ain't a punch in the vagina of life I don't know what is.

"Julianna, I'm sorry. As a heart specialist there is nothing worse than when you realise you can't save someone."

Oh, well, let's make it all about you.

"It's okay. I guess you can't save them all."

"I like to try."

"So, what happens now?"

He's going to make me leave this office. I'm going to have to walk outside with a death sentence hanging over me. A flashing beacon that will tell everyone that I'm different, that my time is up.

"I'll put you on Dr Simmonds list; his secretary will call you. And I'll see you next week so we can discuss renewing your medication."

"Next week? But what if…?"

He smiles, small and sensitive. "Julianna, you aren't going to die before next week. Not unless you get hit by a bus."

I stand, legs not connected to my body. The door to his office is a whole five steps away. I might not make it.

"Buses. I'll watch out for them."

"Make sure you do." His bright-blue eyes twinkle. "If you've got any questions please ring. I'm not sure you've taken it all in."

He might be right there, but I'm pretty sure I picked up the Cliff Notes.

Die. Twelve months.

Kaput.

Finito.

Morte.

I turn at the door, waiting for him to tell me it's all been a sick joke.

"Next week," he adds with a nod. "We've a lot to discuss."

Do we though? Seems to me that all discussion is up.

"Next week," I repeat automatically and then I slip out of the door. I keep my head down past his secretary who I can sense has her sympathetic blinkers pointed in my direction. I bet she knows. Bet they discussed it over tea while they dunked their biscuits.

My feet run down the hallways of the hospital, flying me around beds being pushed by porters, nurses in maroon, old people with sticks.

I run.

I run.

Until my lungs are pulling in icy air, dragging in the clouded sky.

Grey hangs above. Grey exists inside while cars zoom past, taxi's weaving, lights on, lights off. People rushing, late for lunch, late for the office, late for life.

I stand in the middle of it all.

An island of solitude.

Normally after a visit I treat myself to lunch at the wine bar next to the hospital. It's been somewhat amusing to have a posh bar with gastro food next to a building where people fight for their lives.

Joke's not funny anymore.

Instead of the wine bar, I push down the side streets to the ominous Thames running at high tide, pulsing against drab banks, the colour of the water merged with the heavy sky.

On unsteady legs, I stumble to a bench, not even checking for pigeon shit, my shins bashing against the wooden slats as I fall backwards with a bang. *And they all fell down.*

Then I sit.

Stare.

Brain stuck on words I'll never be able to unhear.

Final stage heart failure.

Twelve months at the most.

My fingers wind into the wool of my coat, pulling it tight around my chest, holding all my broken bits together. It doesn't work, the indigo wool doesn't even keep out the January chill.

I should have bought a better coat.

Should have spent more money.

I gaze down the river watching the tide.

My coat will be the first of a long list of things that I know I'll come to regret.

The swell and ebb of the river is like my life, but I can't look too deep beneath the surface of that thought because then I'd know my swell hadn't been high enough, and my ebb had lasted too long.

I can only wonder if my last few months will be full of random thoughts where I consider if anything I've ever bought has served any purpose.

It takes a moment for me to realise the ringing I can hear isn't internal but coming from my bag. Unzipping and peering inside, I pull my phone out and glance at the screen; a small, icy bloom of exhalation frosting in front of my face.

Olivia.

I tighten my grip, thumb ready to swipe to answer, but I can't. Won't. So I shove it back in my bag, hoping the ringing will be drowned out with the zip of the fastening.

It rings again. And then again.

All the while I watch the river flow. I could pitch the phone in the swelling tide, but I'd only have to organise a new one which seems rather a waste of precious minutes remaining.

"Miss, you okay?"

I blink up in surprise. There's a man in a dark-green uniform. Parked behind him on the path is a dustcart, a broom poking from the top.

"Oh. Sure."

I swipe at my face, my cheeks stinging from the cold, sticky tracks having now dried to almost icy rivets.

"You've been sat here for hours, Miss. I've been circling around not sure whether to say anything." He pulls on the edge of his beanie. "You know. It's not my business and all that, but I'd hate to clock off for the night and leave you just sat here still."

"But you haven't?"

He casts a quick gaze over me, and I tug at my coat. Small particles of icy droplets have formed on the surface, turning the purple wool into a layer of mush. Should have bought a better coat, fact.

"You'll catch a death out here."

I nod. God, is that what I'm doing? Waiting for the Grim Reaper to find me on a pigeon poop splattered park bench? That's an unimpressive way to go. I could imagine the newspaper headlines: ***Woman freezes to death in pigeon shit***. A story like that would make the papers; a trashy one, with red title fonts. It would be my fifteen minutes of fame. But I'd be dead.

"If you need somewhere to stay, I know there's a shelter down the road. I think they're still open for the night. I can give you directions if you want?"

He thinks I'm homeless.

Lifeless yes.

I have a home.

With plants in pots. Ferns in the bathroom. A cat that farts.

Oh, no! Barney. Who will look after Barney?

"Miss, are you okay?" He's fingering his walkie talkie like he's about to call for back-up support.

"Sure. Thanks for getting me moving. I could have sat here all night lost in my thoughts." I smile and get up on stiff legs.

My phone rings again. Olivia is almost shouting through the ringtone that I should answer. And I so should. So, so, so should.

But she's going to want me to say things I don't want to say.

It's a conversation I can wait for.

I turn back to the looming shape of the hospital, a morbid backdrop to the twist my life has taken.

Right. Where is that wine bar? If ever a woman hit the day when she needed wine, I'd just straddled the gap.

There it is. I eye it across the road, slipping my gaze from the hospital of unfinished dreams to the place where wine is kept. I know which one I prefer, and it serves chilled perfection and peanuts in bowls. I reckon it's twenty-five steps. That's not that far. I can do that. Taking a deep breath, I step off the kerb, one eye focused on any free-wheeling double deckers that might be coming my way.

One, two, three. I count the steps, keeping myself on track.

It's twenty-eight. I lost that game.

My phone rings again as I push open the door, blasted from inside by steamy-hot air and the bubble of chatter, the clatter of cutlery. What is it about a pub, even a posh one like this, high end with fancy seating and modern edges, that makes you just breathe out a long gust of air? You know what you're getting, it's that familiarity, the known facts of what you face. You smile, order, pay. A drink is put into your hand. You sit, absorb the ambience: the lights, the sounds, the taste of your poison of choice on your tongue. It's always the same sounds. Women laughing, men talking sport. You could be anywhere in the world and the same thing would be happening around you.

I think I'll miss pubs.

Stopping at the door, I analyse the distance to the bar is fifteen steps, I bet.

I can get that far too. Same as I could keep breathing after Dr Francis gave me my prognosis, same as I didn't turn into an ice cube down by the river, same as I crossed the road without getting hit by the Number 14 bus.

Ah! Thirteen steps.

The black leather squidgy seat of the stool is cool as I slide onto it and peel off my limp bedraggled coat. It drops to the floor like a dead animal, all twisted and deformed like it should be by the side of the road, guts splattered.

The man behind the bar, tight-fitted white shirt, slim hips in black trousers, abs to lick visible through the stretch of cotton across his chest, throws a dish cloth over his shoulder. "It's a chilly one." He flashes me the 'bar man' smile, everyone knows that smile, as he breaks the ice.

I nod. Up and down. Up and down. Silent. Is this how it's going to be until the end? I'm going to become a robot of destruction. *I will terminate. I will terminate.*

"A Pinot Grigio isn't it?"

My cheeks warm up, mouth parting. "I only come in here every six months. How on earth do you remember what I drink? Or do I just look like the kind of woman who drowns in Pinot for survival?"

I probably do, and I have no plans to deny it.

He winks, all Irish charm, as I peel some flat snakes of wet hair away from my forehead, feeling the steady spring of frizz set in. "I always remember the pretty ones," he says.

"Oh please." I laugh, shifting back on my stool, gaze lifting. You've got to love a barman's wile. I'll miss that too. "You say that to every woman who walks in. I'm guessing you have a fifty/fifty hit rate with that line."

He breaks out a laugh with a sly grin, shaking his head, his muscles flexing. "It's true. You come in every six months. Always on a Friday. Normally it's earlier than this though." He eyeballs my drenched hair. "You look like you've been duck diving in the river."

Ah, now that would have been a better way to spend the afternoon. Anything other than having *that* conversation, inside *that* place, otherwise known as the prison of dreams.

"Here you go, although you look like you need a brandy to go with it."

Ugh. Cringe. "No thanks. Brandy is the devil's drink. He offers it as a test to see who should be let into hell." I take a restrained sip of wine and then put it carefully on the bar. My fingers are tingling with the cold, my face stinging as the warmth of the bar melts my frozen mask.

The shape next to me pivots slightly. I didn't notice it was an actual person before, because honestly, it's a bit like sitting in the shade at the foot of a mountain.

Navy suit, crisp white shirt.

Beautiful.

Okay, random thought about the stranger, and I've only had one sip of wine.

With a flick of his wrist, he motions for the bartender,

while I catch a glimpse of long, beautiful hands. His face is only in profile, shadowed from the overhead lights, so while the overall first impression is one of startling beauty, I can't actually confirm this as fact until he turns. He doesn't. Instead, he beckons again to the barman. "Excuse me." The barman shoots me a sheepish glance before hot footing it over there.

They whisper, lots of gesticulating and stabbing of pointy fingers at the spirits lined at the back of the bar. The man with the fingers still doesn't turn fully. *Disappointing*. I sip my Pinot, maybe a little fast, as I wait to find out if my guess is true. Eventually, the barman shoots me another glance before sloping off to the bottles he clinks around.

The man mountain in navy doesn't look at me. His attention on the broadsheet he has spread along the bar. Jeez, he'll have to move before the evening rush. He'll be like Moses parting the sea. I don't think he's going to move though, and I feel sorry for anyone who tries to make him. You'd put your back out.

I sit on my stool, twisting slightly from side to side until I happen to glance forward to follow the barman turning mysterious bottles. A dark gaze is watching me in the back mirror behind the bar, one dark and expressive eyebrow curved.

I am not disappointed. No.

Disappointment, what's that?

Midnight eyes; full lips petulant below angled cheekbones. He's a shopping list of perfection.

Michelangelo could be crying in heaven because he failed to sculpt a masterpiece like this.

Face an elegant symmetry, there's a dark soulfulness in the shadows of his face, the hollow curve under cheekbones, the shine of midnight, the plump fullness of lips. I wonder what they'd feel like to kiss?

I've been caught staring. He stares back. It's okay though. I'm going to die anyway. This can't get uncomfortable and cause me to squirm forever because there isn't a forever to squirm through.

The barman comes back and slides me a short glass. "This is what you need, apparently." He shrugs while his face says: *please don't be ill all over the floor after drinking it.*

"Is that so?" I peer into the glass at the purple-hued liquid. "What is it?"

The man mountain shifts, spinning long legs around on his stool to face me. "It's best to just drink." His voice is heavily accented. All: *It'sa besst tooa shust drink."*

Is that French? Shoot me now for not paying attention in French GSCE. I'd go to night school just to learn how to wrap myself around those vowels with him.

Oh wait. I'm dying. French will serve me no purpose on the other side unless there's an Artisan bread stall I need to concern myself with. "*Petit pain, Monsieur*."

Focus, Julia.

I lift the glass, sniffing gently, scrunching my nose as my nostrils tickle, watching those full lips curve at the edges. I tilt the glass at him, feeling very Film Noir sat at the bar talking to a tall, dark, and bangingly handsome stranger. "Merci."

He nods and then turns back to his newspaper. Okay, so maybe not *that* Film Noir.

The first sip is sweet, so I take another, gasping as my insides set alight, pure rocket fuel slipping down my oesophagus. It might be melting.

MY OESOPHAGUS IS MELTING, PEOPLE.

I glance up and find midnight eyes staring back at me in the mirror. It looks like he's chewing the inside of his cheek, but it's hard to focus due to the all-out body burn I've got going on.

Well, if you've got to go, I'd take staring into those eyes any time.

3

A SHRUG IN FRENCH MEANS ANYTHING

WHAT THE SHIT was in that drink? My face is on fire. I can't look in the mirror above the bar in case he catches me checking out the heat damage.

I can't stop looking at him either. My eyes are involved in some major eye-fuckery as I throw him some side eye. Thighs stretching navy. The white cotton is taut around some pretty hefty muscles... those ones in your arms. What the fuck are they called?

That drink has melted my brain.

"Biceps."

"Pardon?" he asks, but it's all *pardonne?*

"Oh. Sorry." My face is nuclear.

I could be used as a clean energy power source.

"I wasn't talking to you." I give one of those British smiles—tight-lipped, containing lots of unspoken words—and then zip my lips shut in case I blurt out any other body parts. Attempting to act unaffected, I stare down at the blurred menu I have positioned on the bar. I say blurred, because what I'm sure was English during my last visit is now in... well, actually, I don't know. I zoom it closer to my face and then back out again. I should put my glasses on.

He turns, man hulk spinning on his stool so he can look at me better. *Please don't look at me, I think I'm purple.* "Are you eating?"

"Not right now." My gaze drops to his lap. It's a total dick sweep. I have no shame.

I think I might be in shock. After all, I've just received some bad news... it's likely my brain will struggle to compute the information it's been given. What was that news again?

Don't know. Don't care. I'm busy working out bulges under navy.

You're going to die, Julianna. Oh yeah, that.

That buzzing fills my ears again and I clutch onto the brass rail around the bar while my vision tinges with black. I'm pretty sure the man mountain sighs. "Would you like to share a meal?" *Would shuu like to zare ameel?*

"With me?" I look up, so navy trousers are replaced with navy eyes.

"We are both sitting here together, no?"

"Ugh." The fire from the drink evaporates, my tongue dries, head pounding around the edges of my sanity. I can't think of a single word I know. "Ugh."

Say no... Say no...

But... Julianna... you're going to die remember? There's a loud voice sitting on my right-hand shoulder, but I can't remember if that's the devil side or the angel side. *You could have sex... No! Dinner! With a beautiful Frenchman. I mean...*

Pretty sure the Freudian slip came from the devil.

I nibble my bottom lip. I've taken too long to answer his question now. *He is beautiful,* I debate with myself. I'm not into insta-attraction. That's for romance books and people who've taken too many drugs and have melted their brain. But he is beautiful, nonetheless.

"I don't share chips."

He smiles. My God what a smile. With his hand leaning on the bar, he waves long fingers for the barman. "A bottle of mineral water please, and then a table for two." He holds up two long fingers like he's talking to a small child.

The barman looks between us and then pouts in my direction. *I know, buddy. I'm not sure what's happening here either.*

The water arrives fast, and Man Mountain pours me a glass and slides it across the shiny wooden surface of the bar. "Here, I think you might need this." His long fingers loop around the glass bottle. "I didn't realise the brandy would put you on your ass."

"Ugh, brandy. I hate that stuff."

"You drank it." An expressive eyebrow lifts. Can eyebrows be expressive? Is that a thing? He makes it a thing.

Despite not moving his stool, he's in my space. The back of my neck is prickling and I'm having to tilt my head to roam my gaze across the surface of his face. And believe me I'm roaming—I'm 4x4'ing that damn landscape with barely concealed scrutiny.

Holding out his hand, he opens his mouth. I guess he's going to do the polite thing and introduce himself to the woman he's just invited to share a meal.

Except, I don't want to be that woman. She no longer has a future. She no longer has anything.

"No, wait." I hold my hand palm up. "Can we, ugh." How to say this without it sounding various levels of wrong. "Not do names?"

Well, that doesn't sound wrong at all... not.

That eyebrow dances, his full lips curving at the edges and making me lean forward unwittingly. There are soft lines around his mouth, lines made with smiles and laughter. Scattered in the skin stretching from the corner of his eyes to his hairline are more crinkles, each one I'm sure has a story to tell.

"No names?" Laughing, crinkling those eyes, he pushes a hand through his dark hair, teasing it into a military stand of attention with his long fingers.

What it would feel like to touch. Silk. Satin. Something soft and ticklish?

With a shrug, he reaches out to shake my hand and my heart pounds as I slip my small hand into his large bear paw.

Another shrug. "No names."

"Sorry, it sounds wrong." God. Kill me.

Oh wait...

A quick internal body sweep ensures my heart isn't about to give up within the next hour or two. That would be a damn shame, he really is gorgeous, and it's been a while since I've been for dinner with a man. The truth is, if I can sit here with a complete stranger with a beautiful smile, crinkles around his eyes, and hair that might tickle, it means I don't have to go home. Don't have to face a stark reality that I don't want to be mine.

The bartender clears his throat. "Table by the window." He points, flicking an accusing gaze over me again that says —*I remembered your drink and now you're going to have dinner with that beast of a man, how's that fair?* In response, I drag my gaze away from my unexpected dinner date and grimace an awkward smile which says in return—*it's okay. I'll be back for another depressing appointment in hell next week and I promise I'll drink all your Pinot.*

"Thanks. I think," I say, already distracted by Man

Mountain turning back to his paper. Without a sign of rushing, and with a surprising delicate touch, he folds it neatly back down the crease and folds it again in half.

Now that is how a newspaper should be treated. Not scrunched into the trash; left abandoned on the Tube; or worse, wrapped around fish.

I could fall in love with him just because he knows how to fold a newspaper.

Okay. I am *definitely* in shock.

Without a sound, he gets off his stool, and I crank my neck to look up at him. He truly is a mountain made of man. Wide shoulders and narrow hips wrapped in a tan belt against his sharp cut suit. Wowser. I don't want to get off my own stool. I'll only come up to his nipples.

A steady gaze on my face, he holds his arm out to help me down. "After you," he says in that gloriously seductive sounding accent.

My feet plop down onto the floor like an elf next to a yeti. "Thanks." I put my neck out to look up as I start to cartograph an ordnance survey of his face just in case I ever forget I saw it.

Does he know how beautiful he is? How did I end up sitting next to him in a bar? The worst day of my life and I end up having dinner with a face like that. Wait till I tell Liv.

The universe is a strange thing.

His lips flicker into a smirk and I know he's assessing how incredibly small I am.

I can't help it, small is good. I get to wear kid's trainers at half the price. I also get ID'd every time I buy alcohol and at twenty-nine, I'm no longer offended.

Across the room, in an awkward silence, Man Mountain waits for me to sit, his hand hovering on the back of my chair, angling it slightly and pushing it in as I bend my legs to sit.

My heart gives a little flutter. No one has ever helped me sit down before. I think my vagina just fluttered too.

This is crazy right? I should be on the Tube. Going to Olivia's so we can whisper about my exceedingly bad news over wine at her kitchen island while my niece runs riot like a wild animal, and my nephew cries with the inflamed passion of a six-month-old that hasn't been given milk in the last five minutes. That was the way today was going to go.

Almost on cue my phone rings again.

Man Mountain's gaze reads my face. "I don't want to be rude," he says, and I want to tell him he could never be rude because his accent makes it almost impossible. "But your phone has been ringing the whole time you've been here."

I fiddle with the fork a waitress puts down in front of me. Her attention is solely on my dinner partner. Who can blame her? She's human, not a robot.

"It's my sister." I peek up to look at his heavenly face. Glory to God, what a face. And it's sat opposite me at a cosy table for two.

"And you don't want to answer?" He steeples his fingers into a cathedral arch, staring at me over the spire.

"Not right now, no." My shoulders drop. "Sorry, that probably sounds awful."

He shrugs, before flashing me a brilliant dash of white in his smile and dismantling his cathedral, in preference to holding his palm out to me. "Shall I answer? Tell you're out for dinner with a handsome stranger."

Yes! Do that! "Tempting, but she'd likely think you were a rapist and/or murdering bastard trying to pretend I was still alive." I squint my eyes at him. "You aren't, are you?"

He laughs. Pure fucking magic. "No."

"That's a relief. Could have got awkward."

The trill of my phone disturbs the moment as we stare at one another. For God's sake, Olivia. Get with the programme; I'm not answering.

"May I suggest switching it off?" He pours a glass of water for himself and takes a sip. I pout my lips into a little kissy shape as I watch him slide his against the glass.

"You could, but it would only make it worse. If I switch it off the police will be out scouring for me in a matter of minutes."

"Oh really?" His eyebrow lifts again. Most people's eyebrows are just furniture on their face. Not his. He uses it as a method of communication, I'm sure of it. "That sounds very..." he rolls his hand, "dramatic."

Shaking my head, I rub at my cheek—tears by the Thames seems an age ago, but I've just realised my makeup would have washed away in salt water. "I had an..." I go to point in the direction of the hospital, but then stop myself. "Do you know what? Doesn't matter. Liv, Olivia, my sister, she thinks she has to mother me all the time, when the truth is she can't help me right now. I don't think anyone can." Unless they have a spare heart just lying around in a cooler box waiting to be inserted into my chest cavity. Said chest cavity gives a little boombababoom, just to remind me off the current issue at hand.

"No?" His head tilts to the side, all teasing evaporating from his face. Instead of the smirk, a beautifully carved relief of concern settles on his features. "Most things are important, no, and it must be important if she wants to take care of it for you?"

"What's important to you?" I ignore the water I should drink and pick up my Pinot.

He shrugs. "Various things."

"Like?" I take another sip, drowning myself into the deep sea of his eyes. My toes can't touch the sand and I know I should start treading water.

"People." He nods to my bag with the endless phone ringing. "Siblings."

"Why are you here by yourself?" This man I'm pretty sure isn't alone often. Even if he wants to be, women probably herd around him like cattle around a trough.

I've just realised I'm the cattle in this scenario. Suddenly, I have a wild urge to moo.

The smirk creeps back across the soft upturn of his mouth. "Business." His sigh mellows my bones. It's a sigh that says—*I don't want to talk.*

"What do you do?"

The dark-blue gaze twinkles. "I sell cheese."

Unfortunately for me I've taken a large gulp of reconstituting wine.

At least it's not my standard Shiraz because that would have made a spectacular mess across the white cotton of his shirt. As it is the ejected droplets absorb and spread.

"Oh my, fuck." My cheeks burn with the heat of the earth's core as I leap from my seat, napkin in hand and start to press the tissue against his chest.

Wow. What a chest.

I keep patting and it has nothing to do with clearing up my mess.

He clasps his long fingers around my wrist, holding it still, turning so his lips are just millimetres from where my face is lowered towards his pecs. "Please, no need."

My legs wobble.

"I am so sorry," I say with needy little pants. My hand is on his chest. His face is near my lips, his breath on my skin.

He gives a small shake of his head, but his hand still

holds mine. "So... cheese," I fluster, as he turns those luscious lips up at the edges in response.

"It doesn't normally have such spectacular reactions, ma petite."

I narrow my gaze, standing up to my full five foot two. "You just called me little." *Thank you Madame Schmidt for GCSE French.* I make a mental note to tell Olivia all was not wasted at school.

He shrugs and lets go of my wrist. "A statement of fact, no?"

Ugh. French. Every answer is a question.

"Sometimes stating facts isn't polite," I grind out.

He shrugs again. "But still, there they are."

So actually, beautiful Man Mountain might be rude. I should probably leave.

I glance out of the window at the dark January night. What am I going home to? Homemade Pot Noodle for one and a farting cat? Or worse, a quick detour via my sister's place to break her heart.

Giving it some sassy hip swing, I stomp back for my seat and flop back down. His smirk grows.

"Brie?"

He laughs and it's rolling hills of sheer pleasure, all green and covered in morning dew. "A little more *compleecated* than that."

I nod. I know all about cheese. And the port that goes with it at Christmas. "Roquefort then?"

That brow quirks again. "You know about Roquefort?"

"Well, I read an article about it once." Okay, I skimmed an article about it once. "And it tastes really good on a poppy seed cracker."

He booms another laugh, making people turn to stare, not that he seems to notice. If he does, his concern is right down on the couldn't-give-a-shit level. He stares out of the window for a brief moment, while I take the opportunity to stare at his profile.

"It's a family business." His words are said with a shrug that I think is meant to say more. "It's a unique process. It costs money, no? But then how do you make money when it costs so much? So, things change."

I nod. I understand this.

He turns back, smile bright and enigmatic. "And what do you do? Apart from sit on stools at bars oblivious while the bartender flirts with you."

Cheeks warm, probably staining a dark pink, I choose to ignore half of his question. "I work for a newspaper." I nod at the carefully folded broadsheet.

"The Times?" The eyebrow does some serious talking.

"Ha! No. A very small press. It's a satirical paper... On Fleet Street." I trail off. I hadn't thought about work after the devastating news bomb this morning. What would I tell Rebecca? Were you meant to hand your notice in? I really knew nothing about this dying business.

"What's wrong?"

"Oh. Uh." My chest is tight again, my heart pounding unevenly. I grasp the buttons on my black blouse. "Nothing."

Man Mountain watches me carefully. "You look like the person who loves to have fun but isn't right now."

My throat tightens and I incline my head, although I wished his character assessment was halfway true. "No offense to the current company."

"None taken."

"How often do you come to London on cheese business?"

Another enigmatic shrug. "Once a month if I can."

"That's a lot of Eurostar."

Shrug.

"Where in France do you come from?"

A wistful smile tilts his lips. "The Pyrenees, a town called Perpignan."

"Down in the south, right?"

"Have you been?"

"No." A tug pulls at my chest. How incredibly pathetic that I haven't even visited the country right next door, not even for the day, or to stock up on wine on a booze cruise. Although saying that, I haven't been to Wales either, or Ireland. Scotland was only for two nights.

Funny that life is always in such a rush to never really do very much.

Maybe it's time for a bucket list.

"It's beautiful. The air is warm, buzzing with bees, and smelling of honey."

"Not cheese?"

Those eyebrows pull together, but a smile flickers. "The view is a haze of purple heather and wildflowers, the wine good." He sniffs his shirt and I snort a laugh, holding up my hands in surrender. "The food is easy, simple, the people relaxed and full of sunshine and vitamin D."

"Sounds like heaven. Vitamin D is in short supply this side of the channel." I side eye the miserable grey sky outside and he chuckles.

"Of course, now it's January, so it's freezing pipes and barren landscapes."

I smile up at him, warmth spreading from my chest down my limbs until I'm all floaty and golden.

"I prefer your original description."

"Moi aussi, ma petite, me too."

The waitress cuts in, angling her hip so she's directly

facing the Frenchman across the table. "Are you ready to order?"

He peeps around her waist, eyes dancing. "My date would like chips, and she doesn't like to share."

My cheeks flame, but I can't help a smile.

"And steak frites for me and a bottle of the 2020 Beaujolais. Mystery woman, would you like anything else?" he asks me and silently I shake my head. I might not manage to eat one chip the way my stomach has tied into knots.

"Eh?" she asks.

"Steak and chips." For the record it sounds soooo much better in French. I'd roll in the words if I could.

"Date?" I ask once she's moved away, after throwing a smouldering pout in his direction and glancing over me as if wondering how I became the mystery date woman?

Lady, I don't know. One minute I was sitting by the Thames considering the end of all things and now I'm staring at that masterpiece in navy.

"Well, it's dinner. We have wine."

"Beaujolais?" I roll the letters around my mouth. "I'm more of a Shiraz girl."

He groans, dropping his head into his hands, fingers pushing through the thick dark waves. "New world grapes? I'm guessing, average five pounds a bottle?" He shudders and glances around the restaurant through his fingers. "I might have to pick a different date after all."

"Hey!"

Laughing, he straightens up and catches my hand in his meaty paw, turning it and examining my palm. My breath hitches and his dark gaze flicks to my face. "Wine is all about the grape, the age of the vine, the water it drinks, the soil it sits in, the amount of sunshine it absorbs." His gaze zeroes in on my mouth and I shift on my seat like I'm sitting on hot coals. "A Beaujolais is a Gamay grape, young and ripe. It's picked and processed and then bottled all within the year. It's a race by vineyards to see who can get their bottle on the shelves first. You never want to drink a bottle that's older than the year before, otherwise that's just a bottle of Gamay with a fancy label." *Fancee labbell.*

"I'll try to remember." God, I sound breathless.

"Then this dinner will have served a purpose."

I breathe in through my nose, out through my mouth. He really has no idea. "Believe me, it already has."

4

ONE NIGHT

"This has been lovely."

It really has. So lovely. Let's be realistic here, I could stare at his face and sit in silence and it would have been lovely. But beneath the stormy eyes, those talking eyebrows, and fuck-me-kissable lips, the man has a brain.

It's done odd things to my thighs.

I've been rubbing them under the table. I hope he hasn't noticed.

"Definitely a perk to London." He smiles over his wine glass. I'm jealous of the glass, the way his lips just skim it.

I'm also utterly deranged right now.

I need to go home. Process the shock. Speak to Liv. I don't know, make a plan for doomsday.

The Man Mountain has made me forget almost everything that has broken my heart today.

"We could have a nightcap." He lowers his wine glass, gently placing it on the table with such grace I'm mesmerised.

Until he clicks his fingers under my nose. "Are you

awake? Or has my concoction finally hit home?" That smirk. It should be illegal.

"What was the concoction?" Are my lips even working?

"Brandy, Chambord, and a dash of grenadine." His smirk grows into something wolfish while I frown.

"Chambord? That's berries right?" I don't know why I remember that being in the teak 'drinks' cabinet we had at home growing up. Liv and I must have hit the supply at one time or another. Clearly hasn't left a mark like the Crème de Menthe did.

Man Mountain chuckles. "What did you just think of? You shuddered."

I heat up from the inside out and shake my head. "Nothing. Just remembering my sister and me tasting all the random bottles in the drinks cabinet." I pull a face. "There was a nasty green one."

"Everyone is sick first time with Crème de Menthe." I can't stop staring at his smile. I've got a serious lip-obsession going on.

"Even the French?"

He chuckles again, and musical bells ring in heaven. "Even the French. You are close to your sister, no?"

His question makes me rock back in my seat. "Yes. Very much so."

"But you've been ignoring her calls the whole time we've known one another." Something about the way he says this makes my chest hollow. He doesn't say, since we met... rather... the whole time we've known one another... like we could always know one another.

But that's crazy.

He's French.

Actually lives in France, apparently in a purple-hued heaven.

And I'm... Well... I'm....

"She's been through a lot. Her husband left." I attempt a French-style shrug. "A few months back. They've got kids, so it's not nice."

"Why did he leave?" Man Mountain's eyebrows furrow together.

I shrug again, nodding slowly. "Apparently he wasn't sure about it all anymore."

"What?"

"Marriage, commitment, monogamy." I pout at the table before lifting my eyes. "Love. If he ever even did love her."

The man mountain stares at me, earnestness chiselled into his expression. "Then I would say he's not worth her being committed too. Marriage ends, but for the right reasons."

"That's what I've been saying." I drain the last of my wine. "I really should go; shall we get the check?"

He motions with his hand at the waitress. "Allow me."

"Oh no, I'll pay my share." His lips press into a line, but he doesn't say anything, so I speak, "Okay, thank you."

That pays me back in kind with a beautiful smile.

Payment is swift, maybe too swift. Smoothly, he tips the waitress for the gratuitous ogling she's been participating in while I've nibbled my chips.

Outside, the wind blusters straight through us, sheets of icy rain smattering against my almost dry coat. I step back against his chest as another blast rockets down the street. It's always colder down by the Thames, always makes me shiver.

Firm hands rub on my arms. "You're freezing, ma petite."

I don't know if I'm shaking from the cold or because I

don't want to leave this place; this magical moment that's been carved out of the dismal reality that surrounds me.

When I walk to the Tube, the magic will break. It will snap in two and this moment will never happen again. It will fall into the folklore of my history that's soon to be complete.

I turn, patting his chest. "Thank you for di—" His lips catch mine. I stumble back, off kilter, off balance, until his arms stretch around my back, pressing me upright and into his chest, while his hands run up my spine creating a shivering tingle.

Kissing.

He's kissing. Me.

Like nothing else could ever exist.

Shock makes my lips open. The tang of wine brushes from his mouth into mine, warm and delicate, Beaujolais grapes really are the best.

Instinctively, I flick my tongue gently, tasting for more. His hand cradles my jaw, strong fingers tilting my face to the angle he wants. And who am I to disagree?

Kissing.

It's a kiss unlike any other. He dives, and I sweep. I shift forward, he edges back. It's a game of chase that I don't want to end. One of us will need to breathe soon, but a challenge rises between us, who can be the first to go without air.

I will. I'll make the sacrifice just so this never ends.

I make little gasping noises as his chest presses against my damp, wool-covered body. There's a tingle down in my toes that threatens to unleash a fire through dry and barren land. I'm the arid hard earth after a harsh winter and with each probe of his tongue a little flower blooms to life. A snowdrop pushing against the January ice, flourishing despite the winter chill.

His lips slow, one long press, then another, and then another. He's going to come up for air and I will be left forever remembering this moment that a perfect kiss broke. And it stops. A deep aching pull tugs deep down in my stomach, my eyes sting—I'd say it's from the bitch of a wind. He doesn't let go of my face. "Mon dieu," he breathes against my skin.

My God.

I fucking know.

My God.

I've been kissed to within the final inch of my life. The kiss of all kisses has made me almost forget that life itself is nearly over.

"Nightcap?" he growls low in my ear and I push back to look up at his shadowed face.

This is insane. I need to get off the crazy train, because it's leading me to a place I shouldn't be going. I've got my ticket for my final destination and it's somewhere I can't take anyone else.

Knowing all this doesn't make 'no' any easier to say.

It teases on my tongue with the leftover tingle of his kiss.

"I should go."

He tugs on my coat, this mystery man, with the eyebrows that talk and the hands that... Jesus Christ, what could those hands do. "You should stay. Another half an hour."

I meet his gaze, wanting to steal another kiss before I run into the night. "Where?"

"My hotel is just across the road." *Otel.* I want him to repeat every syllable. It's like my new, favourite music.

"How many steps?" I grasp the lapels of his overcoat. If he gives me the steps I can work out if I can make it.

Without a beat, his eyes lift over the top of my head. Then he leans back to glance down at my legs, arching a brow. "For you, twenty-five."

I snort a laugh. A magical sound on a day where laughter could have come to a final end.

"Not a step more."

"I'll carry you if it's more."

We count together. One. Two. Three. Un. Deux. Trois.

It's a small boutique hotel: iron railings and a roaring fire in the lounge. It crackles and dances, throwing the room into orange and red. He takes my coat and puts it on the stand by the door. Then he turns back, catching my elbow and whispers in my ear. "Five steps to the sofa by the fire."

I'm warm and liquid on the inside and it has nothing to do with the crackling spit of the hearth fire.

He counts us over, settling me down, tucking me in like a little dolly with a tartan wool blanket. Never have I been tucked with such care. It's like he knows I'm spectacularly broken without me having to say it.

I've always strived for independence. I'm a strong, independent woman and all that jazz.

But right now, I want to be wrapped like a burrito by mystery man.

He turns back and strides with impressively long legs for the bar and I watch him leave, eyes trained on his tight arse encased in navy.

What would the end of days be like with someone like him at my side? I mean, Barney is okay, apart from the farting, but he's never going to roll me up in a blanket, fingers skimming my cheek.

What have I missed out on being a *strong and independent woman?*

Why didn't I realise that maybe the two things didn't need to be mutually separate from one another?

Twelve months to go and no family to leave behind, no husband to cry real tears.

That's a good thing, right? I mean this way I'm not hurting anyone. Not breaking anyone's heart, only my own. Olivia will survive. She's got those two gorgeous kids to keep her going. She'll miss me, sure, but her focus will always be on them, as it should be.

No, this way is definitely for the best.

Definitely.

"You're lost in thoughts?" He comes back and offers me a small glass. It's his concoction again. Oh crumbs.

"Just mulling over life."

I expect him to sit on the other sofa opposite the fire, but instead he settles next to me. Sliding an arm around my shoulder.

"Life... no small subject to contemplate." He takes a sip of his drink and I watch for him to wince. He doesn't.

"I'm thirty next year."

"A babe in arms."

I shoot him a side eye. "How old are you?"

"Forty-two."

"Wow. You're old."

He chuckles and it rocks me against his chest. "And so, you're thirty next year? And what?" He turns slightly, beautiful pouty lips near my face.

Chewing on my lip I consider this. "I'm thinking of all the things I thought I would have done by now but haven't." This is halfway to the truth and I nod, pleased with my efforts of honest conversation.

"Like?"

I tease a smile, sipping delicately at the liquid fire, just wetting my lips and then running my tongue along them. "Well until ten minutes ago I'd never kissed a mysterious Frenchman in the street."

"Ah, well that's a must before you are thirty." The twinkle in his eye makes my stomach tighten, makes me feel brave where normally I would hide.

"And you know, funny fact." I look up at him through my lashes, the sharp angle of his cheekbone, the dark stubble on his jaw. My words want to catch and stop on the way out. They hesitate with a gasp of air, but I push them through. "I've never had a one-night stand."

Who am I? Where is Julianna Brown?

All I know is that I want this. Whatever this is. I know in my gut this is my antidote to my really bad day. He's the antidote to heartbreak, no not even heartbreak, life break.

He turns, gaze on my face, dropping to my mouth, making the taste of his kiss flood back onto my tastebuds. Taking my glass, he leans across and places it on the occasional table by the side of the sofa. Shifting his weight, he slowly moves back, nose skimming my cheek. I breathe in the scent of icy air, wood smoke, and brandy.

"So sad, ma petite." His lips glance mine. A brief sweep, challenging me to back out, asking me if I want to retract my statement, take back my unspoken question.

I don't.

I push my lips against his, the warmth of them, the perfect pressure making me shiver.

"No names," I whisper into his mouth.

"No names." Every time he speaks, turning every vowel and consonant into something exotic, I could disintegrate into a thousand pieces.

"One night." I pull back, holding my gaze firm on his face.

No one can blame this girl. I'm in shock. Just lived through bad news. No one would judge me for this.

I'm a good girl really. Ask Barney, he's my living proof.

All I know is I don't want to go home.

My hands grip the white cotton of his shirt sleeves, sliding over all the things he has hidden beneath. I know it's going to break me apart.

"One night," he confirms, nodding. The deal is done.

Which it is. Done. Signed. Posted in an envelope to my treacherous desire.

Leaning forward, he licks the seam of my mouth and I gasp sharply. "How many steps to your room?" I ask against his lips.

Pulling back, he glances over my shoulder, gaze narrowing. "Non. I'll carry you, ma petite fleur."

Unlocking me from where I've almost crawled into his lap, he lunges forward, lifting me with him, long powerful arms catching me up with ease. Laughing, I clasp my little legs around his tall frame.

A midnight gaze flashes over me with dirty promises of how he's going to end me and then start me all over again and my laughter dies on my lips as I stare back.

A small whimper escapes me as he strides through the lounge area and to the lift, jabbing his finger on the call button.

Maybe now's the time to point out I've never had sex in a lift either.

5

THINGS THAT GO BUMP

My legs cinch around his waist, tongue teasing into his mouth, hands in the dark strands of his hair. I think there's a mirror behind me with my arse in a skirt pressed against it. Don't care.

I sigh a little, daring him to kiss me harder, push into me further. His fingers squeeze my thighs hard and my sigh morphs into a groan. This man, with the hands.

The elevator door pings, and he steps us through, our kiss still a spun dream far from breaking. My fingers work the buttons on his shirt.

No idea who this wanton woman is but I'm loving her style.

He breaks the kiss and I'm close to crying, but his mouth falls to my neck, sucking gently on the skin at the hollow of my collarbone as he balances me against the wall and fishes a key card out of the back of suit trousers.

Those trousers are going to be seeing the floor any moment now.

Any. Bloody. Moment.

The door beeps but not before he's cursed French

obscenities into my mouth and jangled the door handle so hard it might fall off. Wouldn't want to admit that to reception.

That would kill the mood.

The door kicks open and we are through. I don't know what I want more of, more lips on my neck or more hard squeezes of my ass and thighs.

More.

Just more.

The door clicks closed, quiet against the loud carnival I've got clattering in my head. Every touch he places on me sets off another loud round of crashing music and applause.

Who knew kissing could be like this? So all... all... all encompassing. I lose my train of thought as he detaches my legs from his waist and gently lowers me to the ground. I'm unsteady and he chuckles as he holds me upright. I meet his gaze. This should be so awkward. I'm about to get naked with a total stranger.

Nothing about this is awkward. It seems so right it's almost on the point of alarming.

No, I don't believe in insta-connection. I don't even believe in fate, but there is something in that dark-blue gaze that sings in my soul.

And it's just one night. I'll never have to see him again.

"That shirt, it smells of wine. I think you should take it off."

With a boyish grin he silently agrees, unbuttoning the remaining fastenings much quicker than my lame fumble.

I pretend to sniff the air—Okay, I'm not practiced at this stuff, I have to work with what I have here. "I can still smell wine."

He laughs. It booms around the four corners of the

room and around my faulty heart. Picking me up, he stalks two steps to the bed and launches me on it.

I bounce. Actually bounce. He clutches my leg to stop me from ricocheting against the ceiling, pinning me down. Laughter bubbles in my chest; insane, uncontrollable laughter.

It builds. Builds. Like a whistling kettle on a stove.

"Something funny, ma petite?"

"Nope." I smash my lips together, but my chest is tight with holding it in.

"Let me give you something to sober you up." He leans forward, catching my face in a delicate touch from such massive hands. I'm breathless as he stares at me. Truly stares at me, holding my gaze, searching for something, though I'm not sure what. I struggle and squirm, hating that he could still be searching for the sadness he thought he could see in me earlier. He holds me still, continuing to stare deep into my eyes. When I finally lay tranquil, meeting him stare to stare, he smiles. "I'm going to kiss you now."

"I thought you did that already?" My breath hitches.

A slow smile spreads across his mouth. "Not yet, ma petite."

Oh crumbs. What was that in the lift, because it sure felt like he was kissing the fuck out of me?

Leaning forward, he skims his lips up my throat. His hand palms the length of my calf, running up the black, thick tights made for January weather and not sexy times.

I quiver as his hand trails firmly up my thigh, over the cover of my hip, waist, side-boob until his fingers arrive at my chin. The slow smile curving at the edges of his lip makes my heart flip like a pancake. I drag in air. With a delicate clasp on my face, he presses his lips to mine: one, two, three. Tilting my head, he steals inside, unchallenged to explore the dark recesses of wanton kisses while I want more of his tongue inside, hot and slow, sliding against mine. I open my mouth more, dirtying the kiss, relishing every flick and dive.

This kiss is everything. It burns in my stomach. Slow, leisurely, it has me clawing for more, fingers finding purchase on his smooth skin. And oh, what skin. I want to open my eyes to look, to gaze at the fine surface, but I don't want to break *The Kiss*.

I've never been kissed before.

I mean, I have.

But never like this.

Languorous, it stretches time; spinning the moment until it glitters with stars, or maybe that's just the lights in my vision from lack of oxygen.

Oxygen is for losers. Fact.

His fingers drop their hold on my face, but I understand the unspoken demand. Don't move. Don't break the kiss. That's the rule of the moment.

Don't break a thing.

No sudden movements.

His hand lands on my hip, soft yet firm, his thumb pressing into the soft spot in front of my hip bone where underneath I'm sure my ovaries is having a little party.

Angling me closer, he presses tight into my body.

Oh.

Ooooh.

More, ooooh.

My toes curl up as the hard outline of what he's packing under that navy suit presses into my belly.

He breaks the kiss. Rule breaker. Dipping his mouth to my throat, my collarbone, he slips the black of my staid office wear blouse to the side like I'm encased in the sexiest negligee ever made. Every inch of space his lips travel along tingles in his wake, like a riptide after the roll of sand on the ocean floor. I churn into a vortex of desire.

"So beautiful," he whispers against my shoulder, the slow descent of my blouse taking a hundred years. One cup of my bra is exposed, and my nipple pulsates with the need to be touched. It doesn't come though.

No.

Torment is in the waiting. A fact I realise he knows.

My fingers find his hair, tugging at the strands. Soft and silky, the tousled waves slip through my touch. It's how I imagined it would feel, smooth, running like liquid.

"Clothes off, now." I breathe.

My mystery man lifts his head. "Impatient, ma petite?"

"Yes." Pushing him away, I sit up, yanking at the buttons he's been taking an age to undo. Discarding the blouse, I reach around to undo the button on my skirt, and he tuts low, growling almost under his breath. "Stand."

Okay, no *please*. I can take that though.

I scramble off the mattress, legs heavy, strangely hot. It's these bloody tights. Ghastly things. I'm never wearing them again.

He sits, hands on my hips, squaring me between his knees. His toned flat stomach scrunches and I push my knees together making him smirk. I'll let him have that smirk. I'm on fire down there, raging fire.

"Please don't think this is what I normally do," I gasp as he lifts a hand, palming my stomach, running his thumb under the edge of my plain t-shirt bra.

"Does it matter what I think?" He pulls me forward, eyes closed, hands anchored, kissing along the bones of my chest just under my collarbone. I have never been kissed there. Intimate, every delicate bone that creates my form quivers with anticipation.

"No. Yes. I don't know." I feel his smile against my skin.

I think my skirt should come off now. And the tights. Definitely the tights.

Possibly the shoes.

He reaches around me, the side of his face pressed against my belly in the most intimate of holds as he unfastens my bra, freeing my aching breasts. They fall around his face with delight. Glancing up, he meets my gaze and the burn in his gaze dries my tongue so much I close my eyes. Dropping my head back, I give myself over to the stranger I almost didn't meet, gasping as he slips my nipple into his mouth, pulling and sucking deeply, while his hands drop to my ass and give a firm squeeze.

I gasp and moan at once, a sound I don't think I've created before.

Another smile meets my stunned gaze as he moves to the other side.

This must be the French way of doing things. I can sense that if I was to rush, he would slow. This torture of standing half dressed, tingling nipples standing to attention, begging for his devotion, is already my punishment for demanding more.

Once he's administered equal consideration to both my nipples: sucking, kissing, nibbling, he smirks up at me. I'm a wreck.

I've never nearly reached orgasm from nipple play before, yet here I am, quivering and desperate for the next touch.

It hits me with blinding clarity.

I've never made love before. Not really. Sex, yes. Fuck, definitely.

But love? Slow and delicate, an adventure across the unknown landscape of someone else's skin. Never.

When I get home, I'm writing a bucket list, putting this at the top and then crossing it instantly off.

"Turn around."

I do, without hesitation.

His fingers undo the button on my skirt, then the zip, so slow I could die with every notch it undoes. Inch by inch the material, the slinky lining of the pencil skirt, rubs against my hips and thighs as it lowers to the ground. Trailing his fingers in an arc around my body, he brushes them lightly across my breasts. Heaven forbid they get jealous that my ass might get some attention.

"These tights are hellish," he observes, "Don't wear them again."

I nod. I've already made that decision.

Something illicit lights inside me though at the prospect that every day I don't put the tights on I'm doing something he's told me to do.

I know I'll never see him again. I also know I'll never wear one hundred denier tights again.

Lifting my right calf, he slips off my red stiletto; the only splash of colour in my work wardrobe. Sliding off my tights and freeing my toes, he places my bare foot back on the floor and I stand at an awkward angle while my body adjusts to being three inches shorter on one side than the other.

I'm sure he chuckles, but I can't really hear it clearly as he lifts my other foot backwards and repeats the same, leaving me only in black lace trimmed shorts.

He doesn't turn me. Doesn't touch.

Then with the slowest of movements he inches my knickers down. Half an inch one side, then half an inch the other.

It's sheer torture.

Once they are on the floor and unhooked from my foot he turns me. The expression on his face burns straight to my heart. "Beautiful. Just like I knew." That smile. It's everything. Bright like the touch of the sun on the first day of spring.

"Now I'm naked and you're still dressed." He shrugs and I roll my eyes. "Your turn. Stand up."

"No time, ma petite. I need to be inside you."

Now the French start to hurry. They have an issue with timing.

I shriek as he pulls me down, cradling me in the arch of his arms, pushing me into the mattress with his body. This kiss is hot. Demanding. Unrelenting. I gasp for air.

He moans as I scrape my nails down his back, travelling the length of his spine, feeling his muscles bunch around my touch. He mutters in rapid French under his breath. Pushing back, he unbuckles his belt and steps from the bed, sliding off the rest of his clothes.

Then I see him. Perfect specimen of man that he is. His erection bounces free of the confines of his clothing and my stomach tightens right down low.

Oooooh.

He makes swift work of flicking through his wallet for a condom. The whole time his massive dick just standing to attention between us.

I swallow hard as he crawls back up the bed, caging me again in the safety of his arms and one hand sweeps delicate fingers up my thigh, between my legs, his gaze finding mine when he feels how wet I am.

Biting my lower lip, I try to still the wild beating of my heart.

He pauses though, a frown pulling those brows. "I can't

be inside of you and not know your name. Sex, it's truth between two people. You want me to lie."

Well, fuck. Just shoot me in the heart and bury me right now.

I give a small shake of my head. "That was the rule."

He glares and I desperately keep an eye on his erection hoping we don't have a last minute capsize. Nope. Still upright. The towering mast on a ship at sea.

And fuck if I don't want to be that sea.

"So give me a name," I whisper. I'd happily be anyone other than Julianna Brown with the death sentence right now in this moment.

Don't make *me* be *her*.

I watch him.

He watches me.

"Juliette."

I laugh. Is he for real? Could he have chosen a name closer to my own? "Juliette?" I say it like him. *Juuuuliette*

He nods, satisfied with my unexpected baptism. Reaching forward, I clasp his hand and yank him down. "Good. Can you fuck me now?"

"Please?" He arches an eyebrow.

"Please," I beg on a whisper and he pushes straight for home. I gasp, stretching around him. His hand palms my hair, gaze firmly on mine, unflinching, as he pushes to the absolute hilt and I'm pretty sure he's breaching my goddamn cervix.

Fully home, he closes his eyes, serenity flooding his face for a moment until his eyes flicker back open and he shoots me a secret smile that could spin a million promises if only I'd let it.

I stretch my hands above my head, pushing my tits for

the ceiling, meeting his thrusts, waiting for heaven to come and find me.

No names.

One night.

One thing ticked off my imaginary bucket list.

I give myself up, losing myself in the Frenchman, pushing deeper and deeper until I'm crying, toe pointing, feeling him buried deep within me and he's groaning, hips flying, lips smashing.

He collapses on me, winding the little air I have left in my lungs, staying inside me, connected through the come-down. His arm tugs around me tight, holding me close, lips brushing my neck. "Sleep," he murmurs.

"Should I not go?" My chest gives a strange and strangled hitch, but he cranks an eye, arm tightening.

"Sleep."

Strangely I want to. It's so calm, like being washed up on a desert island of zero expectation. Darkness slips around us, wrapping us tight in an unexpected moment.

Later, when his body is spooned around mine, his breath steady and heavy, I shift from under his weighty arm.

I can't look back. Can't look at his sleeping form, long limbs tangled, a sheet around a taut waist. Muscles that could make a grown woman weep.

The magic of being Juliette is fading fast. The short break from reality the man mountain reprieved me with is ending.

I've got to go home. Got to face Olivia. Need to face the truth of all the things.

I pull my clothes on, grab my bag. Tears slip down my face. Such a shame. He really is beautiful.

It was just a moment.

Just one moment.

One night.

As much as I know this, I still stop at the door and glance back, massive Frenchman sprawled across a bed tangled in white sheets. "Thank you," I whisper, and then I steal away into London's pre-dawn grey.

6

SISTERS

"WHERE THE ACTUAL fuck have you been?" Olivia yanks me over the threshold into her home encased in layers of cream. Walking into Olivia's house is rather like being one of those tiny figurines on top of a wedding cake.

I'm trembling, my legs barely holding me up, while her hands grip my shoulders in an almost shake. I know that shake. It's the, *'where have you been, don't you know I'm going out of my mind with worry'* shake.

"I'm sorry. I'm sorry." My lips tremble, my tongue dry and stuck to the roof of my mouth.

"What are you wearing? Why are you in work clothes on a Saturday—" she's cut off from more questions by an ear-splitting screech and a wild form cantering through the hallway where we are standing.

"Aunty JuJu!" The screeching banshee draws to a skidded stop and tilts its head to the side, peering at me through wild, unbrushed, untameable knots of hair. "Naughty JuJu. Mummy said bad words." A finger wags sternly at me, side to side. "Soap words. Never say soapsie words."

Oh, the wash your mouth out with soap threat. Must have been really bad words. I cock an eyebrow at Liv, the younger of the two Brown sisters.

"What?" She lifts her chin in the air and glares daggers at me. "I was bloody worried. I called your phone at least a hundred times, and your office."

"Oh, Liv, what did you call them for?" I sigh, making her cross her arms like a warrior preparing for battle.

"Because you went for a check-up and then never called me."

"You aren't Mum, Liv, I don't have to check in."

"Is that so?"

Okay, this is not the way it's meant to go. I've got far worse things to say.

Bending down, I grab the thigh-high Gremlin and push back its hair, finding my niece buried underneath. "Hey, beautiful girl. Can we play dress up today?"

Paige stares at me through brown eyes I know are the exact colour of mine and a little pang pings my chest. "No hairbrush." She folds her arms, meaning business.

I pull a face. "Well, if we don't have the hairbrush then we can't have the ice cream, can we?"

"Ice cream, for breakfast?" Paige starts bouncing and I can only think she's already got a secret stash of sugar stored away like a squirrel. I glance over her head at Liv whose face has drained to grey, dishwater grey.

"Sure," I return my focus to Paige. "Personally, I love ice cream for brekkie, it's the breakfast of champions."

"Champions!" She fists her hand in the air and zooms off like a superhero dressed only in vest and knickers.

"Hairbrush!" I call after her. "And maybe some of that magic spray I bought you."

Straightening, I level up with Liv. "Seriously, sis, you've got to brush it when she gets out of the bath."

Liv holds her wrist out for me to see. A round, bite-shaped bruise sits on the pale flesh.

"Jesus, she's wild."

Liv meets my eye. "Cut the bullshit, Julia."

This isn't a conversation to have over breakfast, even an ice cream one. But it's a conversation that can't be avoided.

"What did Dr Francis say? I knew I should have come with you."

I launch myself forward, wrapping my arms around her, face pressed into the strands of her ash-blonde hair. "You don't have to be Mum to everyone, Liv."

Olivia pulls back and tucks my hair behind my ear, the most motherly thing anyone has done to me in probably years. "I know. But you're my sister. I should be there with you."

She means because no one else can beyou know, because I'm a singleton of life. But then I guess she is now too. What did getting married and trusting anyone give her, apart from a baby that communicates in upchuck and a wild terrorist that bites?

"Shall we have a coffee?" Her voice shakes.

I wince, twisting my lips. "It might need to be stronger." And that's it. Her tears fall and we cling onto one another, salt water from two different sources creating an unstoppable torrent.

"I can't bloody believe this. I always knew he was shit." Liv splashes more Tia Maria into her coffee. The coffee is long gone. She's basically refilling straight Tia Maria. I mean it tastes of coffee—that makes it almost the same thing.

I stare into the depth of my mug, searching for the answers to the universe, like, how can life be so shit.

Paige's hair is braided into tight French braids. My stomach gave a little squeeze as I did it, even the word French making me shiver.

"Dr Francis isn't shit, Liv," I lift my gaze from my fortune teller Tia Maria mug. "He was lovely actually. Even held my hand." My voice tightens. "You know. When he told me."

Liv grips her cup so tight her knuckles whiten. We will have a liqueur volcanic explosion if she carries on at this rate. "Right. Well, I'm coming next time, I've got questions."

"Sure you have," I smirk into my cup.

"And I'll hold your damn hand."

I can't take a breath. My chest doesn't want to play ball. I try to breathe through the panic, but it won't ebb, won't release the pressure around my sternum.

"Liv..."

She slips off her stool, wrapping her arms around my waist. "I'm not letting you go. You've all I've got."

I swipe at my wet cheeks. "That's not true. You've got Paige and Lenny. You can't let this bring you down, you've got to be the best mum you can be for them."

"I know, and I will, but I'll also be the best sister. I'm going to fight for you, Julia. I'll never let you go. Which makes me think." She lets go of me, reaching for her phone where she fires off a quick message. I straighten myself up.

"What are you doing?"

"Asking Charlie for the healthiest immune boosting recipes she has."

"Ugh. No. I am not drinking any of that green shit. No way."

"Ummmm, naughty word."

I turn, caught in the act of adulting by Paige. "Come here, monster."

She slips to my side and I haul her up, pushing my nose into her hair. "You'll look after your mummy, won't you?"

"Sure. I'm a biggish girl, but where are you going?" Her pale gaze holds mine and I crack under the pressure of it.

"She's going nowhere, ever." Liv slams down her mug. "And that's a promise."

I shake my head at her over Paige's head. *Don't promise things we can't keep.*

"Sweetie, Daddy will be here soon to pick you guys up. Can you go and get your backpack." I hate the way Liv's skin pales. Hate what he did to her with his empty promises and dick that couldn't stay contained.

I've threatened to chop it off, but she assures me it's not worth the jail time.

"I'll just go and wake Lenny." She hesitates, like she thinks I might just disappear as soon as she leaves the room.

"I'll go." I jump down from my stool, my tight covered feet cool against the tiles of the kitchen floor. "Does he need changing?"

"No. I did it before his nap." She shakes her head, leaning over the kitchen counter, sobs shaking her body.

"Liv," I whisper, reaching and brushing her hair down her back. "I'm not going anywhere right now."

"I'm scared."

"Me too. Me too. But I can keep going, I can fight this as long as I can."

Her face tells me otherwise. Liv absorbs facts the way I inhale chocolate. Two years ago, when this all started, she did all the research, things that I never bothered to read up on.

Maybe she should have come to the appointment with me.

But then I would never have...

I shut down the thought of my mystery man and the way things were in his arms.

One night.

No names.

No strings.

And a good bloody job too. My sister's face is telling me all too clearly that there is no way I can dodge this bullet. Damn her and the facts. I much prefer fantasy and illogical random thought processes.

Much better that way.

Without anything more to say, I leave her in small pieces at the kitchen island and tiptoe down the plush carpet to Lenny's nursery. Inside it's warm, calm. In his cot he's wrapped like a little tubby pudding of gorgeousness.

"Hey, sleepyhead," I murmur, running my finger down his cheek.

He's all warm, flushed cheeks, long lashes resting. Six months of cuteness.

"Lenny, time to wake up." I'm louder, this kid can sleep.

Still there's no movement so I lean into his cot, lifting him into my arms. He's wearing a sleep bag, legs all tucked up like a frog, hair damp from where he's been so cosy.

I snuggle him close, breathing in that baby smell that can't be bottled.

I'm a strong, independent woman. But with my nephew in my arms, a bundle of upchuck perfection, I let the barrier come down and I cry for all the things that I will never get to own.

Some paths I guess you are meant to walk, others will always remain closed.

Sitting in the rocking chair in the corner, I cradle him tight, gently shifting us forward and back with my feet, tears landing on the strands of his dark hair, until Liv comes to find me and unwraps him from my hand, leaving me in a rocking chair with empty arms.

"Okay. Don't shoot me down." Alone in the house, I've squeezed myself into some of her jeans, rolling them up three inches—the bitchand a shirt I think might well have been a breastfeeding one.

We are in her living room. I say living. I mean show-room. I shrug to myself. Hell, she can do what she likes. If being pristine brings her joy then I'm all for it.

"Go on." I nod and take a sip of my wine. I think we've made an unspoken agreement that we will drink away the day.

There are days for healthiness.

There are days for wine.

Today constitutes wine. Although she has made me drink some vile green juice her friend Charlie recommended. I heave just thinking about it.

"Don't freak out," she says.

"Well now I will."

"I think you should speak to Mum and Dad."

Kick a woman while she's down, why don't you?

I see what she's done. She's waited until she thinks the wine has oiled the gears of my hatred. Liv doesn't realise there isn't enough wine in the world for that.

Idly, I contemplate if she's serving me a glass of five pound a bottle new world wine.

"Nope."

"Julia."

"No. I mean it, Liv. Please don't bring them into this."

"You're their daughter. Don't you think they will care, want to know?"

I can't look at her. How dare she.

"No. I really don't."

She sighs but I still don't meet her eyes.

"Okay. It was just a suggestion."

I nod. Throat tight.

"I'm changing the subject now; you can calm down." I lift my face and give her my best death ray stare and she clutches her chest, falling sideways onto the oversized couch. "You got me."

I have to laugh. Bitch.

"So. What happens now?" She sits back up and readjusts her hair.

"Now the transplant team will call me. I'll have to go and see them to... I don't know, talk to them about shopping for a new heart..." My joke falls flat. "Is it weird, hoping someone else will die so I can live?"

Liv lowers her glass, face scored with something I don't want to see. "No. I'd go on a murdering spree if I thought it would help."

"Oh my god! And you won't let me cut off Darren's dick, how's that fair?"

"Can I come to it with you?"

I rustle up a small smile. "Liv. You need to focus on you. Please."

"You're asking for something ridiculous." She pauses. "Have you thought about work?"

"No. I can't afford not to work. And I don't want to stop. Why would I?"

"Jules, twelve months..." She drops her face into her hand.

"The only thing I ask is that you promise to have Barney. That's all I want to talk about, discuss."

She looks in alarm at her cream carpet and I snort a laugh.

"Okay. I'll do it because it's your dying wish, but I can't guarantee I won't shave the bastard."

"Don't you dare. His fur is his pride."

We grin at one another. A voice shouting in the back of my head to make all these smiles count for something. Anything really.

"So. Next question."

I groan. "What now?"

"How did you turn up here this morning in an outfit I'm pretty sure you wore to work yesterday morning?"

Oooh. I could do with being swallowed by the massive armchair I'm sitting in. I mean, all this cushioning you'd think it could happen.

"Nothing. You know. I just... needed some processing time. Ya know?"

Liv bites on her lower lip, face scrunching. I'm about to dial 999 because I think she's having a stroke when she bursts out a laugh. She clutches her middle, bending over, heaving in breaths, rubbing at tears squeezing through the corners of her eyes.

"Does processing mean being naked and bumping uglies?"

"What! No!" My burning face is going to speak the truth. "What makes you say that?"

She motions for me to get up and join her by the mirror. We face one another in the reflection, one blonde, one brunette, shadows of one another in our features.

"You should have buttoned the shirt." She motions to where the shoulder strap of my bra is exposed by the fall of the shirt's neckline. Beneath the simple elastic is a purple, mouth shaped bruise.

My mouth drops into a wide 'O' shape as I push my hand against it, my body flushing with warmth.

Even though I'd do anything to keep that mark on my skin.

Another thing to tick off the list. Love bite. Twenty-nine and never had one before.

"I need a piece of paper. It's time to write a bucket list."

Then we both start to cry all over again.

7

FRENCH RED

It's a sad state of life when every day starts with the winking of a cat's anus in your face.

"Barney, ugh." I push him off and pull the duvet over my head. In a weekend that lasted approximately five billion years, the cat alarm is not wanted right now.

The duvet does nothing. Barney looks at it as a morning workout. He's stretching on his Lycra and pinging his headband.

I screw my eyes shut waiting for his next move. A paw slips under the edge of the purple cotton. The cat is Houdini, apart from he gets himself *into* tight spaces rather than out. Tap tap. The paw says—*give me breakfast, bitch.*

"I'm no bitch." I stretch a toe out from the other end of the duvet, hoping to lure him away from my face.

Not a chance. He splurges down, weight on front paws, claws out, just an inch shy of my nipples. The air presses out of my lungs at the heft he has.

You could say it's all fur. It's not. It's all fat covered in fur.

Shoving down the duvet, I scowl at him. Barney doesn't understand sulking. He thinks it means headbutt and purr.

Headbutt and purr.

Headbutt and purr.

Being a cat must be so easy.

"It's five, Barns."

More purring. Another headbutt. "Ow! You just made me bite myself."

He stands up, circles, winking his ass again, and then resettles closer to my face so he can rest a paw on my cheek.

"We've really got to try this diet food. You're crushing my chest."

More purring.

Huffing, I stare at the ceiling and stretch my toes, pinching the muscles in my calves. My eyes ache when I blink, my head pounding. I could blame the bottle of French red I went to the off-licence to buy, but I think the headache has been caused by other things, like dying.

I don't know what happens today. Today is day one in the no man's land called The End.

I'm headbutted again and I reach a hand into the chilled air of the bedroom before swiftly tucking myself back under.

French red.

Okay. I went for an Argentinian Malbec... planned to push the boat to seven quid. I figured dying deserved the splurge, but then I'd stood in front of all the reds and found myself drawn to the fancy French labels. Funny that French labels are class. No bright colours, no lizards or kangaroos. Subtle colours, classy fonts.

I've been trying very hard not to think about one-night-no names with the man mountain.

Thinking, not succeeding.

Because my thighs ache. I keep stretching my legs at the gentle pull of my muscles. My brain is on a porno reel where I think about him lifting my calf and taking off my M&S knickers.

One night. No names.

Someone tell my body that.

There's this little warm flurry in deep places.

He was a bit like a French wine label: classy, unassuming, and smooth as you like as he slipped up and down. In and out.

Barney just wants breakfast. Unconcerned with my part memory, part fantasy, part absolute reluctance to get out of bed and face a Monday on what could be one of my last Mondays, he decides subtle purring and head butting isn't getting him the things he needs—Whiskers—so he pads my face in an act of love, springing his claws at the last moment like a cruel lover intent on revenge.

I throw back the covers knocking him into a spiralling tangle. "Goddamn, motherfucker."

And I'm cussing the cat.

Zombie swinging to the kitchen, I pick up his tin and shake some of the contents into his bowl as he weaves between my legs, our lovers spat momentarily forgotten as he pounces on a kibble that's bounced off the bowl and skidded across the floor.

"Fatty," I tell him, putting back his tin on top of the microwave and then flicking on the kettle.

While it boils, I pull on the cord for the blinds, peer outside and then swiftly lower it again.

I have a wardrobe issue.

At some senseless part of the night during Friday's activities I swore to never wear my thick tights again.

With fair reasoning.

I pull on the cord again assessing the pregnant sky with a critical glance. It's going to have to be what Liv calls 'Work pants'.

Liv can wear work pants because her legs are ten foot long.

I wear suit pants, or smart tailoring, and I look like a prison guard. Or a woman who drives a security van, the type that has 'This vehicle is armoured and alarmed' printed on every side.

Grabbing a mug out of the cupboardit's surface so cool against my touch I think I need to search for icicles in the flatmy heart races, rushes almost, skipping a beat, pounding hard for two, before racing for another three.

My head whirls.

Gasping, I catch my breath, a tiny puff of air wheezing into my lungs. My fingertips tingle, limbs heavy as I stumble towards the small lounge area and head for the sofa, Barney weaving between my ankles. "Not now, Barn."

I can't hear my own voice, maybe I didn't even speak.

Falling onto the cushions of the sofa, I roll onto my back and focus on the ceiling, waiting for the breathlessness and the racing train in my chest to depart.

My skin slicks with sweat, head light.

Pouff. I groan as Barney assumes position. "Feline, I'm s-struggling to b- breathe here."

He answers with a purr and limply, I lift my wrist and scratch his ears.

Headbutt.

My eyes sting and I swipe at them with the back of my hand and wrist. An episode. When my chest is easier, I roll over, knocking Barney onto the floor and grabbing at my diary on the table. I mean, am I even supposed to be keeping these records now? Dr Francis didn't actually say. Kind of seems pointless, but nonetheless I dutifully flip to the first week of the year and add in: breathless, racing, dizzy.

Flipping it closed, I study the new diary. A present from Liv at Christmas, I'm guessing she didn't know it would be my last.

I really need to research more. I'm being an idiot by pretending this isn't going to happen.

Ignorance though... it really is bliss.

So they say.

Flipping the navy cover with its watercolour peacock back open, I scan through the first couple of pages.

What was she thinking? *Affirmations for success... yearly focus target...*

Yes: **I don't want to die**, and: **Live beyond twelve months.**

Chuckling, I write my answers on the dotted lines.

Health goals: **Reach thirty.**

Career aspirations: **Not to get made redundant before I die (maybe hand notice in – not sure – need to research).**

Happy with my responses, I flick through the rest. December. November. October. Will I even see those months? Should I rip them out now?

I should have asked Dr Francis more questions on Friday. Maybe I could ring him. He did say he'd be in contact this week. I could call and say, 'Hey, it's only Monday, and I've already had a turn'.

Barney's high-pitched pip of air from his butt pulls my attention. "You repulse me," I tell him, but he just licks the end of his tail, face turned away from me. He's had all he needs today. Well, until six-thirty this evening when we begin it all over again.

Flipping through the pages again, I settle back on the self-help twaddle at the start.

This Year's Goals

Tapping my teeth with my biro, I consider the prospect. Liv would be horrified if she knew all this stuff was in this diary after the news we'd just got.

We.

Funny her and I were always my *we,* yet I probably haven't been hers for a long time. And that's the way it's supposed to be. The way I want it to be. Right now, she's no longer getting ready for work as a hyper efficient personal assistant. She's busy changing nappies and wrestling the terrorist to pre-school. Doing all the things that she chose in her life, no matter how much Dickweed Darren let her down.

I grind my teeth and consider that prison sentence again. Would they put a dying woman in prison? I'm willing to take the gamble that they wouldn't. That man no longer deserves a penis. Maybe if he was a eunuch, he'd have more time to contemplate what a total asshat he is.

Now... Mr Mysterious Frenchman. He should definitely keep his penis. He knew exactly what to do with that.

I need to stop thinking about it. It's not a one-night stand if you obsess about it after.

On a whim I write on the top line of the Yearly Goals section: **Have sex with a Frenchman**. Tapping away at my teeth I consider this and then write: **Have a one-night stand**, beneath it.

Then I put a line through both.

Oooh. The love bite. That goes on the list too followed by another concise line cutting through the words.

~~**Love bite.**~~

There you go. I've only been dying one day, and I've ticked three things off.

Swiftly I add:

Go to Wales, Scotland, and Ireland (Don't worry too much about Ireland).

Get kissed at the top of the Eiffel Tower.

(Damn, there he is back in my head again. Mr Dazzling Dick.)

Go in a Hot Air Balloon.

Have a McDonalds for three meals in one day.

Drink a bottle of the most expensive champagne.

Swim with Dolphins (okay this one is cliché and I can probably let it go, but now I can't cross it out because it will look like I've done it. **NOTE TO SELF – DON'T WORRY ABOUT THIS ONE.**

And that's it. That's all I have.

Throwing the diary on the floor, I roll over on the sofa and pull the throw resting along the back over me. Barney opens an eye. He loves the blanket a little too much.

Reaching for my phone I fire off a text.

Me: Sorry, Rebecca, not feeling good. Going to take the day off sick.

The dancing dots beneath my message flicker to life.

Rebecca: Okay, darling. See you tomorrow?

I can't even face a response, so I send a thumbs up and then drop my phone to the floor.

Then I pull the duvet back up over my head and wait.

What I'm waiting for I don't want to contemplate.

"Don't you make me kick down this door!"

I sit up, trying to work out where the fuck I am.

Ah. Lounge.

Hammering lands against the front door.

"I mean it, Jules. I've battled the whole way down here with a buggy. Do you know what the Tube is like with a buggy? Hell, I tell you." The letterbox jangles. "Hell," Liv shouts through.

Trying to focus, I can't believe I've fallen asleep after only being awake for the sum total of half an hour. I stand up on unsteady legs and stagger for the front door.

"Use your key," I shout back.

"I tried; you've got the damn chain on."

She's right, I do. And who can blame me.

"Liv," I sigh and open the door. "What are you doing here?"

She's swinging Lenny in a car seat that unclips from the buggy base, and unwittingly bashes him into the door frame. "I called the office to see if you wanted lunch and they said you weren't there. That you're sick." She assesses me with a laser beam top-to-toe body sweep. "What's wrong? Have you taken your medication?

"Why didn't you call me?" *Ah, shit. Medication...*

"I did. About a hundred times. Seriously, Jules, you can't be playing Dodge the Call anymore. Not now." She pushes into the flat, plonking the car seat in the middle of the room like a roundabout. I can see her flicking her sweeping gaze over the plain walls, piles of books, old newspaper prints and... last Thursday's pizza. I block her view of that before she launches into a spiel about mould spores.

"What? So now I'm officially dying, and no longer

possibly dying, I have to answer every call that comes to my phone?"

She bites on her lower lip and my shoulders slump.

"Sorry. I was just tired, and..."

"You couldn't face it." She focuses on my face and not the dismal clutter bomb explosion of my small and perfectly messy home.

I nod.

"Does Rebecca know?"

"No! I don't even know what I'm supposed to do." My fingers tingle again, my breath coming a little faster.

Liv glances at Lenny on the floor. He's asleep, blue dummy dangling from his puckered lips. "What do we always do?"

I breathe in, stretching my chest cavity, focusing on the air coming in and the air flowing out. "We take one step at a time."

Liv smiles and shakes her blonde hair over her shoulder. "Exactly. And how many steps is it to your kettle? I wasn't joking about the Tube, it was hell. Now make me a brew and then get ready. We might as well go for lunch now I've found you."

"Lunch where?" I turn, brightening at the prospect. Maybe today could be my three McDonalds in a row day.

"We'll go to Charlie's of course."

I groan and slope towards the kitchen. Fuckety fuck fuck. More wheatgrass and some hay smoked tofu for my sins.

I should have drunk more of that French red. Much more.

8

NOTTING HILL HEALTH FOODS

"What is it?" I stare at the shot glass, peering at the murky liquid. It looks like pond water, I'm not going to lie.

Charlie perches her hip on the edge of our table. "It's turmeric and spirulina."

"Oh, well that doesn't sound too bad."

"Just all the healthy stuff." She gives me a sympathetic smile. The same one I've been seeing for two years now and then she leans over to squeeze my shoulder. "We are all here for you, Jules."

"Thanks." But what I mean is, thanks that's lovely, but I kinda need you to be here for Liv more.

"Enjoy your lunch, ladies." She edges her way off the table and goes back to behind the bar where she starts assaulting the coffee machine, clanging on levers and muttering darkly under her breath. In her standard white t-shirt, black apron and black trousers she's wearing the only outfit I've seen her in for the last two years since she sunk all her inheritance money into a health food restaurant in Notting Hill.

"She okay?" I nod my head in her direction and Liv

shoots me the universal eyeroll and tight-lipped *shut the fuck up and I'll tell you later*.

I glance back over at Charlie. "You guys have been friends such a long time now, it's crazy."

Liv shrugs. "Yeah. I don't know what I'd do without them all, or you. The last year would have been truly awful if you hadn't all pulled me through."

Her face falls, her eyes watering a little, glistening under the retro lights swinging from the ceiling of Charlie's restaurant.

I give her a small smile and then sip back some of my health shot. "Oh, holy crap, that's awful." I mumble around the liquid pooling in my mouth.

"Shhh, don't say it too loud." Liv waves her hand at me, but she's not the one with a mouth full of… actually I think it is pond water.

I widen my eyes at her. I. Am. Not. Swallowing.

She glares at me. The longer I hold it in my mouth, the more I think it's burning away my gums and possibly the enamel on my teeth. You could use this stuff to unblock sinks.

Ugh sinks. I'm going to puke.

I shake my head.

She nods.

I shake my head again just as Charlie looks over to our table. "Food won't be long." Her gaze drops to the glass. "How is it, Jules? It's delicious, isn't it? I have it every morning for breakfast. Great for your heart and circulation, and all sorts of inflammatory conditions."

I thumbs up while Liv widens her eyes even further until she's doing her best mascaraed Bambi impersonation.

Fuck's sake.

I swallow, trying hard not to gag as the liquid slips down.

I should have gone to work. Telling Rebecca that I was going to be leaving one way or another would be better than this.

Lenny who up until now has been sitting quietly in a highchair giving the kiss of life to a breadstick decides it's time to have in on the action and throws the soggy snack onto the centre of the table next along.

"Gosh, I am so sorry." Liv jumps up with a napkin and swipes up the sloppy mess. The two women, large white wines and power suits, both offer her tight-lipped smiles and I hate them for the way they see her. That she's just a mum who can't control her kid.

Up until nearly four years ago she looked just like them. Before Dickweed Darren put a spanner in the works by starting a family with her he 'wasn't entirely sure about'. Damn, I hate that bastard.

With red cheeks, she sits back down and tucks her silky hair behind her ear. I pass Lenny another breadstick. "Go at it."

He drools a smile and then presses the overbaked bread against his gums.

Checking where Charlie is, I quickly pour the rest of the health shot into the pot plant next to my chair. Thank God, Charlie is all about the green. Her restaurant resembles more of a greenhouse, but she assures anyone that comments that the added oxygen in the air makes for a relaxing experience.

I suppose if my breathing gets any worse, I can always come and hang out here every day.

Thrusting the thought to the back of my head, I refocus on Liv. "How's the rest of the guys?"

She smiles. "Fine, you know, busy. Actually, we are going out next week. Well, I say out, coming here for a catch up. Why don't you come?"

I suck my teeth. "Liv, they are your friends."

"*Our* friends." She's being kind. She wants to share, like all good sisters do. "They love you; you know that."

"That's wonderful, but you know, I don't think I'm really in a place to socialise right now. Hell, I couldn't even get to work."

Liv straightens up, her graceful body strengthening. "So, what you going to do, just sit at home and wait for the worst to happen?"

"No," I pout back, "I've started a bucket list."

"A bucket list? Why?" She straightens her knife and fork, considers the remaining folded napkin before doing the same to that too. "You aren't going anywhere."

"Liv. That's not actually a helpful attitude right now."

"And hiding in a small poky apartment with a smelly cat is?"

"What exactly else should I be doing?"

Here it comes... the R word.

"Research. You need to be prepared for when the transplant team call, have a list of questions ready. You need to speak to Dr Francis. Didn't he want to talk about your medication."

I open my mouth to stop her, but she holds her hand up.

"There's other stuff too. You need to look into sick pay. Will you still get paid when you have bad days?"

This makes me snort. "I'm lucky to get paid as it is. I think sick pay is taking the piss."

"Ah, but you still have to live, still have to pay your mortgage."

"Rent," I correct.

"Same thing."

It's really not, but I don't bother correcting her. When I'm no longer here, the flat currently my home will be rented by someone else. It's not like there is an estate to finalise.

"Also, did Dr Francis give you any idea on how long you will be functioning like this, when things might change?"

I grasp her hand and squeeze tight. "Liv, stop. This is just the first day. We don't need to have everything spread-sheeted, calendared, and organised right this moment."

She doesn't look convinced. In fact, she looks like she wants to get her laptop out to start crunching numbers.

"So anyway, tell me about your girls' night." I swiftly change the subject before she can get her phone out and start the 'regime'. "What's the occasion for the Notting Hill Sisterhood?"

"Rachel is having future mother-in-law issues. We decided she needed wine."

I cock an eyebrow while my stomach rumbles and I eye Lenny's breadstick with the rabid zeal of a starved wolf.

"Ooh, sounds fun." I stare her dead in the eye. "Sign me up."

Charlie swings back with two big bowls of salad, more garden feature than actual food. "You coming next week, Jules?"

Liv smirks and spears at her salad, peering into the dense forest with the tip of her fork.

"I'll see," I nod vaguely, "I'm not sure when I'm going to hear from the hospital." This will be my excuse from now on. I'll officially never have to socialise again. Yay for me.

Charlie pulls a seat from the empty table the other side of ours and plonks down. With only two tables occupied to keep her busy I guess she needs a break. I look around the restaurant. Come to think of it, I've never seen it with more than two tables full.

Ah. I see now the unspoken messages Liv was trying to tell me earlier.

"You okay?" I ask Charlie. The Notting Hill gang might be Liv's friends, but that doesn't mean I don't care. As reluctant an adoptee I might be, they've looked after me the last couple of years since I got sick.

Got sick.

I probably needed to rephrase that now. *Got sick* kind of implies that there will be a recovery.

"Oh, you know. I'm thinking of doing a special wine night or something, try to pull in some new faces." She nods, plastering a smile.

"Wine and cheese?"

Liv arches an eyebrow. "Cheese? Are we in the seventies? Do you want pineapple on sticks too?"

Jesus, I've got cheese Tourette's. Next, I'll be suggesting a French-themed night in a vegan health kitchen.

"Sorry, I kind of forget the vegan thing." I spear a hedgerow of salad and shove it in my mouth before I can say anything else or get asked anything else.

Charlie smirks, her dark eyes dancing. "So how was your Friday night, Jules?"

"Fine. How was yours?"

"Depressingly quiet." A grin starts to stretch across her face. "Bet yours wasn't."

Liv throws her head back laughing.

"You bitch, I told you that in confidence." I glare at her.

My cheeks burn while Liv claps her hands together making Lenny squeal. "I'm just so excited you weren't at home reading a book."

"You told Charlie?" I glare at her then swiftly turn to Charlie. "No offense, Charlie."

"None taken."

Liv is biting on her lip, pretending to wipe Lenny's soggy, crumb-covered face.

"Exactly who else have you told?"

Her face says it all.

"Great!" I put my fork down. "Liv, that's not cool."

"It is. Sooooo cool. My boring big sister got seduced by a sexy Frenchman... be grateful I haven't taken out an ad in The Times."

I scowl, my forehead aching with the ferocity of it. 'I don't think The Times allow adverts for that kind of thing."

Charlie leans in, across the table. "So, tell me, is it as hot as it sounds?"

"Stop it guys, I already feel dirty enough." This is a blatant lie. I don't feel dirty at all. I feel hot as hell every time I so much as allow myself to think back to Friday, "and I'm never going to see him again. It was one night. I don't even know where he comes from, his name, or anything."

This much is the truth.

Well, I know he's from Perpignan in the Pyrenees, but I've looked on the map and it's a bloody large town to search for a one-night stand in.

Not that I would search for him.

Of course not, that would be silly.

That would make it a Not a One Night Stand.

Okay, stop thinking about him now.

No... now...

Liv and Charlie are staring at me grinning, so I flip them both a double zap sign.

Right, salad.

My phone rings and my gaze automatically locks on

Liv's. I grab my bag off the floor and fish my phone out. Unknown number.

"Hello?"

"Miss Brown?"

"Yes?"

"This is Dr Simmonds' secretary from Queensborough Hospitals."

My heart races. Good racing, not bad. "Hi."

"I'm just calling to arrange an appointment. How are you feeling?"

I'm taken aback, eyes stinging.

Then it hits home. For the first time I actually get it.

Doctor's secretaries are never nice. Living on a power trip, their professionalism is almost cutting. She's just asked how I am.

Which means I'm actually really bad.

9

REALITY WEARS DARK CLOUDS

"Darling, I've been so worried." Rebecca ushers me into her office like she's the queen inviting me into her palace.

"Sorry."

"Sit, sit." She motions me down and then pulls her own chair around. Her heels are six inches high and as slender as a matchstick.

Rebecca taught me all about heels seven years ago when I arrived straight from university, optimism painted like a fresh coat of paint on my future. I'd worn ballet flats which she'd looked at with such abhorrence I might as well have turned up in carpet slippers. *Darling, heels are your power tool. Your mind might be brilliant, your ambition might be endless, but heels stop everyone in their tracks and give you the chance to speak.*

Clearly, I'd tried to explain feminism to her and I'd held off on the heels for the first week. Then I realised that as the only woman on the team my lack of dick shaped appendage and sporting knowledge wasn't going to get me anywhere.

So, I went and bought a pair of heels that made my eyes water when I wore them.

The office shut the fuck up the next day.

So maybe I won't get my feminist badge after all, but do you know what? Whatever works. A woman can't fight everything.

Rebecca has that look on her face. It's her calm, concerned, *tell me everything* look.

I slump down lower in the leather seat, skirt sliding. "Don't look at me like that."

She nods, head tilted, lips pressed straight. "What look?"

"That one!" I point at her face. "You want me to spill my guts."

"Spill your guts? Julianna, you're so vulgar sometimes. You can't spill your guts in here, you'd ruin my Persian rug."

I grimace at her and she licks the top of her cherry-red mouth.

In her mid-fifties, Rebecca Livingstone is simply the most put together woman to walk on earth. She arrived once in the middle of a rainstorm and stepped into the office without a single hair out of place, not one drop of water on her coat. I'd asked her how she'd done it. My own hair looked like I'd got out of the shower and I'd already been in the office an hour before her. She looked at me, directly in the eye and said, "Darling, I made them keep the car running out front until the rain stopped."

It wouldn't have crossed her mind that a car idling for an hour on a busy London, already congested, street would have burned another little hole in the ozone.

She's not inherently evil, just... well... from a planet where they don't worry about the ozone and drive around in cars with drivers at their beck and call.

Rebecca Livingstone is the last in a long line of Livingstone's on Fleet Street. The family made their money with the railways during the Industrial Revolution. A picture of Great Great Great Great-however-many Livingstone hangs in the dusty boardroom. He's got a handlebar moustache and looks like he may have had pervert tendencies. I try to keep my back to him at all times just in case he's looking at my tits.

His son, Rupert Livingstone, was what they would have called a 'cad'. He cared nothing for the business of trains and industry. He wanted to influence people, ride the shit out of those in charge, and mock his peers. So, he did, pouring all his money into where I now sat.

Satire Weekly. Yep. What he lacked in imagination and brain he made up with in hard cash.

Satire Weekly.

It was literally titled what it was.

It's enough to make you cringe when asked what you do and where you work, hence my by now well practised 'A satirical newspaper' because that's what it is folks.

Not that any of that matters.

Days are numbered, and not just mine.

"Do you mind if we just leave it?" I try to smile at Rebecca. Despite her lack of concern for the environment, she's looked after me well, especially the last couple of years.

She eyes me. "We can, for now."

I sigh deeply. "Thank you. How were things on Friday afternoon?"

She flashes me small and even white teeth beneath cherry lips. "Well, the building is still standing. Alan and Reece didn't punch each other during the final print release, and we started the print run at three this morning as we do every week." She clicks her tongue against the roof of her mouth. "Proving that we can manage without you, so you should probably take that long overdue holiday I've been suggesting." I wave my hand at her, but she carries on. "For two years."

"I don't need a holiday." I smile brightly, ignoring the fact stamped on the back of my brain that I'd soon be on a permanent vacation to the other side.

"Everyone needs a holiday. Sunshine, cocktails, sex." Her smile turns sly. I think she might be describing her own weekend.

Then I remember mine and a faint heat warms my face.

"I've got to go back to see Dr Francis one afternoon. Is that okay?"

She pounces like a cat on a mouse. "So soon? But you only go every six months."

I nod, face free of any thoughts I have locked away, any truth that might want to print on my skin. "Yes, but he needs to talk about my medication, and it took longer than my allocated appointment time last week."

"Darling, Julia, I don't care how many times you need to go to the hospital. You could go every day if you needed to. I just want to know you are okay. I couldn't cope without you, you know that. How would I deal with all those men?" She says men like it's a dirty word. Which to her, these guys probably are.

Satire Weekly is staffed by a motley crew and let there be no denying it.

Shame we are going to fold soon, because sadly while the world has moved on, Satire Weekly is still firmly languishing in the Industrial age.

"It's just as well I'm not going anywhere," I lie barefaced.

"Good, good. Now, I've got lunch today, darling, with that investor." Her eyes glint and I try not to scrunch my face. Rebecca knows a lot of old money. They have different ways of discussing things than the rest of us. "I probably won't be back. Can you make sure the building is secure?"

My face falls. I can see it in the reflection of the window.

"Don't worry, darling, I'll make sure they all know they have to leave on time tonight."

I offer a tight smile. "Sure, not a problem at all. I don't have anything else to do anyway."

She stands up, pushing her chair back to the other side of her ornate desk. "I thought so. I'll bring coffees and pastries tomorrow as a treat."

Getting up, I smooth down my shirt over my trousers, noticing Rebecca flick a glance at my lack of skirt. She shakes her head but doesn't say anything.

"Anything else? I'm going to go and check the print room?"

"No, no, that's all."

My hand is on the door as she calls me back. "Darling, better check the print run. I'm not sure if I might have made a teeny bit of a whoopsie on Friday."

A deep and painful groan lodges itself in my throat. "Sure."

Without another word, I launch from her door, heading straight through the office half-filled with the editorial team, to the stairs to the underbelly of the building.

"Jules, where you going?" Flynn, one of the ad managers, calls after me.

"She's fucked up the print run again," I shout back over my shoulder, not stopping to see if he's heard me or not.

. . .

Two hours later I trudge back up the stairs, using a wet wipe to rub dust from my hands. We are the only newspaper to still have our print room on the premises—which I think says it all about the number of copies we sell.

Today though we'd be two thousand copies short of what we should have been, because someone, and I'm not casting blame here, but someone—*Rebecca*—managed to delete a cell in my spreadsheet which means our American copies haven't printed.

Not a car crash in itself, but the plates have already been changed. One way we make money is to loan out our printing capacity to other small prints.

So, Satire Weekly was palleted and shrink wrapped by the time I got down there, while Chicken Monthly was whizzing through the printer.

I fall into my chair.

"How bad?" Flynn flicks a rubber band at me.

"Just two thousand short thereabouts."

He winces.

"Question is, will any of our readers in America even notice if their copies don't turn up?"

"Probably not," Flynn snorts. "Bigger problem is will our advertisers?"

I rub at my forehead. At least I hadn't thought of dying for two hours. Plus points and all that.

A cold cup of coffee is sat in front of my computer. "Thanks for the coffee."

Desk partners sat opposite one another, we've created our own little hot drink gang. Doing a drink run for the whole team took far too long, so about three years ago when he started we set ourselves apart on an island of Nescafe.

"You're welcome two hours ago."

"I'm away this Friday too. How the hell do I get her not to press anything while I'm not in the office?"

"Another Friday? I'm beginning to think you are going away for dirty weekends." He wiggles his fair eyebrows at me. "Are you? Should I be jealous of someone who isn't your cat?"

I stick my tongue out. "Leave Barney out of this."

"What? I'm being serious here. I should know if I've got to share you with anyone else other than your feline housemate."

"You," I wag my finger at him. "Aren't sharing me with anyone."

The loud but undeniable sound of someone breaking wind across the office halts our conversation.

"I hate this place," I mutter under my breath.

Flynn grins and it's so damn smug. "You don't. You love us all, otherwise you would have left years ago when Glamour magazine tried to headhunt you."

"Believe me, I'm still ruing the day."

"Remind me again why you didn't take it?"

I lob a ball of Blu Tac at him. It will be back on my side of the desk later in a never-ending game of catch we've been playing. He doesn't know why I didn't take the job. No one does apart from Rebecca.

She did me a solid back then and I will be loyal to her until my dying day.

So not long then.

Unless we fold before then.

Right as I think it, I have the blinding idea. I'm going to make it my dying wish to get this damn place online. Leave them with a legacy that will live on.

Ignoring Flynn and his achingly punchable face, I boot my laptop and pull it closer.

Right. How am I going to do this?

First things first though, I'd better do something about this American disaster.

"Juliette? Anyone know a Juliette?" Ray is shouting through the office. It's dark outside, half-five and I really want to go home.

Rebecca lied when she said everyone would leave on time.

Lied.

Instead, they are sitting around chatting about the Premier League and every time I happen to give them a glare, they all put their heads down and start working again.

"No women here, mate," heckles Alan. "Oh sorry, Jules, I'd forgotten you were a girl, what with the trousers you've got on. Did you get them from a special uniform outfitter?"

"Fuck off, Al, shame you can't make your column as funny."

His smile drops and I smirk.

All of these guys are too long in the tooth. Relics from a previous life when sexist jokes weren't just politically correct but actively encouraged. Probably part of the hiring process even: *Give us your best one liner... there were two blondes and a lightbulb.*

Flynn and I are the youngest blood, and I'm nearly thirty for God's sake.

"So, no Juliette?"

Is Ray taking the piss? It's only been the six of us for years now.

Oh. Wait. Wasn't I Juliette on Friday...?

No. It can't be.

My legs knock under my desk despite me sitting down. Flashes of long fingers and warm skin heating my face.

"Where did it come from?" I ask, getting up, unsteady and trying not to show it.

Ray peers at the label. "Hell, if I know."

"Not where it actually came from, you bloody idiot. Do you have X-ray vision? I mean who delivered it?"

Was he beautiful with midnight eyes and talking eyebrows?

"Dunno, courier on a bike."

Before he can resist, I snatch it from his grasp. "I'll make sure it gets sent back to wherever it came from." The label really does only say Juliette. No surname.

Ray snatches it back. "No problem. I'll just bin it."

I watch in horror as he tosses it in the trash bin under his desk.

"Right. That's today done, everyone home!" I shut my laptop without closing it down properly—I'll pay for that tomorrow—and pick up my purple coat off the back of my chair. "Come on, guys, I want to get out of here."

I'm met with a load of groans and general unwillingness but eventually I herd them all out of the office.

Once we are outside and I've waved Flynn off from offering to wait and walk with me to the Tube, I dash back inside.

The dark building is scary as shit at night, but I run straight for Ray's desk and grab out the small brown-paper wrapped package.

Call me crazy but I'm sure I'm Juliette and I'm sure this package is for me.

A pull in my gut is telling me so.

I slip back out into the January dark, contraband tucked under my arm.

Only when I'm home, kettle shooting smoke signals into the sky do I open it up.

It *is* for me.

My mystery-one-night-only-no-names-man remembered the one thing I told him about myself. I work for a satirical newspaper on Fleet Street.

The only satirical newspaper on Fleet Street.

Inside is a beautiful hardbound copy of Romeo and Juliet. No note.

It makes me grin, heat flooding over me.

Carefully putting it on the side away from the kettle, I go and grab my diary and add to my list of yearly goals.

Read Romeo and Juliet instead of pretending I have.

10

B NEGATIVE

"Dr Simmonds won't be long," the secretary behind the wall length counter says. "The nurse will be with you in a moment to do your checks."

Liv squeezes my hand tight, and I clutch it back while I try to look around the waiting room at the other patients. Are we all waiting for hearts? All of us cooling our heels in a waiting game.

And it is a waiting game.

So far, for me, nothing has changed. Every morning I wake up feeling roughly the same, the more convinced I've become that they've made a mistake.

It happens.

"How you feeling?" Liv whispers.

"Fine." I look at an older man, probably mid-fifties. His wife is holding his hand. Every so often he pats it absent-mindedly. I wonder if he's been waiting long, or if this is his first time here too. His wife rests her head on his shoulder and wraps her arms around him like she's worried he might disappear.

"Julianna?" I turn at the call of my name to where a nurse with peroxide hair and a wide smile is holding my file.

"Hi."

"Want me to come with you?" Liv asks.

"So you can see how much I weigh? Not a chance." I grin down at her, hiding the pound of my heart behind my smile.

"I already know how much you weigh."

I pull a face and turn for the nurse. "Hi." My voice wobbles, uneven.

"Don't worry, this is just standard stuff."

I nod, not clear on what standard stuff is. I follow behind her into a room where she closes the door. "Simple checks, Julianna."

"Jules, please. It's a mouthful otherwise."

She smiles and motions for me to sit, logging into her computer. Why do they have paper files and computer files? That seems a waste of time and resources to me. Glancing quickly at the screen, she opens the file and then hammers her pen open with a resounding click.

"Bloods first. I can get them sent off and the results should be back before you leave."

"What are the tests for?"

"Just checking inflammation levels, iron, general things like white blood cells etc."

I nod. "I'm B negative." I tell her, mainly just to show that I do know something, anything.

Her face flickers but she keeps on the smile. "That's always good to know. You'd be amazed the people who don't know their blood type."

"I didn't, I have to admit."

"So quick blood test, ECG, then we will put you on a

running machine to check your oxygen use during physical activity. Swiftly followed by an MRI."

"MRI," my mouth falls open. "Today?" Then I focus on what else she's said. "Running machine?"

She laughs and shakes her head. "Don't worry, you don't actually have to run, just walk."

I glance down at my shoes and she follows my gaze. "We really should tell people to wear trainers."

My heels are black today, a statement piece.

"I can take them off." I frown at the fifteen denier tights I've got on. They have to so much as be in the same vicinity as a rough surface and they run with an instant ladder. I'm spending more on tights the last month than I am dinner. "This is going to take a while, isn't it?"

"Sure is. I hope you brought snacks."

"My sister needs to collect my niece from nursery at two thirty."

The nurse tilts her head from side to side. "It could be done that quick, but honestly I doubt it."

"Why is everything done today?"

Her smile stretches, commiserating and sympathetic. "If you're a straightforward case, you should know today whether you go on the list or not."

"Really? Today?"

"We do try to. It's nice for people to leave with a positive outcome." Her gaze drops to my notes again and that little flicker sets her lips straight at the edges. "Right, come on then. Let's get going and get you on the scales."

"Do we have to start with the scales?"

She chuckles and shakes her head. "That's what everyone says."

• • •

Back out in the waiting room, I flop down next to Liv. "We are going to be here hours. You need to go and get Paige."

She scowls at her phone in one of her hands while the other rocks Lenny's buggy back and forth over the shiny floor. "I'm trying to get hold of Darren."

"I don't want you asking him for help, just because of me." I fold my arms, the bit of sticky tape in the crease of my elbow pulling on the fine hairs. "I've got to have an MRI yet." I swallow hard. "Apparently they do everything in one day and then tell you if you're eligible or not."

"He's her dad. He's supposed to help with things. I'm not leaving you."

"Do you know how long an MRI takes? Forever."

"I know. I was with you last time you had one." She shoots me a *shut the fuck up* glance, but I'm not going to be put off.

"I'm a big girl."

"I'm your sister."

"Exactly. And you'll still be my sister later when I get to your house and you pour me a nice glass of wine."

Liv shakes her head. "Nope."

"Yes."

"Nope."

"Miss Brown." We both look up at the towering Roman God standing before us in a doctor's coat, stethoscope hanging around his neck.

We both inhale a collective breath. I'm thinking more Men's Health Magazine cover model than heart transplant surgeon, but either works for me.

Yep. Either.

I glance at Liv who I think has something in her eye

she's blinking so fast. "Miss Brown?" he asks again, looking between us.

"Yes," we both answer at once and he grins wide. More blinking from Liv.

"Which one?"

"Sisters." I point between us. "But me."

He comes closer and crouches down in front of us. Jesus, Doc, we aren't five.

"I heard you had to rush off to get your child from nursery. I thought I could do," he looks at me... just about noticing my existence. *Hello! I'm the one who needs a heart!* "Your sister's appointment in reverse."

"That is so kind." Liv's hand flutters to a blotch of flushed skin at the base of her throat. "But doesn't she need to have all her tests?"

Dr Dreamy straightens from his crouch. "Come with me."

We both stand to follow, like sister like sister, neither of us looking at anyone else in the waiting room.

He motions us into a bright room, warm sunlight slanting through blinds. "Please sit."

Two arses hit plastic chairs.

"Please don't worry. We run a very fluid clinic. As I'm sure you can imagine we get a lot of people in various states of health. Some of them we see on wards, those that are too ill to make it to consultation." He smiles, gaze darting at Liv. "But you, Julianna, are lucky that you haven't got that far yet."

Lucky?

He peers at my file, flicking through the pages. "I spoke to Dr Francis last week on the phone. Can you give me a quick rundown?"

Ah, the please tell me in your own words just how shit it's all been.

"I had meningitis two years ago." I shrug. "The heart problems started quite soon after. I had trouble feeling like I was getting enough air. The doctors who treated my infection were stumped so I eventually got sent to the heart team. There they found out the meningitis had caused..." I try to say the word, almost feeling Liv roll her eyes next to me.

"Cardiomyopathy?" Dr Francis suggests.

"Yes, that. You'd have thought I'd have got something I could actually say." I smile rubbing at my hot neck.

"And your symptoms now?" He flicks to another page. "How have you been the last couple of weeks?"

"Fine, all good."

Liv elbows me and his smile flickers in her direction. He's a beauty to look at, blonde and blue-eyed, and I know Liv will be coming to every appointment from now on if he's the one sitting in the doctor's chair.

She giggles.

I'm dying here. Now is not the time for flirty giggles.

"Sorry." She pulls the neck of her jumper away from her throat, that flush burning up her skin, "She lies. She will tell you she's fine when she really isn't at all."

I elbow her back. "Cheers, sis."

Dr Simmonds chuckles. "It's okay. Our tests find most things, even little white lies."

I scrunch my face. "Okay, so the breathlessness is getting a little worse, nothing I can't handle though. The irregular heartbeat is more frequent too."

He nods.

"But really I don't feel too bad. I think Dr Francis made a terrible mistake with my diagnosis."

His smile drops. Ah, it's time for the sympathetic look.

"He didn't, Julianna, but..." He flicks through my file again, scribbling something with the nib of his fountain pen. Liv clutches my hand sensing this is the moment. "If your tests come back positive, which I think they will, it doesn't sound like your further organ damage has spread too far. Although we will be looking at your lungs, there is no reason why you can't go on the list. I'll confirm later on." He smiles widely at Liv. "But you can go on the school run now knowing the news looks positive."

We both sag, relief rushing through my veins, making me feel lightheaded, in a good helium sucking way.

"However." My stomach lurches. No... no however, no caveats, no if's... "Julianna, you have one of the least common blood types. Not rare that it doesn't happen, but rare that your wait might be longer."

"How long?" My question is a breathy little gasp.

The answering shrug is not what I want to see. "We really don't know."

"Dr Francis said I only had a year left." And there's that sentence again that sounds so ridiculous to say.

"Then it will be your job to keep yourself in optimum of health. Our job is to get you that heart as quickly as possible if and when one becomes available." I don't like the IF word. It should be banned from the dictionary.

"That's good news right, Jules?" Liv turns and grasps my hand, a light shining in her eyes I don't want to put out.

"Yeah, that's good news." I swallow hard. "Right, can you go and get my niece, and I'll see you later."

"You sure?" Another squeeze of my fingers.

I nod. My throat too tight to talk.

. . .

It's almost dark by the time I'm ejected from the hospital. I've been prodded, scanned, and made to runthe nurse lied.

Good news. All my organs are doing what they are meant to do.

Bad news, I got the distinct impression they didn't plan to see me again anytime soon. Still, it's okay. I've only done one of my remaining twelve months. There is still time.

Time.

I trudge through Waterloo under the big clock, feeling it echo in my bones. Tick and a tock. Tick and a tock.

Most women my age are starting to think of their biological clock, maybe hearing it start to speed slightly. The only clock I can hear is the mechanical one inside my chest, winding and cranking.

Stupid fucking heart.

"Juliette!"

I keep walking, head down. I need to get home. Need to put my pyjamas on. Need to Netflix.

Denial comes in the form of compulsive binge watching.

Dawson has been up the Creek without a paddle; The Queen has held onto her Crown; all the Vampires are dead, well the ones I like anyway; and I've jumped off the Bridge of Ton.

"Juliette!"

A pressure pulls on my sleeve and I whirl around ready to sock the person daring to touch me. It might be busy in the station but there is no accounting for weirdo's these days.

Ooooh.

I stare straight up into deep navy. Wide and sensual lips curve down at me as my mouth gapes open.

"Juliette!" It's him. Mr-One-Night-No-Names. Mr All the Feels.

Oh, good God. *It's him.* Stealer of dreams and Pornoland's lead star.

"You ran away." *Zhuuu raaaan awaaay.* That's his opening line? Did I do him a favour or is that displeasure in the turn of his mouth?

My heart races, a little flutter that doesn't feel all that bad. My stomach tightens as memories of moonlit skin on skin play front of house in my brain. "I'm sorry."

He has a firm grip on my elbow, a hold he seems unwilling to break. And that's fine with me because his touch is damn electric and he's only holding my arm.

He steps up close, uncaring of the people weaving around us and my breath snatches in my throat, puffing out as a little gust of air. "You left without saying goodbye."

I stare up at him, eyes roving over the face that's a perfect landscape of smooth, olive skin and dark, expressive eyebrows. I want to charter the land for my own.

Shaking my head, I try to lose my random thoughts.

Keep it together, Jules, we've fallen down this rabbit hole before.

"Ma petite Juliette, I have thought of you often."

Wheeeee, down the rabbit hole I go.

"You have?"

"Oui, of course." He rubs at his jaw. "Too often, I think." His smile is rueful and utterly time stopping. Not heart stopping, but time itself.

He's thought of me too? B-list Porno or Pornhub?

In no hurry to go anywhere, his broad back acts like a boulder parting the sea of evening commuters. His lips curve into a cheeky grin that gives birth to a dimple I didn't know existed.

Leaning down to my ear, he brushes his lips against my earlobe. Right here in the middle of Waterloo train station—the man has no boundaries at all. I shiver, remembering all too well his lack of boundaries and where that leads. "I thought I might have done something wrong," his finger trails my cheek, "but I see your blush and know that cannot be the case."

Ooh, this guy is smooth. So smooth.

"Well…" I try to think of a suitable answer for why I ran away from him, stealing into the dawn like a thief, but I can't. He chuckles and it echoes straight through me, lancing my core, making Pornoland all the more desirable. I need a season pass, make no mistake.

"Do you have plans?"

I look up at his question.

"No,' I blurt, but then pull myself together. "But I can't be doing." I point between us. "Again."

He laughs, throwing his head back. Angels weep. "I had in mind a drink."

My face begins to burn. "Drink makes sense." And yes, I do want a drink with him, Pornoland hasn't portrayed his face quite right. Today he has a slight stubble on his chin, there's a faint shadowing under his eyes.

"You look tired," I state. His gaze washes over me.

"And so do you."

Well, that's to the point, but then so was I, I guess. "You're in London again?"

I don't know why this fact gives me a little warm burst in the chest area. The man's beautiful, too beautiful, but he was also a one-night stand which doesn't hold any future. I don't hold any future.

The stark reality hollows me out like a scoop of ice cream falling from a spoon.

"So sad still, ma petite," he murmurs in my ear and I tremble down to my toes. Why does he turn up on days when the very worst has happened?

Maybe that's his thing. He's a distraction from the end of all things.

"What are you doing at Waterloo?"

"Heading home." He sighs and I sigh with him as he runs a hand through his hair. His suit, grey this time, is impeccably cut, as sharp as a knife edge. His overcoat black, a dark green scarf loosely hangs around his neck.

He looks like an investment banker, not the maker of cheese.

But then I suppose cheese is a French thing. Maybe they do it differently there.

"What are you thinking of?" His smile teases the edge of his mouth.

"Cheese."

He laughs, hands sliding down my arms and he leans in to kiss me once on one cheek before slowly kissing the other, minty breath gently brushing my face, cooling the tip of my nose. "I am so pleased to see you again. I didn't think I would."

"Me neither," I sigh, but in my heart, I don't know if this is the truth. I can't stop my smile. It's addictive, like a rainbow from behind rain clouds.

"Dinner?"

"Only dinner?" I confirm.

He shrugs. "If that's what you wish, ma petite Juliette."

11

MOONLIGHT

"Close your eyes."

I don't want to.

If I close my eyes then I won't be able to see his face, and I'm currently filling the spank bank.

My mystery man has removed his suit jacket, loosened his tie and rolled up his sleeves. His olive skin is illuminated by candlelight as he leans on his elbows and watches me with bright eyes from across the table.

I want to fuck him on the table. Let there be no mistake about that.

Sadly, we are in a little bistro and I think it would be frowned upon.

I'd suggested the Wetherspoon's pub in the station, to which he'd looked at me with such horror I'm surprised he didn't run for the Eurostar right there and then.

He sighs while I continue to stare at his face. "Sorry," I mutter and then dutifully close my eyes before swiftly cracking one back open to make sure he doesn't run away. He arches an eyebrow and I drop my shoulders and close my eyes properly, trying to relax into the moment.

"Now, wet your lips and lick them. Just a little taste."

I lift the wine glass hoping not to drop it across my lap, or totally miss my mouth. There's a low chuckle and then his warm hand cups mine, thumb brushing my knuckles. "Here." He guides the glass to my mouth. "No cheating."

I taste the wine on my lips, giving a little lick as prompted.

"Now take a longer sip and hold it in your mouth."

I do as he asks, my body feeling warm, intimate, despite the public setting.

"What can you taste?"

I think, not wanting to rush my answer and then swallow. "Tobacco, berries." I lick my lips. "Earth?" I open my eyes. *Earth...* Seriously, is that the best I can come up with?

He laughs, his eyes dancing.

"I amuse you." I sit up a little straighter.

"Only in all the very best ways."

"Thank you for the book." I dive off the highest springboard into the pool of awkward conversation, because I don't think I can sit here and pretend that we didn't do what we did. We did do it, in a very ground-breaking, earth-shattering way.

He grins, and I think I might be in love with that dimple. It's so cute in someone so suave and smooth. Ducking his head down, he loops his fingers around the stem of his wine glass. "You didn't give me a chance to say thank you. I felt unchivalrous."

"And you like to be chivalrous?" I arch an eyebrow.

"I try."

"With all your one-night stands?"

He smiles into his glass. "Now you are asking leading questions."

"And..."

"You were the one who said, 'No names."

"I did." Slut move 101. "Not my usual modus operandi."

That smile grows into a smirk. "And neither is it for I to be unchivalrous."

"With your one-night stands?" I go there again, just because it feels good. Our eyebrows match one another in a battle of the arc. "So, I'm Juliette?"

Her name sounds dangerous on the tip of my tongue.

"To me, yes." His smile falters into seriousness and my heart splutters with it.

"Who does that make you?"

He shrugs. "Juliette's Romeo?"

"They both die." It's meant to sound light-hearted, but it doesn't.

Another shrug.

We both sip our wine.

"What time is your train?"

He glances at his watch. "An hour ago."

"Oh." My mouth dries.

He shakes his head as if to say, *no big deal*. "So, Juliette, tell me about satirical newspapers."

My cheeks flush. "I can't believe you remembered that."

"I can't believe you're surprised." Ugh, this man. Everything he says rings like a poem.

"What else do you remember?"

His gaze burns down to the marrow in my bones. "Everything."

"Me too."

"So, tell me. Newspapers."

Roll me in those r's because they sound like heaven.

"Well, it's kinda boring."

He snorts. "Kinda boring. That's no way to live life."

Too late she cried.

"Well, it's not really what I thought I would be doing now."

"Non?"

"No." I shake myself into focus, ignoring the illicit pull of his Frenchness (is that a thing. I'm making it one if it isn't). "I left university thinking I was going to set the publishing world alight, that I would have this amazing career, would be written about in the broadsheets how I'd discovered all these breakout authors. 'The woman who finds the greatest writer of our time'." I air quote around my former dream.

"And you haven't?"

I shoot him a withering glance. "No, I work in a dingy office surrounded by disgusting dinosaur old men for a newspaper that no one wants to read anymore."

"So, change?" he gives his shrug.

"I can't."

"Why?"

"Because, Rebecca, my boss. She needs me." I stare into my wine, unwilling to meet his expressive stare. "She makes so many mistakes. Even last month she fiddled with one of my spreadsheets and managed to accidentally not print two thousand copies." Lifting my glass, I glug down more of the amazing red. Probably a bit too amazing judging how quickly I've been sinking it. "We can't afford to lose two thousand readers."

His fingers steeple together, reminding me of our first dinner, his thoughtful *I'm going to read you like a cheap and loose magazine* look.

"That's not all on you though, Juliette." Even though that's not my real name, I love it. I like being her, sitting and having sophisticated dinners with a sophisticated man.

"I've thought of you." Someone take the red away from me. Truth bubbles with the tang of fermented grapes. "A lot." I tuck my hair behind my ear, gaze down. "I was telling the truth you know. I'd never done anything like that before. But somehow, from that night you've put a smile on my face at a time when I wasn't sure that would happen again."

"But you still look sad." He reaches across the table and slips his fingers over mine and I shiver in my seat. "Look at me."

I do, meeting his dark-blue, incandescent stare. He doesn't speak and neither do I.

What am I doing?

How did this happen again?

"It seems like fate to me, ma petite." He rolls the words making them swim in my head with the wine. "The chances of two people meeting in two different places in one very large city, no?" He shrugs. "Fate? Maybe destiny."

I snort a giggle. "Destiny?"

He doesn't answer my schoolgirl giggle, merely watches me, making my mouth dry. "So, what happens now?" My gaze falls to his lips—stupid, treacherous gaze.

His smile expands, enigmatic. "I'd suggest a nightcap, but you made your rules very clear."

He's thrown that gauntlet down.

I feign innocence. "Oh, does nightcap mean something else in French?"

"I think nightcap is a bilingual expression of understanding, no?"

My heart thuds. Pulse beating in the base of my throat.

"And if I said I'd like a nightcap?"

Am I really doing this again? Am I crazy?

My pulse is shouting yes. Yes. Yes. Yes.

Maybe it is fate. Maybe this man is supposed to appear

like magic and make all the bad things evaporate with wine and happenstance.

He pulls his phone out of his pocket and holds it between us, balanced on the surface of his broad palm. "Your word, ma petite."

Go home... go home...

I meet his eyes.

"Yes."

He snatches his phone away, swiping the screen. "One thing." The eyebrow tells me this is important, and I nod, swallowing.

"Yes?"

"No running away."

"But that's not the rules."

"This time is my rules."

I swallow again, harder this time, expectation lighting through me like fireworks on the 5th of November. Light me up, Guy Fawkes, I'm on a slippery slope to Doomsday.

Question: What is a one-night stand called when it happens twice?

Answer: Fate.

He taps the screen and then puts his phone back down, his gaze landing on mine with expectation. "Ready, Juliette?"

Yes, Juliette is ready. I stand, pushing back my chair. I grab my coat and bag. Chuckling, he does the same, throwing down notes onto the table for a bill we haven't even asked for.

"Shouldn't we...?" I gesture at the table and the five twenties he's put down for wine and chips.

He grabs my elbow, tucking me into his side, holding me firm. "No time, ma petite, I've been thinking of this for a month." He leans closer to my ear, this unexpected Romeo. "Now I just need you."

And I need him. It courses through me, a river of desire I didn't know I was capable of. "How far to the hotel?"

We rush through the bistro's doors, blustering into February like the rest of January didn't happen. Like a month hasn't passed since we were last right here on the cusp of something unknown.

He turns me, tilting my chin with his forefinger and thumb, brushing my mouth with his, pressing firm, stealing little pockets of air from deep within me. "You taste like sunshine and berries. August heat and the moon at midnight, a cool blast of water from the lake at noon."

I pull back from his lingering kiss and whispered words.

"I taste like a lot." I blink up at him, hand pressed against his chest.

He drops his forehead to mine, inhaling deeply, "All my favourite things." One of his hands tucks hair behind my ear as his gaze drills into my secret places, my thoughts and feelings, the scared bits of me that don't know what anything is anymore. "How did I find them all here in this dismal place with grey skies and concrete and glass?"

"I don't know,' breathlessly, I pull him back in, slanting my mouth over his, my body scorching as I shift against him. "How far is the hotel?" I ask again.

Grinning against my mouth, he flicks his eyes open over my shoulder. "Fifty steps.' The grin becomes crooked. "And a Tube."

I snort, pulling him close. *He remembered.*

We end up back at the same boutique hotel as before, its black railings comforting and familiar.

Romeo explains to the staff that he's missed his train. There's lots of shrugging and good-humoured enthusiasm from the girl behind the reception desk. I hide behind his back in case I've got a neon sign stapled to my forehead that states One-Night Stand.

He grasps my handno drink, no firesidestraight for the lift where he pushes me back against the mirror, squeezing my thighs tight and making me moan. "Oh God," I groan into his mouth and he murmurs at the back of his throat.

"I don't know where you've come from, ma Juliette. He pelts kisses across my skin, teeth nipping my throat. "But mon dieu, I'm glad you're here."

With every plant of his kisses, the desolate days of January slowly unwind, painting them into bright splashes of colour, yellow instead of grey, pink instead of black.

He carries me to room one-hundred and three, opening the door easier this time. Practise makes perfect so they say. I know just what I want to practise. I want to become a master in the field of screwing him inside out.

"No running." He demands with a kiss.

"Not running."

"Breakfast is a condition of this." As if to prove the point, he places me on the floor, edging back, putting space between us that rushes like icy water.

"Breakfast." I grab him back. *Don't break the rules,* my kiss insists. *The rule is your mouth has to be on mine until one of us is about to pass out from lack of air.*

One of the better ways to pass out, I think.

Anchoring my elbows into the cups of his palms, he lifts me slightly so he can carry me, edge me back further into the bedroom. I let him lead, willing to see where he wants to take this, what he needs from me.

By a chair he turns us, sitting down and drawing me onto his lap, fingers dancing at the nape of my neck as he keeps my ravenous mouth on his. My skirt gathers around my thighs as I straddle his legs and I pull at his tie, sliding it down gently so I don't tighten the knot. I dot little kisses at the unbuttoned top of his shirt, planting kisses that grow into a heady kiss of tongues and clashing teeth. His hands run down my spine making me arch and straighten like a cat.

Damn, Barney.

I push him from my head. He can survive one night without an extra-large serving of Whiskas.

"Where have you gone?" Romeo pulls back, hand slipping through my hair, gaze intent.

A grin breaks on my face as I shake my head. "Sorry, was thinking my cat hasn't had dinner." I peck another kiss on his mouth.

"Your cat? You're thinking of your cat?"

"Sorry, it won't happen again."

His kiss tells me it won't happen again. His tongue demands complete focus and adherence. *I can do that*, I answer back, sweeping mine against his, diving deep into warm places.

"Is this crazy?" I ask, words just bubbling.

"What?" he asks my throat as I lean back.

"This. Us."

Lifting up, he meets my gaze and I warm into a molten pool of hot metal at the rawness in his gaze. "Only time can tell, ma petite."

His fingers reach for my black blouse, ending further conversation. He probably thinks I only have one outfit. It's not my fault Friday seems to be our day. Good news is I have on my best underwear. Strangely, the hospital visit, which was my reason for putting it on, seems far away. Like it could have happened in a different life.

Which I guess I wish it had.

I block the thought as he gently and painfully slowly undoes the buttons, cool fingers dipping inside the material. He leans in following his lips along the same path. Until he stops and pulls back.

"Juliette? What is this?" With the tip of his middle finger, he runs southward on the pink scar down the middle of my chest. Not old enough to be hidden in the moonlight, it stands out in stark relief. A crimson splash on alabaster.

"An accident." I lie, but it sits uneasily on my stomach. "It's nothing." His midnight gaze watches me. "Are you taking this blouse off today or tomorrow?" I tease, knowing I'm setting myself up for the most pleasurable form of torture.

I rush, he slows.

A delicious dance. A two-step between us, unique to the way he makes me feel.

"Are you rushing me?"

"No!" I bite down on the inside of my cheek, fighting my smile.

With his hand, he lifts my hair, brushing it over my shoulder, running it through his fingers as he straightens up and pushes us close together, his lips dancing at my ear. I drop my fingers to his shirt, unbuttoning one fastening after the other, smoothing my thumbs along the warm skin of his chest.

I need to be skin on skin. I arch myself while his dark eyes watch me curve, the articulation of my body begging for more.

He moves my blouse an inch and I growl in frustration, his answering chuckle vibrating against my neck.

With his shirt open, I rock back and unloop his leather belt, running it through the buckle and unhooking the fastening of his suit trousers.

Flashing the devil's grin, I slip from his lap and come to my knees on the floor, shining a smile up at his shadowed face. Moonlight floods the room, bathing the surfaces it touches in pewter. His fingertips brush the crown of my head and I lean up, unzipping his fly and easing his trousers and boxers down with a gentle pull of his hips.

His gaze is all hooded burning desire and power rushes through me, waking me up to the strength I have inside me. Dipping my head, I lick his length, savouring the smoothness of his skin. That ripple of power tickles down my spine as he sighs, slumping back a little, his long arm still stretched towards me, heavy hand on my shoulder.

"Juliette," he sighs, "You have the most exquisite mouth."

To prove I do, I slip him in, hollowing my cheeks and flattening my tongue to encase around him. His thumb brushes my cheek and I look up to find him watching, lips parting as I lower my gaze to suck him back in again.

The power is all mine. I've never been one for oral, but that might have been because it's never made me feel like this before, like I'm queen of the world and he's going to fall at my feet on the whim of my lips and mouth.

I quicken, taking him deeper, flicking with my tongue, pulling a little harder until I'm roughly pulled up and away, his hands under my armpits.

"You're an enchantress. I can't stop thinking about you, remembering the way it felt inside of you." He yanks at my blouse and I squeeze my eyes shut in case a button pings off and blinds me for life.

Thank God for good underwear.

He mutters in deep and lyrical French as he palms the lace of my black bra, thumb lightly pinching my nipple through the delicate material as I arch my back away from him. He's making me a ballerina, pulling a languid dance out of me I didn't know I knew the steps to.

Hoisting me with his upward movement, he straightens from the chair and strides for the bed. I wait for the bounce, but this time he lowers me carefully, like I'm a goddess he's going to worship.

And he does, loosening my heels and dropping them to the floor, muttering in appreciation as he slides a hand up my leg. "I prefer these tights" He kisses my inner thigh, and his hands slip up the outer edge of my hips. Lifting, I wriggle free, relishing the skim of his slightly rough palm on my skin as he pulls down the tights. There's a distinct ripping sound as they come off my feet.

"What's the possibility of us meeting by chance twice?" I gasp as he presses a kiss to the inside of my knee.

"Fate, Juliette, fate."

What I want to know is if *Fate* will bring us together again, because this tastes like an addiction I don't want to recover from.

His stubble scratches my jaw as he stretches up to kiss me. I angle my hands to cup his face, holding him still so I can stare in his eyes.

There it is.

Something deep, twisted, and moreish that tells me I might want this over and over and over again even though I don't know his name.

"Romeo's should be naked," I whisper in his ear using my foot to push off his trousers tangled around his ankles.

"Juliette's should be less demanding," he counters pressing me back into the mattress and hiking up my skirt.

"I have to be demanding. I might never see you again."

He looks up, perplexity shadowed in the circles under his eyes. The skin that I know crinkles. "Want to know my name, ma petite?" he teases in my ear and my toes point, my knickers almost pulling themselves off my body in a bid to get to where I crave to be.

Yes, I want to know his name. His address, birthday, star sign. Yes, I might even want to know if he'd like a date next time he's in town... a proper date where we arrange it, maybe he brings me flowers... or I him, let's not be sexist here, and then we spend hours sparring in meaningful and enlightening conversation...

But Julianna Brown who might have wanted those things doesn't exist anymore. It's a future that no longer belongs to me, with hope, brightness and optimism dusted like fairy magic.

"Yes." I gust with an exhalation as he dips a finger under the elastic of my knickers, slipping his touch through my desire, gaze darkening as he reads my body's reactions. "No!" The finger pushes inside, twisting and pressing, filling me as it rubs along long unexplored sensitive spots.

"No to this?" He pulls his hand away from between my legs and I almost cry. A frown scores his face.

"God no. No to names. Put your hand back right now."

Chuckles rock his body, but he obliges, and I writhe against his touch, groaning as his thumb circles my clit, his fingers dancing and alternating: one, then two, then one. Oooh one again to make me gasp as it encroaches further.

Let there be no mistake. I am going to come.

I hold on hard and fast, my hips moving with the strength of his arm and hand. The wave builds in my toes, racing up my legs with the bursting velocity of a dam that's been breached.

"Come, Juliette." I know he's watching me fall apart, the moonlight illuminating every emotion on my face. I know it, but I can't let the knowledge change anything about it.

I shudder hard, clenching around his fingers while his lips, which should feel foreign but instead seem like something else, catch my gasped moan.

"God, that feels good." I capture his face, hungrily kissing his lips.

"Every part of you feels good." He shrugs out of his shirt, thrusting it to one side as he cages me in his arms, holding his weight from me as he settles between my legs.

"How good?" I smile up, trying to stop the wide grin that wants to escape.

"Better than my English will ever allow me to express."

"Tell me in French then." I wiggle down, trying to connect us, but he holds firm.

"I will, hold that thought." Pecking a quick kiss to the end of my nose he eases away and stretches from the bed, long lithe body flexing in pewter and pale gold. Streetlamp and moonlight.

My French lover under a London starlit sky.

I giggle as, with condom in hand, he stalks towards the bed. "Do you speak French, Juliette?" he asks, cocking his head to one side.

"Non." I snort a laugh that he pounces on with a kiss.

"Just as well, ma petite, I'm about to turn the air blue."

And with that he pushes deep inside me and I'm pretty sure heaven has just landed on earth.

12

VALENTINES FOR THOSE WITH AN ACTUAL BROKEN HEART

"Tell me about your home."

"Hmm?" He plants a sleepy kiss on the top of my head as I sprawl across his chest. Last time I stole into the dawn, untangling myself from the warm knot of his legs and arms. Tonight, my legs wouldn't move me if I wanted them to—I'm not even sure they are still attached to my body.

I point my toes and stretch, just to make sure, not at all disappointed when his hand runs up my thigh.

"Your home. What's it like?" I lift my head a little and rest my chin on my fingers. "I mean if you had got on the train and were nearly home by now."

He chuckles, rocking us together. "I wouldn't have been home yet. First would have been the Eurostar, then a short flight from Paris, and then a taxi ride."

"Wow. Can't you fly direct from London?"

"Of course, but I have contacts in Paris too, so I'd normally stop to see them, check everything is okay."

Mmm... cheese intrigues.

"And who is your contact in London?" *And why does it*

sound like we are talking about the Mafia and not cheese production?

"Harrods."

I laugh, but then when he doesn't laugh back it quickly dies and I push up a little straighter. "Harrods. You sell your cheese at Harrods?"

"Oui, Mademoiselle. As well as direct to some restaurants in the country."

"What restaurants?" I narrow my gaze a bit.

He shrugs, which let's be honest isn't an answer at all.

Okay, he can keep his cheese secrets. I've got enough of my own. "So, what would happen when you get home." I'm about to lay back down, my cheek needs to be pressed against one of his firm and vast pecs, but I have a thought that perhaps I should have asked before dinner, maybe even a month ago. "No girlfriend waiting for you is there?" Wincing, I try to avoid eye contact. First the no names, then the belated relationship status update. I'm not entirely sure why he shouted out to me across Waterloo. I'm clearly a woman of loose morals.

Oh, I know why. We've just had mind blowing sex twice, and I'm pretty sure we are an exact, surprising, but undeniably perfect fit.

He tilts my chin up, so I have to look at his honest and disarming smile. "No girlfriend."

"Phew. I'd have had to send her some apology chocolates or something."

"I told you at dinner, I'm a chivalrous man."

"Where you had your tongue earlier isn't thought of as chivalrous in numerous countries."

He laughs, bellowing it at the ceiling and shakes his head. "Where have you come from, amant croisé étoile."

I shift under his gaze. "What did you call me?"

Using his strong hands, he grasps me under my arms and lifts me, so we are nose to nose, my short legs knocking somewhere around his naked knees. "My star-crossed lover."

In response my stomach sinks. I'm a doomed lover.

Which is why it's perfect I've found someone like him to have sex with, twice. Okay, twice tonight. I won't have to worry about hurting anyone when this ends.

Maybe we did meet in that bar for a reason after all.

"So, no girlfriend." I settle back down, stroking my fingers along the valleys and hills of his chest and stomach. The man is built.

"Non, I'd go home and check on Maman."

"Maman?"

"My mother."

A Mummy's boy. How endearing.

"My father passed away eight months ago. She gets lonely."

I reach up again so I can see him. "I'm so sorry, for you and for her. Was it sudden?"

He nods. "A heart attack. I thought at the time it would be better, no? No lingering goodbyes to break her heart. But it broke anyway." He offers me a fleeting smile and then leans down to kiss me on the lips.

"That's awful." A tight band weaves its way around my chest.

"So now I take over." He sighs, staring at the ceiling.

"And you don't want to?"

A shrug. Which I'm learning can mean anything, everything, and nothing all at once. "It is what it is."

It is what it is. That sounds like a motto for life if you ask me.

His smile grows, that dimple coming back out to play.

"And you? I don't need to worry some jealous boyfriend will track me down?"

"Nah. I doubt he will go all the way to the Pyrenees to find you." I manage to stay serious for a whole two seconds before he grabs me, fingers wedging in my ribs and rolls me over, his knee pressing between my thighs and making me all warm—again.

"So funny, ma petite?"

"I try."

"Let me show you how incredibly serious I can be." His gaze intensifies, the glow from the bedside lamp casting half of his face into shadow.

"How do you plan to do that?"

I squeal as he rolls me again, catching one of my nipples in between his lips. Okay. I can take *Romeo's* serious any day of the week.

Dawn is starting to filter through the edges of the thick brocade curtains, I'm still spiralled across my Two-Night One-Night Stand like a cheap sweater on the floor of Primark.

My stomach has been rumbling for at least an hour, waking me up from my light sleep. I've been dreaming of the Tube ride home in my work clothes sans tights.

Another walk of shame.

If I left now, I wouldn't have to face the morning rush.

I haven't even got a hairbrush, let alone a toothbrush.

Oh God. I'm going to have morning breath.

I should leave.

Definitely leave now.

"I know what you are thinking." His finger trails down my spine.

"You do?"

"You're planning an escape."

"Wasn't. I was considering my lack of toothbrush."

"Easily rectified. Reception will send one."

Well, I suppose... "My tights are in tatters on the floor."

"Your skin is beautiful and shouldn't be hidden from view."

I peek up through my mess of dark hair and catch a sleepy smile flit across his face.

"My..." Goddamn it. Where have all my reasons gone?

"It's Valentine's. I need to book another train; we could have breakfast."

"I need to feed my cat."

He cranks an eye open. "I need to meet this cat."

My cheeks flush. "I think that would be in breach of the no name rule."

He inclines his head and I tighten my embrace of his chest, inhaling the warmth of his skin. "This hotel is beautiful. Do you always stay here?" The room is a classy old-fashioned affair: heavy dark-stained furniture, opulent furnishings. On the opposite wall is a large gilt-framed mirror on which I will always see, captured in a snapshot in my memories, the sight of our limbs entwined, fingers clawing skin.

"Oui, my father did too. Maman and he came here as part of their honeymoon."

"Ah, that's romantic."

And he was lying with me in one of their beds... shut the thought down, Julia, it won't get you anywhere.

"I thought the French hated the English."

His sleepy smile quirks into a grin and on a whim I press my lips to the dimple on the left curve of his mouth. "Only for rugby."

"That's not too bad."

"And football." He presses a lazy kiss onto my forehead. "And Hundred Year wars."

"Anything else?"

"Oil, maybe fishing rights across the channel." He chuckles, wrapping me in strong warm arms. "Weekenders who never learn the language."

"Okay, let's stop now. I'm beginning to feel vilified."

His face is earnest, a mask of brooding sincerity. "Non, never you. You are worshipped."

I begin to flow from the inside out. My skin painted gold as I bask under his words of praise. To be worshipped is a wonderful thing. Even if it's by someone whose name I will never know.

"So... breakfast..." I can do breakfast with him, even with unbrushed hair and tightless legs in February. It would be worth the goosebumps to bask under his golden glow for a couple more hours.

He snatches me forward, pressing my tits against his chest. Warmth licks along my skin. "Breakfast later," he murmurs against my mouth. I ignore the rumbling of my stomach and decide kisses should be made a national food source; very low in calories and great for the hips.

A phone rings, shattering the building heat and he curses in French, dropping his face into the crook of my neck. I run my fingers through his silky, dark waves.

"Shouldn't you get that?" I ask as he does a steadfast job of ignoring the piercing ring and recommences the torture of my nipple with his tongue. I say torture in a loose context kind of way.

Torture because nipple play is definitely one of his strengths and it makes me ache in other deeper places.

"I really, really don't want to."

I stare at the ceiling over the top of his head as the phone rings off and then starts again. It's extinguishing little fires all over the place.

"Damn it to hell." He pushes away from my pliant body and I snatch up the sheet as cool air brushes along my sensitive skin. Grabbing his phone, he swipes the screen and then launches into a barrage of ferocious French, every word the angry strike on an old-fashioned typewriter.

He stands, butt naked. Arse like a fucking peach. Long legs flexing, he has muscles in his back I want to photograph and frame on my wall.

Really wish I'd paid more attention in French because I don't understand a word he is saying, apart from the fact he is rather cross about something.

Hanging up, even my limited French telling me he didn't say goodbye, he throws the phone onto the chair we sat on last night and then sits down on the end of the bed, clutching his head in his hands and dropping over his knees.

"What's wrong?" I have a yearning ache to know his real name so I can provide some comfort from the torrent of anger he has coursing through him. As it is I lift onto my knees, dragging the sheet with me as an elaborate robe. I put my hands on his curved shoulders and plant a kiss to the warm spot where neck meets shoulder.

I wait, the flicker of strong muscles running under my touch until he turns, an enigmatic smile drifting across his face.

"Nothing, ma petite. Unfortunately, I have to cancel breakfast."

"Oh." It hits like a punch in the gut.

Stupid Julianna.

"Sure, not a problem at all." I smile, gathering the sheet around me further, covering my exposed skin.

His smile falters, that beautiful seriousness taking its place. "I am truly sorry."

"It's fine, we don't owe one another anything. Not an issue. I have plans this evening anyway." I clamber across the mattress on my knees in the opposite direction to his naked perfection and struggle off the bed in my self-created wedding dress of bed sheets.

"Juliette," he snaps.

Oooh, no. No one snaps at me... well apart from Liv.

Using my hand as a shield between us I edge away. "I'll get dressed quickly and be out of your way."

"Juliette." He pounces up from the bed, crowding into my space. I'm not sure if he realises he is still naked. His dick is just swinging out there, brazen as you like. I, on the other hand, am slowly morphing myself into an ancient mummy with a hundred thread count Egyptian cotton. With his large hands he grasps my shoulders, holding me back from edging towards the safety of the en suite. The midnight gaze watches me, waiting for something.

"I am so glad I saw you yesterday." A smile flits across his mouth. "At first I thought you were a mirage because I'd thought of you so often."

I nod. "You always turn up just when I need it." My words feel empty though and I hate the space in them.

"You're cross?" He crouches down and I can't help but do a swift dick sweep with my gaze.

"No." I sigh because I'm really not. How can I be cross when this isn't meant to be anyway? "I guess I'm just disappointed."

He smiles, fingers squeezing my knees. "I can feel your rules crumbling, ma Juliette."

"Well, they aren't now, are they?" Forcing a smile, I

reach forward to kiss his lips. "Thank you for another lovely evening."

"Thank you," he whispers against my mouth and it awakens something hungry and needy inside of me.

I don't want to walk away from him, but I have to. He's a stranger in a hotel room. Nothing else.

"I'll do you a deal." He catches my chin and makes me look at him.

"Uh huh." He's the breaker of deals. He promised me breakfast and my stomach is grumbling.

"We meet one more time. One more chance for fate to tell us that this is meant to be something other than anonymity in a hotel room, and you tell me your name."

My mouth flaps open. "But..."

"No buts. I have a feeling here." He lightly punches his stomach and I feel it in my own, it's a hollow pit of expectation. "It tells me that to walk away from you is wrong, but I can sense the boundaries you have in place." He lightly pushes his index finger in the space above my heart. "The first moment I met you, I could see them."

"Don't." I push his hand away. He's too close to my bitter truth.

"Next time you tell me your name. Next time you let me in."

"I have let you in."

He shakes his head, lips turned down. "No, you haven't."

"What if I can't?"

He shrugs. Bloody Frenchman.

"Okay. Next time." I agree knowing that there can't be a next time.

Time is ticking along. I can feel it within me, using the

same force as the hand on the clock at Waterloo keeps moving. Tick. Tock. Tick. Tock.

"Next time, ma petite. I think you will be mine."

He kisses me again as the awful truth awakens inside of me and no matter how much I try to push it back down I can't quite manage it.

I am already.

This man with the hands, the eyebrows that talk. The achingly beautiful seriousness that shifts into a breath-taking smile with the rush of a breeze.

Yeah. I could live for another hundred years, be the oldest woman alive and I'd still be thinking of him living under my skin, the warmth of him against the warmth of me.

Yep. I really am a fool.

13

FATE IS A MEAN MISTRESS

"Come on, Jules." Flynn gives me his best puppy dog eyes across the space of our conjoined desks. "One glass of wine."

"I told you already, I can't."

"Give me one good reason." He holds a finger up, pouty lips sulking at the edges.

"I've given you five already."

Flynn smirks. "Tell me again. You give me five and I will stop asking."

"One. I have to go and get Paige's birthday present, which I've left until the last minute. Two, it's unprofessional in a workplace to go for drinks that constitute a date." He opens his mouth up, but I stop him with my hand. "Three, I've got all this digital stuff to do. I've got to show it to Rebecca next week for her approval for me to show the board. I'm running late with it. I'll be working all evening. And four, I just don't like you in that way."

"Ha! You said five."

"Sorry, four and five are the same, I should have said that."

Luckily, we are stopped by the clack of Rebecca's heels. Louboutin's today, the red of the sole to match the red of her silk shirt. "Jules, a word."

Flynn frowns at me and I glance up at him. Why does it sound like I'm in trouble? He shrugs, but it has none of the appeal of a French shrug.

Stop it. Stop thinking about *him.*

Rebecca ushers me in. "Julia darling, I've been watching you."

"You have?" Okay, bit weird but we can roll with it. "I promise I said no to Flynn if that's what you are worried about and heard him asking." I pull at the edge of my blouse. "I know that would be frowned upon."

"What's that, darling?"

"Flynn... uh." I stop talking.

"Oh, he's asked you out again has he? I have to say, Julia, you've done well to avoid his advances all this time. I put his desk there just so he'd give you a little sunshine."

"I can assure you all he's given me is a migraine."

Rebecca tinkles her little laugh. "So, tell me about your plans for this weekend?"

Oh... that's what this is. It's the Friday afternoon pity chat. Ha-ha! I do have plans.

"It's Paige's fourth birthday, so Liv has a party planned at her house."

"A day with the Notting Hill set. All married and settled down, are they? Smug and satisfied?" Rebecca views monogamy the way that I view raisins; unnecessary, total waste of time (and calories) and maybe a trick of the devil himself.

"Nope, I don't think so."

I've never stopped to ponder on just how Liv has managed to surround herself with people as equally useless in love as her. I find myself shrugging, my mind automatically slipping to a mysterious little pocket of France where a man I unexpectedly miss lives. It's been six weeks since our night of Boutique Hotel Heaven and I'm pretty sure fate has decided twice is enough.

Damn you, fate.

And damn me for being a stubborn bitch. What's a number or name swap between two people who have shared bodily fluids?

"Okay, so listen." Rebecca straightens her spine and recrosses her legs, flashing me the vibrant red of her soles. Her fingers clasp a diamond pendant around her neck, and I sense something in her that I've never seen before. I can practically smell it. Uncertainty.

"So, I don't want you to be upset."

My smile tightens on my face. "That's not a great start."

"I know how desperately you want to get us digitised."

"Rebecca, I'm not doing it because I'm bored; it's the only way for us to survive."

"Yeees... that's the thing, darling. We might not try. The board are in discussions to fold."

I stare at her, my mouth hanging wide open. "What?"

"It's not definite, not at all, but I just wanted to talk to you about it. You've been here such a long time, given so much of your creativity and drive to me, when really you probably should have left ages ago and gone somewhere better."

I rub absently at my chest. I know and she knows why I've stayed. "I want to be here. It's a massive part of my life."

"Julianna, there is so much more to life than being here with a needy ex-socialite and a bunch of crusty old men."

"Don't be so harsh on yourself. You're more than an ex-socialite."

"I wasn't talking about me, I meant Flynn." She grins, a splash of bright-red lipstick. "I only hired him because I thought you might like him."

"Rebecca!" I'm honestly shocked. "That's no reason to hire a person."

She scrunches her face, her practically lineless and ageless skin crinkling for a moment. "It didn't work anyway, did it?" She taps her ruby nails on her desk. "It's such a shame you don't date. It's not good for you to be living in that flat with that awful cat."

"For the record there is nothing wrong with Barney, and I do date. I just don't feel the need to waste my time on pointless hours spent with someone that I probably don't like that much."

She narrows her gaze, analysing, and I pull at my hair, fiddling with the ends. "Hmm, why? You're a good-looking woman. I just don't get it."

I shrug... brain... France... again...

With a deep sigh I slump back a little in the chair. "I guess I spent too long trying to be the good girl."

"Good girls are a bore, Julianna. Be bad for a change."

I nod, although I know the ticking death sentence hanging above my head has limited opportunities to re-acquaint myself with my bad side. She's been locked up a long time.

"Would you mind if I head off? I've got to get to Hamleys to get Paige's present. I've left it until the last moment again."

"Sure, sure." Her gaze meets mine, devilish flash in the depth of it. "Want to take Flynn with you?"

Shaking my head, I get up and smooth down my skirt. "Don't mind if I pass."

"Have fun at Hamleys."

I shoot her an evil stink eye. "No adult ever had fun at Hamleys ever."

"Have a good weekend, Julianna. Don't eat too much jelly and ice cream."

Like she thinks that's the highlight of my weekend... oh wait.

"Rebecca?" I stop and turn at the door.

"Mm?" She's pretending to look at something important, but I know she has Vogue under the paperwork—I can see the thick edge of the glossy mag.

"Don't sell yet, will you? I really want to get us online."

She looks up, defeat on her face. "We wouldn't be selling, Julia. We'd need to close. No one wants to go into business with us. And who can blame them?"

"But if we were online and current they might. You could get that place in the Bahamas after all."

Rebecca claps her hands with amusement. "Darling, I already have one. God awful place with those mosquitos."

And there you have it. A different breed of woman altogether.

"See you Monday." I slip out of her office and grab my stuff, quickly shutting down my computer before Flynn can ask me for that glass of wine again. I need to hit Hamleys and get home. I'm tired. More than tired. I'm exhausted, and there is no chance in hell that I can let Liv see that tomorrow. I'll hide it for as long as possible before I let her see the truth that time is slipping away.

"Bloody Hamleys bear," I'm grumbling under my breath as I get out of the cab. I was going to do the Tube, but my chest felt too tight. I couldn't walk because of my heels, rather than the exhaustion pulling my body down until I'm almost parallel with the pavement. So, I went for a black cab and joyfully spent ten quid stuck in a three mile traffic jam.

Damn heels.

And damn dying.

And damn, damn Hamleys bears. I should have got one off eBay.

Stopping myself, I draw in a deep breath. This isn't who I want to be. I don't want to be an aunt who wouldn't travel to the moon via Mars if it meant getting the bear my niece wanted. Liv, Paige, and Lenny, they are all I have really. And Barney. The least I can do is throw myself into an oversized and overpriced toy store to get her the perfect teddy bear.

Right. Let's. Do. This.

I look up at the store and briefly wonder if you can go in swigging from a bottle of wine. I'm distracted from the famous drummer boy symbol by a shadow rushing towards me, a cloud on an intent gust of wind.

Hands clutch my elbows, but instead of screaming or fending for my life with my handbag as a weapon, I'm shuddering, breathing out a long held bated breath.

Breathing the same air as... as...

"Henri Carré." His lips crush into mine, and I moan a deep and toe-curling sigh.

Fate, you wily beast, I thought you'd let me down.

It hits me how much I've been craving this moment, desperately waiting without wanting to give meaning to the ache festering under my skin. The grey of my world bursts into colour with the press of his lips.

Henri. The perfect name.

Henri.

I pull away, blinking up into his wide smile.

"I knew it was meant to be." He presses his words

against my mouth, my cheeks, and I'm disarmed by his open and frank emotional capacity.

In return I do what I've been trained to do in my role as British middle-class citizen. I shift from foot to foot until he chuckles, rumbling it inside of me until I'm all jelly and warm.

"And you are?" He prompts with a curve of his eyebrow.

"I'm Julia. Julianna Brown."

His eyes dance. "I was so close with Juliette."

"So close!"

His hands rest on my shoulders, burning through the loose knit of my cardigan.

"Did you really believe it was meant to be?" I whisper.

His smile, it's so beautiful, so earnest, it's like the first bloom of a daisy under the May sunshine. "I never had any doubt." He tucks a wayward hair behind my ear. "So where are we going?"

"We?" I frown.

"Yes. I said, next time you let me in."

Jeez, can he remember every word we've ever said? I glance at his chest. He's not wearing a suit today, just a white shirt rolled at the sleeve and tucked into immaculately tailored trousers at the waist.

"Are you answering with that wandering hungry stare of yours, ma petite?"

I pat his pecs—because why not?

"I'm still adjusting to seeing you again. Here. Outside bloody Hamleys. What are the chances?" I pull back an inch. "Wait a minute. You aren't following me, are you? Fate isn't fate if it's had a helping hand."

"Me?" Holding his hands palm up he looks up at the

sky. "I'd never mess with fate. She's a mean mistress if you don't do what she wants."

I love how he talks. He's like a poet, every word lyrical and layered with emotion and integrity. I've never met a single person like him in my life, he's unique.

Unique. One of a kind. He's been sent to me for a reason. I see that now.

I wind my fingers through the waves at the nape of his neck and pull his mouth down to mine, hungrily seeking that warm, succulent taste that sets off fireworks in every cell of my body. Uncaring of our standing outside a toy shop, I slip my tongue into his mouth, seeking him out. In return he greets me back and long needed oxygen explodes in my chest.

Then I pull back and smack him on the chest. "It's been six weeks. I didn't think I'd see you again." My eyes sting, unexpected and unwanted, and I blink the tell-tale salt water away.

"I'm here now. So where are we going, or is it a mystery?"

"What time is your train?" I really, really need to buy this damn teddy bear, but then I also need to spend any grasped moments with my mystery man... Henri. I taste his name on my tongue.

He shrugs.

Damn that man.

"Would it alarm you if I told you I was here for the weekend?"

I register his words, letting them sink in, like dropping low into a perfect temperature bath that encases you in luxury.

"A whole weekend?" My eyes are wide.

"Is that a good-scared look or a bad-scared look?"

"A whole weekend?" I repeat.

He laughs, tucking my hair, thumb brushing my cheekbone. "The whole weekend."

We are causing a massive obstruction on the street, but still he leans down and brushes my lips with his. "What do you think?"

What do I think?

Oh, who cares. I'm pretty sure this is one of those life defining moments where you aren't supposed to think. Like the first night we met. Or the time after.

Basically, I haven't thought since we met.

"I think yes." I launch myself into his arms, wrapping my legs around his waist, peppering kisses on his face. He smells of spice and smoke, sunshine, lavender fields and all the unknown things I will probably never know.

He smells of what I hope heaven will be.

"Get a room." I crack my eyes open at two teenage girls in tracksuits who strut by.

"I will when I'm good and ready!" I call after them to which one gives me the finger over her shoulder. Youths these days, don't they have any respect?

Henri grins and lowers me to the floor. "You know if I'd known you'd be so happy to see me, I'd have come back weeks ago." His smile is taunting.

"You're really here for the whole weekend?"

"Yes."

"And you want to spend it with me?" Let's clarify this point.

"Yes."

"I've got to go in there." I point to the inner circle of hell, which is screaming children rolling on the floor because they can't have the toys they want.

He crooks his arm. "Then let's go."

"Oh shit." We've only walked one step and already there is a clanger in the plan. "It's my niece's birthday tomorrow. I'm so sorry." I smack myself on the forehead and make him smirk.

"That's fine."

"I can see you as soon as the party is over if you'll wait for me?"

He slips my small hand in his giant one and I give a little shiver when I remember what those hands can do. "No, I mean I can come with you, that would be fantastic."

I stare at him wild-eyed. "But then you'd have to meet my sister."

"Are we going in there or not?" He tugs on my hand.

"I don't know." I'm rooted to the spot while he leans in and whispers.

"Just one step at a time."

14

BARNEY'S BEST FRIEND

"So, THIS IS IT." I push my key into the brass lock trying to remember if I picked up yesterday's knickers from the bedroom floor. It's not always top of my to do list.

I'm not sure how we got here. From Hamleys, to the hotel where he checked out, to my place.

All because I said, 'I'll let you in'. Turns out it was also a physical invitation to share my home for the weekend.

That's not crazy right?

Oh God, it is crazy.

I don't even know this man.

"Julianna." He says my name and it's like every worry just evaporates out of my brain. "You're overthinking it."

"Overthinking it?" I practically gasp, clutching my chest, and it has nothing to do with faulty valves. "I don't even know you."

A full-on panic attack tinges the edge of my eyesight black, and I can barely register him putting his hand over mine and turning the key. "You know me."

A screeching barrel of fur launches at our legs. I'm late to serve dinner. My bad.

"And this is..." Henri tows me into my own flat by my elbow. My feet trip over themselves without the need for Barney's incessant winding around my ankles, and his *I'm going to claw your eyes out while you sleep* miaow.

"Barney, stop! God, I'm so sorry, Henri."

"The famous Barney." My eyesight clears just in time to see Henri swoop Barney up, turn him on his back and rub his fingers into the mass of fur on his belly.

"No! Your hand." I wait for a splattering of blood to decorate my hallway, but instead I'm met by a steady hum of a contented purr. "Oh. He normally hates everyone."

Henri puts him back down on the floor and Barney starts to weave a figure of eight around his ankles while also shaking his tail. Oh, dear God, is he scenting him?

I shoo him away with my toe. "That's one way to break the ice."

Henri smiles, leaning against my hallway wall. My stomach somersaults like a gold medal winner. "You seem so nervous, ma petite Julianna."

"I am."

"Why?"

I swallow, a lump forming in my throat that feels rather like an ancient brick. "I don't have people over often."

A small line furrows between his brow. "Why?"

I raise my shoulder and then let them drop. "I dunno. I work long hours. Then of course there's always the fact that Barney might maul someone to death." I shoot a sheepish smile which says: *please don't ask anything more.*

Barney is trying to climb his long legs like a tree. Can't say I blame him, been there done that. My cheeks scorch.

"So will we spend all weekend in the hallway?"

Whoosh, even hotter. Henri steps closer, peeling himself off the wall, now my favourite work of art, and runs a finger along my warm cheeks. "I can stay in the hotel if this is too fast for you."

Julia, please don't be that girl—live a little... before it's too late.

I push down whispered memories of the past. "Well, I guess it's not that fast. We've known each other months now."

He stretches a smile that could stop traffic. "Exactly."

Grabbing his hand, I pull him down the short hallway and into the main living space. He stops at the door. "Wow, this is very..."

"Small." I fill in for him. It is and having a massive Frenchman in it is shrinking the cubic square foot by the second.

"I was going to say grey."

I try to see it from his eyes, turning to take it in. Okay, so there are a few grey things. Walls, cushions, sofa, I wouldn't say it's totally grey.

I launch for one of the scatter cushions and hold it up. "This is mustard."

Henri shakes his head. "That's not what I mean."

I know it's not. "I've got ferns," I whimper.

He slowly turns on the spot. "The most beautiful woman I've ever met, and she lives in a square box." His eyes meet mine. "Ma petite, fate really was bringing us together for a reason."

I narrow my gaze. "I'm not a pity subject. I like my life. I like my home. It's exactly what I need and that's all that matters."

His eyebrow speaks for him.

"So would you like a cup of tea or something?" When in doubt, offer tea. My childhood training taught me that much.

He smirks. Bastard. "No, Julianna, I do not want a cup of tea." His gaze turns smoky, and my stomach drops as he paces to where I've put some cooling space between myself and my unexpected visitor.

"What I really want is to fuck you on one of these boringly grey surfaces to bring it all to life a little."

"What?" I don't get to protest any further because he has me in his arms, his mouth seeking mine, licking at the seam begging for entry. "Liv is going to call any moment," I pull away to gasp. His hand runs under the cotton of my blouse, brushing my skin and erupting me hot and cold all at once. His mouth finds mine again. His kisses taste like little droplets of heavenly nectar. "She's going to be furious when that bear turns up. It doesn't match her colour scheme." Another word-stealing kiss. I'm out of air. "It's bigger than Paige's bedroom."

"I have no concern." His lips drop to my throat, teeth on skin. Gasping, I drop my head back and his fingers make light work of my blouse, pushing it and my cardigan into a pile on the floor. Reaching behind, he unhooks my bra, teasing it gently off my shoulders, and then drops that too. My nipples harden at the exposure, at the unexpected, delectable delight of being freed in the middle of the living room on a Friday afternoon. They pebble and wait patiently for a touch. It doesn't come. He stares at them from under thick, dark lashes. Slowly, he lowers his head and pulls one into his mouth. Instinctively I arch my back, my lessons in ballet recommencing at his touch. One of his hands runs around the curve of my spine, supporting me or holding me closer so he has full control; either way it's making me quiver.

"Henri," I gasp his name, it falls from my lips like I've never not known it.

"What is it?" He lets go of my nipple, glancing at me, eyes dark.

"Sofa. I think the sofa should be the first grey surface."

Chuckling, he sweeps me up and stalks for the IKEA special before lowering me down like I'm a goddamn Swedish queen on a throne made of manmade fabric. With his big palms he rolls me onto my front, my face and tits crushing into the cushions. The zip of my skirt fills the air, his thumb running down the V-shaped opening along the edge of my lace knickers.

God, I love his hands.

Crave his touch.

He swears in French before swiftly converting to English. "What is this cat doing? Can't it see I'm busy?"

I snort into the sofa. "He's hungry. Here, let me feed him."

I go to push up, but his hand holds me down. "I'll go. You must stay where you are."

My last shred of feminist rights shrivel inside me and die a sad and lonely end as I heat with scorching fire through every blistering part of my body.

"Tin on top of the microwave."

Cool air rushes across my back as he moves away.

I wait with bated breath as the clatter of biscuit hitting china and the wild miaow of Barney tells me the beast has been sated.

That's good. It only leaves the hungry beast inside of me in need of attention.

I almost kick my feet into the sofa with excitement as I hear him pad back towards me. The sound of clothes hitting the floor has me turning around. Smooth, tanned skin is revealed as he drops his shirt and trousers to the floor, the heavy clasp of his belt clanging against the floorboards. My tongue tingles with dryness. He really is here... in my flat, and I think he's about to do something pretty damn spectacular to me on my own sofa.

Right now, I feel it.

Life.

I can feel what living is. It's in one moment to the next. One breath that leads to another. One touch, one sigh, one glance, creating a perfect moment that is imprinted forever.

That's what life is. Moment to moment encapsulated right in that very second. There is no past and there is no future. It's in the breath, the focus, the intention to just be.

I turn, a heaviness throws itself over us like a warm blanket, offering the ultimate comfort. He doesn't moan at my breaking of the rules. Instead, he falls silently to his knees dressed only in his boxers, his abs crunching. I'm half-naked on the sofa, something new and unexpected, but all I want is his kiss. It's a burn, a desire, a question that needs to be met with an answer.

His lips meet mine and I feel something else. Not life. No, that is coursing through me, pumping my poor damaged heart.

No, I feel something else. It's a tang on the end of my tongue, a four letter word that also begins with L.

And that's crazy. So damn crazy, because I don't know anything about this Frenchman knelt by my side like a knight of old at a holy shrine, but I know between us flows something unexpected and unique.

"Henri," I whisper his name, my lips still grazing his.

"Mmm, ma petite?" Eyes closed, he's worshiping me, and it smooths across me like a healing spell.

"I think I want you to take me to bed."

His eyes flicker open and meet mine. Then he nods and stands, lifting me in his arms.

. . .

"I haven't fed you, I'm a terrible host." Somehow, I've wriggled down the bed, my head resting on his ribcage, our feet nudging tit-for-tat under the covers. His fingers are trailing that magical path along my spine.

"Terrible." *Te-ree-bl.* He leans down and pecks a kiss on my forehead. "But believe me I've eaten." That cheeky grin with its cheekier dimple comes out to play and I bask in its sun.

"I'll make us something." I push my lips into his chest. "In a minute."

"Tired, Julianna?"

"Yes." I press my lips together. I'm so damn tired, it's almost seeping through my bones, but I wouldn't change it for a moment. This man was made to do that to me, of that I'm pretty sure, and it would be a heathen mistake to waste a moment of it, no matter how tired my limbs feel or how strong the tingling in my fingertips and toes is.

Stupid heart. Pump oxygen like you're meant to.

"But not that tired," I add when I've left it so long he probably thinks I've fallen asleep. I don't know what they feed them in France, but this man has a stamina I never knew existed.

"This cat weighs a ton, I'm sure." Henri groans and tries to shift his legs, but Barney has them captured.

I giggle and try to gently kick him off but Barney's not having it. "He likes you."

"I'm glad."

"You've passed the test."

"You get to my age and you worry you'll meet someone and have to win over their children, non. Never did I expect to win over a cat."

I lift up onto my elbow. "Is that what we are doing? Winning one another over?"

His gaze clouds, but that's okay, because my heart has just sunk. Whatever this is, and believe me I know it's epic, it can't ever truly be anything. I have nothing to promise and nothing to give. Anything less than that would be a travesty for a man as exceptional as this one.

"I don't know." He sighs and with his free hand he rubs at his hair.

"It's okay. I'm not expecting anything, proposals or suchlike. I mean, as I've said, we barely know one another."

He eyeballs me from under one arched brow. "And how long do two people have to know one another before they know?"

"Know what?"

A French shrug. Perfect timing.

I shake my head, biting down a grin. "I'm learning your shrugs, Henry Carré."

With a deep rumbling chuckle, he rocks me backwards and forwards, until his smile falters and the laughter dies on his lips. "Truth is though, I don't know what I can offer right now."

I breathe out a sigh of relief. "That's okay; me neither. Can't we just keep this fun?"

Please say yes. Please say yes.

"Believe me I have fun."

So, why's his face shadowed?

Wriggling up his body like I'm climbing a pole, I peck a kiss on his mouth. "This doesn't look like fun."

Sliding his fingers in my hair he holds me in place. "And when I'm shouting your name?"

"My name or Juliette?"

He flashes a grin. "Both. I like you both equally."

"Cheeky." I meet his gaze. "So you like me?"

"Very, very much so."

"But this can't be anything, because..."

"Maman needs me, right now. She's not in a good place."

"I'm not asking you to move here, Henri. Jesus, I haven't even offered you breakfast yet."

"I know, but I got this feeling, it tells me I'll always want more of you."

I hold my breath. He feels it too.

I force myself to remember that I'm dying. "So, let's just enjoy this. When you are in town, you can come and find me." My cheeks flame. "You know... if you want."

Swallowing hard, I hold still as he trails a finger down my cheek. "Can I tell you a secret?" he asks.

"Sure." I laugh off key. "I can keep secrets, the cat not so much."

"I was supposed to go back home Thursday evening. I got all the way to the Eurostar and then just couldn't get on. I couldn't believe I'd been here for three days and hadn't seen you."

My heart beats unevenly.

"I thought you said it was fate?"

"Fate needed just a little longer."

Mulling on this, I chew on the inside of my cheek before saying, "I'm glad," for which I'm rewarded with a showstopper smile.

"Me too."

"So. Let's not overthink this. It's just what it is."

Deep down I know one day he will come to London and I will no longer live here. Tears prickle my eyes and I pull upright into sitting so he can't see.

It seems so unfair.

"And if I fall in love with you?"

He reaches for my cheek and my whole chest empties: no air, no heartbeat, nothing.

"Don't," I whisper, but then plaster on a wide smile. "Right, let's get some food. I'm famished."

From the corner of my eye, I catch his critical glance over me. "You look like you haven't eaten."

"I have."

"What did you last eat?"

"A Pot Noodle."

"What is that?"

I explain and groaning, he throws back the covers and stretches his legs over the side of the bed. Have I mentioned his legs and just how mighty fine they are?

"It's just as well I didn't get on that train."

"Is that so?"

He catches me up in his arms and tosses me over his shoulder, bare naked ass to the ceiling.

"It is very much so. Now what food do you have in the fridge?" He strides for the kitchen and I could stop him and tell him I don't have any food in, but his beautiful dick is bouncing just in my line of sight and after all I am only human.

15

LOVER

Liv: I'm expecting a teddy bear explanation. You know they couldn't get it in the house right?

I giggle and show Henri my phone. Breakfast is brunch at a small Italian café he found five minutes away from my flat that I didn't even know existed. He has a paper laid out, sipping an espresso.

I don't need a paper because I'm staring at a masterpiece.

"I think the bear is going to put me in your sister's bad books before we've even met." He smirks a little sexy lip hitch. I want to tell him that if he just does that in her direction I'm pretty sure all will be forgiven.

"Don't worry. I shall distract her by introducing you as my part-time continental fuck buddy and all will be fine."

He shakes his head and refocuses on his paper and I refocus on him. There's a slight smattering of dark hair that traces from his hands up to where his jumper is pushed up his forearm. It's major arm porn.

Arm. Porn.

He's here. Like really here.

In an orgasm giving, non-boyfriend capacity.

I smirk to myself as I catch sight of us both in an old-fashioned Peroni beer mirror. Yep, some girls get all the luck. My reflection shines back at me. There's an almost forgotten pink stain on my cheeks, my dark hair is down, a shadow against my scarlet cardigan I have on. Henri found it most amusing when I'd put on my weekend Converse and only came up to his nipples. Those heels do serve a purpose after all. Considering he'd only seen me in my black work attire until now he seemed oddly satisfied with the change.

"So, tell me about this party." He folds his paper carefully reminding me of the first time we met.

"Paige, she's going to be four." I wince. "I should warn you, she's a little on the wild side."

"How so?"

"You know, unbrushed hair, talks like a Neanderthal mainly in grunts and screams."

Henri reaches forward and tucks a wayward lock of my hair in place. "Sounds like a fun party."

"Oh, I can guarantee you Liv will have tried to put her in a posh party frock, and she'll be tearing around in her knickers and vest by the time we get there." I slurp my milky coffee, looping my hands around the warmth of the mug. The day isn't cold, but my fingers are numb almost. Pushing the observation away I ask, "Have you got any nieces or nephews?"

That shadow flickers across his. "One, although I think Maman has given up hope of her kids having anymore."

His gaze flickers to mine and I instantly look away. There is no future in that conversation at all.

"Brother or sister?"

"A sister." A firm press of his lips makes me want to know more. I lean forward waiting for more titbits about his life like a puppy waiting for training snacks. "She's not keen on settling down. Lives in Paris."

"Ah, Paris." I stare wistfully out of the window.

"You like it there?"

"Never been, but my heart tells me I would."

Henri's face folds in distaste. "Too touristy."

"More so than London?" I laugh louder now, waking up the waitress from her doze behind the counter.

"I think so. There are some good places to eat, but you have to know where to look. Everything else is cheap tourist fare."

"Heaven forbid cheap tourist fare." I grin into my coffee.

He mutters under his breath in French. I'm guessing disparaging remarks about said tourist fare while I muse on his words. "So, your 'contact' you stop in and check up on in Paris is actually your sister.

He meets my gaze again. "Very perceptive."

"I try." I smirk back but then I drop the smile while I try to piece my mystery man together. Sure, he's sitting right here, and I could ask him, but I have a feeling his answer would be very evasive and French if he wanted them to be. "So, you go from here, to Paris, and then on to your home all to see your sister?"

"Yes." He pretends to read the paper, his fingers curling a little into gentle fists.

"You must be the best big brother in the world." I take another sip of my coffee. "You are the big brother right?"

"Yes,' he repeats, looking up in surprise and I point to myself.

"Big sister. I can tell the signs." I try to smile but it sits lopsided on my face.

"Well, my little sister is the devil's mistress in disguise.

And your sister sounds relatively sensible, no? Apart from marrying a man not worthy of her."

I get that empty sensation in my stomach again. "She went off the rails once. When she was fifteen or so."

"What happened?" He links his long fingers together, expression expectant.

"It was my fault. My parents were really strict: always wanted us to do better, to do more. I rebelled against it." I chew on my lower lip. "Then I guess Liv just copied me. She got in a bad crowd, usual teenage stuff. Mum and dad blamed me; their perfect blonde angel was ruined because of me. They'd always been tough on me anyway. I never got the rope that Liv later used to suspend herself from disaster with."

Henry tilts my chin with a finger, and I look up in surprise, not even realising I'd dropped my gaze. "Then what happened?"

I do my best French shrug. "I moved out. They wanted to blame me for things that were half their fault. If they hadn't had been so bloody awful to me then I wouldn't have behaved the way I did and then Liv wouldn't have copied me. Words were said." I swallow hard. "I haven't really spoken to them since. Maybe the first couple of Christmases, but I quickly realised they had nothing really to say to me. They didn't get me."

"And who are you, Julianna Brown?"

Another impressive shrug. "I don't know."

"You tell me that you used to rebel, but yet you live in a flat devoid of all colour. That wrap is the brightest thing I've seen even close to you, and you talk about your cat like he's a live-in-lover."

"I do not," I protest.

He stares at me intently. "I'm interested to know where this firecracker went."

"Two years ago, I got meningitis. I nearly died." The words just blurt across the checked tablecloth between us. "It made me think that maybe what they'd said all along was right. Maybe I didn't take things seriously. Maybe I didn't strive for the best. Hell, by this point I was fully ensconced at Satire Weekly, a job that was pretty much going nowhere, as I found out yesterday when my boss told me we were going to fold."

"What! No satire! And I've been enjoying my subscription so much."

"What?" I frown over his side of the table.

He lifts his shoulders and drops them. "I wanted to know what it was all about. Call it an unexpected interest in satirical literature." His midnight eyes stare at me unabashed.

"You paid for it?" I grin up at him, wanting to get rid of the heaviness that has fallen on our unexpected weekend dalliance. "Wow, I must have been good in bed."

"Now that I can attest to." He glances at his leather strapped watch. "Which makes me think. How long until this party?"

"Why?" I bat my eyelashes.

"Because I want you on that sofa and I can't wait until tonight.

Well, if he puts it like that. I stand and grab my coat, and march for the counter where I pay for the breakfast before he can say otherwise.

"Are you coming?" I call out when I get to the door and he's still picking up his paper. "Time is of the absolute essence here."

"Ah, ma petite, you know I don't like to rush."

My legs turn to jelly and I can only wonder if I can walk home at all.

By the time we are at Notting Hill and standing outside my sister's slate-grey front door my legs are still trembling. "What are you so nervous about?" Henri chucks my chin, a smile teasing his mouth.

What am I so nervous about?

"I don't really know," I state truthfully. The last couple of hours have been magical, unreal I suppose in many ways. "Who are you when we walk inside there?" I just need clarification on this point.

"You don't want to introduce me as your lover?" he asks, his finger running down my cheek turning me to a shivering goo.

"Lover?" I can barely say the word, it seems so foreign. It's an exotic notion to have a lover. Us British girls we have 'boyfriends', 'that bloke I like', and at a push 'fuck buddy'.

None of those explain Henri properly.

I shake my head, scattering my confused thoughts. "You're right. I'm overthinking it. This is just fun, right?"

His lips find mine, warm and sweet. "The very best kind of fun." Another kiss. "Now can we knock on the door. I want to see the huge bear I bought."

I laugh into a kiss, unable to pull away from his warmth, the taste he has. We don't need to worry about knocking because the door pulls open, Liv standing there, her mouth as wide as the Dartford Tunnel. "What on earth?"

"Hi," I duck my head, "Sorry we're late." She's not staring at me. She's looking straight at Henri, eyes and mouth wide circles. "And this is my lover."

What the fuck?!

"No! Oh God, sorry, that's not what I meant."

Henri roars a laugh and then steps up towards Liv. "Olivia, I presume? I've heard a lot about you." He holds her arms delicately while he kisses her on both cheeks. "It's a pleasure. I'm Henri." His accent seems even thicker if that's possible and I'm not sure if he's laying it on just a little.

"Uh." She has nothing. *I know, Liv,* he rendered me speechless the first time we met too.

"Are we coming in?" I prompt.

"Sure." Flustered and adjusting her loose fit sweater, she steps back to allow us in. Henri stoops a little as he ducks through the door. I hold onto the waistband of his jeans and follow behind, needing some anchorage in the moment. Until Liv pulls me back by the elbow. "What the hell?" she hisses. "Who the fuck is that?"

There's a slash of betrayal in her expression and my stomach flips. I think I've just traversed the Sister's Coalition Agreement.

"It's Henri. I told you about him in January." I whisper back, knowing full well he is too close not to overhear the start of my interrogation, because believe me this is only the start. I'll still be under it when he's back in gloriously sunny France and doing what he does with cheese.

Her eyes widen. "That's love bite man?"

From behind I can see his cheeks curve. Yep, he's listening alright.

"But you haven't seen him in months?"

I wince. "That's not strictly true."

Liv's onslaught of hostile attack questioning is ceased by the screech of Paige as she skids into the hallway so fast she leaves track marks in the thick carpet. She shudders to a halt and stares up at Henri. I sigh. "Jeez, you could have brushed her hair."

"I tried. She was waiting for you."

Paige looks like a character from an awful cartoon movie she made me watch one Saturday afternoon. Wearing just knickers and with her hair hanging in her face in knots she looks like she should live with dinosaurs.

"Happy birthday, my beautiful." I drop to my knees and hold my arms wide for her to jump into, which she does with a crushing blow to my chest.

"Easy with Aunty Jules," Liv warns, and I glare at her. Henri's gaze is on me and I can feel it burning through the layers of my skin as he tries to see inside my locked treasure chest of 'sad'.

"It's my burfday," Paige tells me, holding up three fingers.

"Wait." I uncurl a fourth from her tight fist. "You need an extra one because you are..."

"Fithe," she explains through her hair.

"Four. You're four, and the most beautiful thing I've ever seen," I tell her earnestly, because thankfully, she is all her mum and very little of her dickhead dad. Snuggling in closer I whisper in her ear. "Where's the big bear?" Which makes her bounce in my arms.

"Mummy gots it upstairs. She said bad, bad words."

"Did you make her have soap?" I ask, trying to brush her hair back and balance her in my arms.

"I twieds, but she said her drink was soap." She scrunches her nose, sniffing out the obvious lie.

"To be fair, it probably tasted like soap, so shall we let her off?"

Paige nods, wide eyes luminous. "She's sad."

Liv's cheeks colour when I glance up at her.

"I know," I whisper. "Shall we get dressed for your party to cheer her up? Look I wore your favourite red cardigan." I make a show of swinging the long line knit around my thighs.

She eyes me approvingly and then looks at her mum before giving me a slow nod. "Sorry," I say to Henri. "I've got urgent auntying to do."

"Don't mind me," he smiles and all three of us girls just stare at him dazzled. "Although. I want to see my bear."

Paige's eyes widen. "It's amashing."

"Oh, I know." He nods with all seriousness and then turns to Liv holding up the bottles of wine he insisted we stopped to buy, to which I'd agreed, not knowing it was going to take forty minutes of perusing labels. "I've bought some wine, shall we?"

I breathe a sigh of relief that he's going to face the kitchen audience by himself. Sure, that makes me a bad person, but if I sporadically shout 'lover' again at anyone today or this lifetime I'd spend all eternity remembering it. Bad enough I've said it once to Liv.

As I carry Paige up the stairs, her strangling around my neck like a limpet on a rock, I consider the word *lover*. What is that? Someone you are sexually active with? Someone you are fond of, maybe too fond? But lover sounds like it should be fun, and while this isbelieve me I'll die a happy woman remembering how Henri woke me up this morning with his mouth in unexpected placesit feels bittersweet too.

Maybe if I wasn't dying. Maybe if he wasn't living in France with his grieving mother, then lover wouldn't be the right word at all. Maybe it would be more.

I catch myself smiling in the ornate white mirror on Paige's bedroom wall. I already know that I don't think

Henri would ever have a 'word'. He simply just is, and I can let that be. Let this be.

I think.

After some pretty swift administration with a hairbrush, a wet flannel, and some serious wrestling into cotton, I take the birthday girl downstairs where she is applauded like a duchess. "Remember the ice-cream," I whisper in her ear before she scampers around the kitchen island to twirl for Liv.

"Biggest bowl ever." She motions a massive circle with her arms, and I cringe. I don't think there will be that much bribery ice-cream in the house.

"Want your present, princess?" My eyes flit to Henri who's stood looking various levels of sexy with a glass of red loosely gripped in his fingers. Somehow, he makes holding a glass sexy. Now that is a life skill and make no mistake about it. Liv's friends, Hailey and Charlie, are staring at him with no regard for manners, while Rachel is trying very hard not to look because Peter is standing right at her side. Instead, her face looks contorted mid-aneurysm. "Everyone met Henri?" I grin and I'm met by nods.

"So, what do you do again?" Peter asks, puffing his chest. Bless him for trying.

"My family own a cheese business." Henri smiles and takes a sip of his drink, shoulders relaxed.

I'm still sure cheese is code for mafia.

"Oh, I love cheese," blurts Hailey.

"Hey, I thought you were vegan," Charlie shoots at her but then cracks a grin. "It's okay. I've heard the cheeseburger rumours."

"And what do you do in London?" Liv asks. Interrogation 101—don't let the victim relax for one moment. His gaze flicks to me and my cheeks warm. I'm what he does when he comes to London.

"Any chance of a glass of wine," I mutter to myself getting zero response.

"I visit restaurants who purchase direct from us. We are a very innovative business and when our clients have ideas we like to try and build on them."

"But cheese is cheese right?" Peter asserts.

Henri flashes his best enigmatic smile. "Indeed, it is."

Definite mafia.

"So, petite princess." Henri turns to Paige. "Is your aunty giving you your present?"

Oh crap, yes.

"Here you go, munchkin." I hand her over the gifts that Henri helped me buy just yesterday afternoon. It feels like a lifetime ago.

Imagine if you could live a lifetime in every day.

I'd probably do anything for that right now.

Henri squats down next to where Paige is savagely ripping at paper. "Here, pull this bit." He helps her and a large lump forms in my throat as he ducks his head down.

To live a lifetime in one day... maybe that's all I've got now.

One day at a time, each one as full as possible.

Seeing Henri crouched with Paige, his face animated as she wrestles the correctly sized Hamleys bear out of the paper along with various books, pyjamas, and a tiara that Henri insisted on, I feel the source of my life ebbing away from me.

I will never have this.

Never have birthday parties for my children.

Never watch their father interact with them.

All too soon I'm mourning a life I've forgotten to live

and the evidence of that is six-foot-four with a dazzling smile who's currently talking to my niece like she's the most important person in the room, possibly the planet.

God, I've been a fool.

A total fool.

Too scared by nearly dying, I've now forgotten to live at all.

"You okay, Jules?" Liv links her hand through my arm, tugging me into her side.

"I'm sorry I didn't tell you last month when I saw him again. I just..."

"It didn't feel real?"

"Can you blame me?" I offer a dry snort of a laugh.

"No, not at all." She pulls me slightly to one side, but she needn't worry about us being overheard; Paige is making a terrific amount of noise, and everyone is clapping as she puts on her tiara and declares herself the queen. "But you know this is dangerous territory. Have you even told him?"

Henri's eyes flash up to mine right at that moment and my stomach dips at the smile he gives me. It's full of unspoken words that make my pulse race in my veins.

"It's just fun, that's all. He's not interested in anything serious, he's told me."

We both watch as Henri concedes to being Paige's royal pony and crawls around on his hands and knees while she yee-haws—not very royal if you ask me.

"You sure about that, Jules? Forgive me if I'm wrong, but you've never brought home a man who's done *that* before."

"I've never brought home a man."

She touches her top lip with the tip of her tongue before laying down her trump card. "My point exactly."

16

RAIN

Liv throws her arms around Henri, Lenny squished between them. "Next time you are in town make sure you come and say hi." She blushes and tucks her hair behind her ear.

Maybe she can have him when I'm gone.

The thought blasts out of nowhere. What was that?

"I will, if Julia invites me again." He winds his arm around my waist and kisses the top of my head.

Liv meets my gaze and we both know the unspoken words. I force them away though because I'm absolutely one hundred percent fine and can't see it changing any time soon.

"Come on, it looks like it's going to rain." I cast a glance up at the dark sky. It looks rather like my emotions feel. Like they could burst at any point and just pour down. My throat still feels thick from singing happy birthday to Paige.

So many last things.

I snuggle into Henri's side as we meander down the road. The familiarity he weaves over me is on the level of being profound.

"You're quiet, ma petite." He breaks the silence as the stars start to shine above us. "That sadness has grown today, no?"

I shake my head. "Not sad."

"I hope not. Otherwise, I would think I'm doing this weekend date wrong."

"A weekend date? You're making this shit up now."

With a low laugh he stops and pulls me around, hungry lips finding mine, his body protecting me from the chill in the air.

I want to freeze frame this. Kisses under starlight.

"I could kiss you as a full-time job." I breathe out a shuddering breath when he finally returns ownership of my lips; not that they feel like mine, all warm and buzzing.

"You feel it don't you, Julianna?" He smooths my hair.

"Feel what?" I ask, but I know.

Without words he presses my palm against his chest.

"The bitter irony I've found you here, the one time in my life I am stuck where I am. Fate plays cruel games. She gives with one hand and then takes with the other."

I can't argue with this. It's fact.

"I think irony is a running theme in my life." I force away the dark brooding clouds in my head and force a smile.

"Care to elaborate, ma petite?"

Yes. I'm dying, but somehow you are this magical being that's manifested into my life just when I thought it was over...

"No."

A large droplet lands on my forehead. "Oh shit. We will get soaked." My dress, beautiful as it is under my cardigan, is not meant for British chilled downpours.

Henri grasps my face, tilting my chin. "This conversation isn't over, but right now we need to..." his smile flashes. "Run!"

"Nooo!!" I try to hold him back, but he has my hand and tows me along, my legs pumping to keep pace. The droplets turn into a cold torrent, slipping over my skin in chilled rivets, sneaking under my dress, mashing my scarlet cardigan into a soggy layer.

"Let's get in here, under a tree." I point to a small park with railings. "I can't run like this." We are too far from the shops and the shelter of doorways.

He swerves in, his dark hair smattered in soaked waves, his olive skin glistening under the streetlamps, blurred with rain drops.

"Henri, I can't run." My chest. Oh my god. So tight. The beat uneven, as if it can't remember how to make a rhythm, a useless drum kit in the hands of a child with chopsticks and not proper drumsticks.

He turns, waves scattering more water. If I wasn't struggling to breathe, I'd be admiring his soaked chest. Without hesitation, he swings me up in his arms and paces into the park, cursing as he searches for a bench under a tree, which of course there isn't because—bird shit.

Folding his legs, he settles us under a large oak, it's newly unfurled spring leaves providing a light canopy against the onslaught.

"Bloody British weather," he growls.

I chuckle, but it comes out strangled as I try to rid myself of the drums, the beating, the band of panic and failure.

"Julianna, what is it?"

I shake my head, hiding in his shoulders, fingers winding in what the elements have left of his lambswool jumper.

"Julianna." Firmer this time, he holds the back of my head as a great wave of emotion rolls over me, breaking on a shore of resistance in one sob, then another, then another.

Strange I haven't cried since that day after Dr Francis' appointment. Now it wants to surge up and out of me and into his arms.

"Shhh." Gently he rocks us. His trousers must be ruined in the mud, yet he cradles me closer; lips on my hair, my ear, my cheek, anywhere that he can gain access too.

"Sorry," I mutter when I can finally breathe.

"Don't apologise."

I could sit forever under the gentle sweep of his hand.

There is no forever.

"Shall we go back to Liv's? Does she have a pump?"

What pump? Oh, he thinks I have asthma. That ice-cream scoop hollows my stomach again.

"No, no. Let's just go home," I say, and he pulls back slightly, the left corner of his mouth lifting a tiny wedge.

"Home." He nods, and his eyes flash. "Tell me, ma petite, will I have to carry you the whole way?"

"No. I have a better idea." I scramble for my handbag and fish out my phone, trying to protect it from the persistent rain. I flick the screen and type. "Down the road there's a late-night café. We could stop in there instead of trying to make it all the way to the Tube." I try to peer through the park at the road. We are a little way off the main streets and there's no traffic, no cabs.

"Coffee at midnight. I think I'm turning you French."

I snort a laugh and it's the perfect medicine to eradicate any lingering side effects of my turn. I flex my fingers and rotate my ankles one by one to check their circulation. All seems in order, so I shut my worries down into a deep, dark place to think about another time. I'm sure as hell not going to waste Henri time on it.

That tick of my internal clock vibrates loudly. A scream of frustration builds in my chest.

"Julianna, what are you thinking about?" Henri clutches my face, pulling me closer until we are nose to nose.

"Nothing."

"Liar."

I breathe a little weak exhalation, saying, "Just that I wished I met you sooner," and then drop my gaze. "Sorry, I know it's not what we discussed. This is just a thing, a casual... fling." The last word is a stretch to say.

His lips seek mine, still warm. His tongue sneaks into my mouth, stealing my half-mumbled thoughts and words like he can read them directly from the source rather than what I'm attempting to say. I lean into him, sighing with the perfection of it. His hand grasps my knee, running across the damp rain washed skin.

Eventually he pulls away and I'm breathless for all the good reasons and none of the bad. "I wish we had too."

"This is crazy right?"

He pulls back slightly. "Would you be saying that if we'd met at your local pub or met at work? How quick would you fall in love with me then?"

I freeze at the L-word. Did he mean to say that? A slip of the tongue?

I try to read the expression on his face, the shadows, a solemnity that makes the world stop turning.

"The moment I met you."

He nods.

Is that what this is? Love.

It can't be. I can't offer love because it isn't mine to give.

I'm no longer me to give. I've got a date with destiny that no one can avoid.

I clamber off his lap and then hold out my hand. His face darts with an expression I can't read. "Come on then, show me how to be French." I laugh, forcing it out into the night sky. "Because I'm sure as hell ordering a cup of warm, sweet tea."

His face is adorable.

"You should try it; it's good for the soul."

I take a sip of the coffee, ready to pull a face. I don't have a personal vendetta against the drink; in fact, I like a latte with my breakfast. This is no latte.

Henri is standing behind the counter of the small café. His almost dry shirt sleeves pushed up. The jumper got discarded somewhere with disgust and some muttered guttural French.

Midnight eyes watch me carefully as I wet my lips and lick. I purr like a cat under his satisfied smile. I'm a quick learner and I'm learning Henri's ways like an A-Star student.

"It's sweet." I meet his eyes in surprise.

Samantha, who should be on the other side of the counter but is instead sitting with me, takes a sip of hers. I smile smugly as she fails the lick and taste test. Ha. See. A-Star student.

Henri is behind the counter because when he'd seen her assaulting the coffee machine with barely concealed disdain he'd started offering pointers to help. Enough pointers that she'd then said, "Do it yourself then," and stropped her ripped jean-wearing ass all the way around to my side.

"This is what we would have after dinner to settle the

digestion." Henri's focus is all on me, not the punk-haired twenty-something next to me. I twinkle like a little star in response.

"After dinner? How do you ever sleep?" It's sweet. I take another sip to reconfirm, but there's a smooth power there.

"No one sleeps straight after dinner, ma petite."

"I thought the French ate late?" I ask. "Isn't that a European thing?"

He nods, his smile telling me he's pleased I know this. "Yes, nine." A shrug, but I'm looking on aghast.

"Nine! I'd be passed out in hunger on the floor."

"Our workday is entirely different. Well, how *we* run things is. I guess in the cities things have changed, maybe to keep up with the modern world, but the flow of our life will never change entirely. You have to remember it's so hot in the summer. We work early, then break, work again late afternoon, and then eat our meal late."

"Still going to bed on a full stomach. My Nana said you should always have three hours before sleep," Samantha tells him.

"Believe me, there is plenty of time before the end of the meal and sleep." His eyes are on me and I light into a slow but steady bonfire. One puff of wind and I'll be burning like a beacon in the sky.

I am more than happy to occupy that time before dinner and sleep with him.

"Our evening meals are different to yours too. A meat-based dish, something simple, followed by a salad, then a coffee, and a small slice of something sweet to finish off."

"What? You don't have your salad with your main meal?" Samantha blasts.

Henri looks repulsed, a grimace turning his kissable

mouth down at the edges. "Why would you want to mix all your flavours? The salad is to palate cleanse, to savour."

I want him to savour me, and I'm pretty sure we should be getting home now. Home. Funny word. It's ringing with a different note in my head. I glance at the time on my screen. "It's midnight!"

"Do you turn into a pumpkin?" He smirks and Samantha chuckles. I throw her some major side-eye. Back off bitch.

"No, but don't you have to get a train in the morning?"

He waves his hand dismissively. "Whenever."

God, I hate the little tightening in my stomach.

"So not first thing?"

His eyes meet mine. "Non, unless you want me to?"

I think we both know the answer to that. I down my coffee in one. He's right, it's perfect, but I can think of other things equally perfect, and I can definitely think of things to do to fill three hours before sleep.

Sleep is for the weak anyway. I can sleep when he's gone.

The thought hits me in the stomach but I ignore it.

The Tube takes forever. I bounce my legs the whole way. The walk to the apartment is a sprint. Neither of us talking, fingers tightly bound. It's a race to satisfaction.

We burst through the door. "Cat," I shout as I start peeling off my wet clothes.

Henri launches through to the kitchen, mutters to the cat, blasts some biscuit into the bowl like bullets against china and then races back. Hands reaching for my face, clutching me in close and tight, pressing his mouth to mine. I tug at his shirt, fingers quicker at the buttons as I throw it to the floor in record time, and he cages me against that warm and smooth olive skin. "We should have come home hours ago. Just given Paige her present and left. What a waste," I mutter with small kisses, pressing one after the other on his lips.

"Plenty of time." He hauls me up and steps for the bedroom, kicking the door shut on Barney.

Hours later I'm fulfilling my new favourite role in life as a jumper across Henri's chest. His fingers are dancing that path down my spine that makes sleep impossible, although I think the coffee might have put paid to that anyway.

We lay in silence listening to the odd car rumble down the road, distant from our cocoon of satiated safety.

"Are we leaving this to fate again?" I ask his chest.

I know he's going to want eye contact for this, and the fact I know that fact is life altering. He lifts me as expected, hand cupping around my ear. "Do you want to?"

"Do you?"

"I asked first."

"No."

"Good."

He seals the deal with a kiss.

"Henri, I can't offer any more than this." My eyes sting, emptiness flooding my limbs until they are laden and heavy.

"I know. And neither can I." His lips press into a firm line and I wished I knew what they meant.

I don't ask. What would be the point? I lie down and settle back into my favourite place, waiting for dawn to come.

17

WHAT'S AT THE END OF THE RAINBOW?

Goodbyes are my new most despised thing. The middle of April and all I can hear is the tick and the tock, the tick and the tock.

Henri hasn't been back. We've had the odd telephone call, late night, me snuggled under blankets, Netflix forgotten. He's busy. His voice strained, a tightness running through the lyrical notes that hasn't been in existence when he's here.

I might not see him again. I know that.

The ice-cream scoop has been replaced by a razor-sharp Stanley knife that every so often casts me down with a quick flick of its blade.

"How's it looking?" I ask. Dr Francis is reading my charts. He's got me on the outpatient ward today so he can monitor me for longer. Three hours longer.

"Julianna," he starts and I physically wince.

"That bad?"

"I'm worried about your oxygen levels. It's just not high enough. They are far too low, in the seventies. How is the breathlessness?"

"Fine," I say, smile tight.

"Uh huh." He reads on a bit more. "Nothing from the transplant team?"

Why is his face so grey? What does he know that I don't? I kind of figured I'd got all the bad news back in January?

"Ankles swelling?"

"No, just the usual tingles." I answer honestly and he sweeps a swift glance over me, reading my previous lie.

"We need to decide whether to operate on the valves again." He perches on the end of the bed and it's a death bell of warning.

"Again? You said before that it wouldn't work again."

With a thoughtful nod, he puts my clipboard to one side. "And I can't say it will. I'm just wondering if it's worth the risk."

"What's the risk?" I push up higher on the creaky bed.

"It could make things worse; the heart could be put under just too much pressure."

"Then what?"

"It really depends how the heart reacts. It's a strong machine, Julia, but it's only an organ. The stress of the anaesthetic could put you into arrest."

"A heart attack?" I gasp.

"Or it could be total failure and you don't come around again, and if we don't get to revive you, the heart won't start again."

"Wow, that's some risk. I don't think I'd want to take the chance."

He looks at me with such earnestness. How does he face this as a job? "Julia, you could go into arrest at any time. Your stats really are very low."

"But I feel fine."

"Do you?"

Damn him and his mind reading.

A gust of a sigh blasts from my lips. "No. I'm really, really tired. It's getting harder and harder to get through every day. Work is a slog."

"That's because your heart can't cope. It's under enormous pressure. Enormous." He repeats the key word for emphasis just in case I missed its importance the first time.

"Do I need to stop work? Will that help things? You told me twelve months in January."

He shakes his head and rests his hand on mine. "No, Julia. I said a few months, twelve at the most.'

Silently I absorb what he's saying.

"That changes things," I mutter. "That changes things a lot."

Pulling my knees up to my chest, I drop my head onto them as hot tears burn my eyes. It's only April. I haven't done anything yet, been anywhere.

Henri

His name whispers through my brain.

"I'll leave you to get dressed. I'd like to see you again in two weeks please." With a motion he rubs my sobbing back. "I think it's time to talk about end-of-life care so please can you bring your sister?"

I swallow down a rising tide of vomit pressing my eye sockets so hard into my knees they ache.

I can't answer so I nod. The pull of the bay's curtain on its rails tells me he's gone. A woman in pieces left alone to have a private moment. How many times has this trained medic seen people just like me? To know when to go, or maybe to now be immune to it? When I'm alone I sob, hard and fast.

. . .

"Oh my god, what on earth is wrong with you?" Liv pulls me into her house, her Dyson is still running in the lounge. "I've been so worried about you, why didn't you call straight after your appointment?"

"I..." I heave, my chest has a boulder pushing down on it, my ribcage unable to move. "I saw Dr Francis."

Liv's face falls and she tugs at the Marigolds on her hands. "Okay, what did he say?"

I can't repeat the words. Can't find the vowels and consonants to articulate them. So instead I cry. "Oh, sweetie." She winds her arms around me and crushes us together. "What are we going to do?"

I shake my head and press my face into her neck. "There isn't anything to do, Liv."

"I'll make tea."

My watery grin breaks through like weak sunshine after a storm. "Tea would be good. Although I might need something stronger. I'm going to call Mum and Dad."

Liv's alabaster skin sickens to a dove grey. "Fuck. This really is it, isn't it?"

I nod. "Yeah, sis, I think it's time to start realising the fact." I walk for the kitchen, her zombie ghosting behind me via a detour to the humming vacuum cleaner. The space feels good. I don't have to see her heartbreak while I'm crunching through my own. I turn the kettle on, ready for the next bombshell. "Dr Francis wants you to come to my next appointment in two weeks because we need to discuss end-of-life care."

I meet her gaze and she stares at me in horror. "What does that even mean?"

I lift my shoulders to my ears. "I actually don't know." Then unable to stand up any longer, I crumple to the floor.

. . .

I'm curled on the plush armchair, a sweet cup of tea balanced on the arm, a coaster underneath of course. I don't want to die right this minute.

The ring of the phone at my ear is making nausea climb up my throat again, but I look across at Liv and her eager smile stops me from hanging up.

After five rings I think maybe I'll just be able to leave a voicemail, but just as I'm mentally high-fiving the fact the line connects. "Hello."

"Hi, Mum, it's Julia."

There's a sharp stab of silence. "Julia, how unexpected."

I scrunch my nose and then inhale a bolstering breath. "It's okay, I'm not calling to chat. I know that's not our thing."

"Julia, please."

I cut her off. "I have something to tell you that's important and I just wanted you to know without Olivia having to be the one to tell you. I want to protect her from that. Are you sitting down? You need to sit down."

"Just a minute." I hear a shuffle. "Okay."

"There's no easy way to say this but I'm dying. It's been ongoing since I was ill a couple of years ago, but, well, uh, yes well, that's it really."

Across the room Liv's face crumples.

There isn't a single sound from the other end. I'm about to hang up when I change my mind.

"You and Dad treated me really unfairly all those years ago. I was a young woman, enjoying herself. I didn't do one thing that any other person my age wouldn't have been doing. Olivia made her own choices, she still makes her own choices, and we are still the very best of friends. All of this, all of this distance, the shame you made me feel. It's on your parenting not on me. And do you know what, Mum, I can go to the other side, I can die, knowing that fact is true. I'm a good person, always have been, but you tried to cast me as a monster so you could blame someone for your own mistakes. If anyone should accept the blame for Olivia's behaviour it's you and Dad. You should have let us live, not held us down."

With the end of my splurge of words, I hang up before she can say anything: tell me I'm loose-moraled, weak willed. Whatever other shit she's told me before.

I gasp for air, adrenaline running through my veins. My heart is way too quick.

Liv pads over the carpet swerving Lenny onto his play-mat as he drools like a champ. "I'm so sorry, Jules. Sorry they blamed you. Sorry that I was so stupid. I always make out that I'm the sensible one, the grown up one, but really it's been you all along. Look at the damn mess I'm in, living in a house I can't afford with two kids, married to a bastard who left."

"But look at the kids." I point at Lenny trying to roll over but only getting halfway and then flopping back like a blob of jelly. "And do you know what, Liv. I know this is hard for you, I know you've always tried to maintain something with Mum and Dad, but I don't care, and I'm sure as hell not going to spend the rest of my time thinking about them. Same as I'm sure they won't think of me, even when I'm gone."

"What do you want to do with the rest of your time?" She slips her fingers in mine and gives a little squeeze.

I chuckle low and gruff. "I think my options are running out. I haven't got time to get married, have children, or earn a million pounds."

"Why the hell didn't you tell me you've been feeling worse?"

I raise my brows. "So you can live the ordeal with me?"

"Yes! We are sisters."

Leaning forward, I wrap her into a tight hug. "That we are, but you are your own woman too. You've got lots of lovely friends, and your wonderful children. Pretty sure you'll find a decent man someday... you know if you search under all the rocks and kiss all the frogs."

Ice-cream city, my stomach hollows.

"You thinking of Henri?"

"Would it be sick and twisted if I was?"

"No. You like him."

"Come on Liv, I hardly know him to *like* him. You can't *like* someone you've only spent a matter of hours with and have kissed more than you've spoken too."

Liv purses her lips in response and then swivels to face me. "Who says?"

"Uh, everyone, the universe."

"Come on, Jules, look at me. I did things the right way. Went to uni. to get a glittering career, just like we were told we should. Met Darren who promised me everything, but who sadly gave me nothing, except the kids." She pauses, face twisted, too many lemons in her lemonade of life. "Now I have no career, will probably have to move out of my home and I'm a single mother. Don't get me wrong, I'd do anything for these kids, they are my everything." Her gaze drifts to Lenny who has his whole fist in his mouth. "But do I wish I'd done things differently? Hell yeah, sometimes." Her face drops, splashed with colours of guilt and remorse.

"You wouldn't even have to think thoughts like that if Darren wasn't such a dickweed."

Liv snorts a laugh. "But you see my point."

"What are you suggesting I do? Call Henri and ask if he has time to see me just one last time?"

A stretch of silence elongates between us, pulling thoughts into my head that I want to block but can't. Dr Francis' words mainly.

"What do you want to do, Jules?" Liv's voice filters in and mixes with concepts such as *end-of-life care* and *dangerously low oxygen.*

A tight weave of panic plaits around my chest but I push against it, fighting. I've got to keep fighting. Dr Francis was only giving me his side of the coin. I've still got that small sliver of a chance that I might get lucky.

That's my end of the rainbow I've got to hold on for. So, what do I do while I wait?

I meet my sister's eyes. "I want to live, because I really don't think I have. How sad is that? I've been so scared since the virus hit and all this started that I've forgotten how."

"Julianna!" Liv blasts and I rock back. "You haven't been living since Mum and Dad blamed you for the fact I started shoplifting and doing drugs. You weren't to blame, I was."

"It's irrelevant now."

"How can you even say that? Your life is almost up, and you haven't lived it, all because of me."

"Utter codswallop." We meet one another's eyes and then burst out in laughs. My laugh is so deep it might bring on my need for end-of-life care. My belly aches as I try to calm myself down.

"I'm going to find Henri."

"You mean call him and ask if he can visit?"

I shake my head. "No. That's not living. I don't know

how many weeks I have left, but I'm going to make every one of them count."

Like rain drowning out the sun, Liv's laughter morphs into tears. "I can't believe this. You seem so fine."

I reach for her hand. "I know it looks that way. It's exhausting keeping this up though, because truth is I'm not. I'm tired, Liv, so damn tired. Every breath... it doesn't give me what I need. I can feel it. There's this empty hunger in the place of where vitality should be."

"I don't think I can do this, Jules, don't think I can watch this, live through losing you."

I hold myself together, my hand that isn't holding hers wrapping around my middle. "I'll just slip away eventually. I think that's how it works."

Who knew talking about dying could be so pragmatic?

"Henri?"

"I'm going to find where he lives."

"And then?"

"Then I'm going to go there."

"And then?"

"Then," I pause. "Actually, I have no damn idea." A giggle builds in my stupid, useless chest. "I think I finally understand this living malarkey. I can almost imagine the kiss of the French sun on my skin, can taste its warmth. I have no idea if he wants to see me, sure I could ring and ask, but that doesn't sound much like an adventure to me."

"But wait," her face falls, "you can't travel, Jules. You'll need insurance, medical cover, God knows, I'll have to research—"

Holding up my hand, I cut her off. "Insurance? Olivia, I'm trying to live, not die of boredom while you create me a risk assessment."

She gives me the look, the, *you'd better not let me regret this* look. Then she sighs and shakes her head. "I'll get my laptop."

"What for?" *Please, God, not a spreadsheet.*

Shaking her head she stalks for the kitchen. "So we can google cheese."

Well, that makes much more sense than turning up in Perpignan and knocking on doors until I find that perfect specimen of Man Mountain.

Am I doing this, really doing it?

My gut tells me yes and my heart is nodding along. Both in perfect sync for the first time.

I'm really doing this. Adrenaline hammers my veins hard and fast.

"Will you look after Barney?" I call after her.

Later when I'm home, after I've played my favourite role of Aunty and put Paige to bed, smelling her clean and combed hair as we snuggled for stories, I pull out the peacock diary. At the bottom of my bucket list, I write: **Find Henri.**

Right at the top, I poise my pen, waiting for the right word. Then in capitals I put: **Live.**

18

THE SUN IS A MANY SPLENDORED THING

SWEET JESUS. I cling onto the handle attached to the ceiling of the taxi as it weaves through the streets. I'd love to be able to look at the town, but it's a blur through the window. My non- English cab driver appears to be a Formula 1 racing pro, while the rest of Perpignan seem to be Sunday drivers. I screw my eyes shut as we zoom up to the rear end of a red Renault.

I'm going to die in this taxi before I even get to see Henri.

Breathe, Julia, and don't look, it's better this way.

Unable to decide if I should just rock up to Henri's cheese dynasty and knock on the door, I've taken the slightly easier option of booking a hotel.

We pull up outside a sandstone square building with bright-blue shutters. The double-fronted fascia is covered in hanging baskets screaming an array of colours. Leaves and petals sway in a gentle, rhythmic dance. I stare out of the window of the death cab and take it in. It's as beautiful as the man who lives in this town. *Petite auberge de la ville.* I only booked it because it said 'little' which made me think of Henri, but now I can see it rather than just a gallery of images on Google, I know I've made the right choice.

Beautiful. How had Henri even managed to smile coming to London from here?

This is the place for smiles.

The cab driver flings open his door, not all that concerned whether it stays on its hinges and saunters around to the boot, cranking it open and tossing out my small cabin bag. Scrambling out, I get my purse ready.

"Combien?" I ask, using the last of my remaining French after, yes, no, and thank you.

He rattles off an intelligible string of words, but I just about catch "Vingt."

Diving into my purse, I peel off the fare and a tip. He nods his head and lowers back into his cab, screeching away from the curb. Twenty seems cheap for an airport ride to me, but I guess if you drive that fast you can fit in unlimited trips a day. He must be loaded.

Taking my time, I turn around. I'm actually here, although I can't quite believe it. Right up until I got on the plane, I wasn't quite sure I would. Now I'm here, it's the best decision I've ever made. The air is warm, sweet with flowers, and a hint of fresh coffee. Voices are chattering, birds are singing, and my god the sun is shining. Lifting my face, I seek the golden rays.

According to Google, Henri's cheese empire is out in the countryside, so todaywell until I'm brave enough to go and knock on his doorI'm going to relax, recharge, and do some exploring.

A little spark runs through me. I'm here, I've done this. I've stepped out of the box to life. Hauling up my bag, I walk into the cool reception of the hotel. The marble floors are slippery under my sandals and I almost ice skate myself to the reception desk. Trying to be discreet, I slide open my phone and glance down at my ready primed screen. "Bonjour comment vas-tu? J'ai une réservation." I do not in any way make it sound French. The lady, sixties and smart as a shiny new pin, shoots me a spearing, shrewd look.

"Would English be better, Madame?"

Wouldn't it just. With a thankful smile I nod. "Please. Sorry, did that hurt your ears?"

"I've heard worse," she clips in heavily accented English.

"Oh, I don't know. I might succeed them all yet." I grin in a vain attempt at friendliness. In vain because this woman can only be friends with blocks of ice.

Tapping fuchsia nails on a keyboard, she glares at the screen. "Mademoiselle Brown?"

Ah, I've been downgraded from Madame. Oh well.

"Oui," I answer.

"Room fifteen. Breakfast ends at seven sharp."

"Seven!" I exclaim, but then clamp my lips shut.

"Evening meals, should you wish to dine with us, are served in the restaurant. You will need to make a reservation."

"Okay, thanks." I almost bob a curtsey. How can such a beautiful building house such a miserable old crone? Mysteries of the universe and all that.

"Thank you. I'm going to go exploring." She hands me a key with the biggest wooden keyring on it I've ever seen. I see the game here, make it so big that people can't put it in their pockets and walk off with them. This way all keys are left at reception and she knows who is in and out. "Merci." I take the key and force it into the back pocket of my cropped jeans.

Leaving the sour-faced old coot, I seek out room fifteen,

although the smell of coffee is making my stomach growl with the zest of a bear straight out of hibernation. Well, it's sure too late for breakfast and nowhere close to dinner, so I push on for my room, determined to get back out in the sunshine and find a small café to eat at.

The room makes me exhale a low and steady breath. Unlike the dim and cool interior of reception this is something else entirely: feminine and delicate with whites and blues, sheer voile curtains brushed in a breeze through the open balcony doors. "Oh my," I breathe out loud, my own voice bouncing back at me. Stalking for the curtains, I pulled them to one side to be greeted by the most spectacular view of streets winding off into the distance, framed by a vivid blue sky. Down below a canal or maybe a river, if there's a difference, serenely cut through the street.

I think I'm finally in love. Eager to get out there, to walk those winding paths, to touch and feel all the things, I plant my suitcase on the bed and tear open the zip. Grabbing my hairbrush, I yank it through my hair and tie it in a high ponytail before squirting myself with some perfume. No time for showers, I want to explore. The shoe situation needs more thought though. I go back to the Juliette balcony to look at the pavements. As much as I love my gladiator sandals, I will fall on my ass in them. I pull out my Converse and tie them on, before realising the look is putting me into the 'man pant' zone. Flipping through my capsule packing, I tug free a cotton dress and quickly swap my jeans and t-shirt, pairing the low-cut trainers with a sundress. Now I look like I'm on holiday. The cardigan I needed when leaving England can stay firmly behind. I throw it onto a high back chair.

Right. This is it.

Life.

I pause at the door. The unknown stretches in front of me. There's a little voice that says, *Julia, you came here to find Henri, not buy knick knacks.* But I push it away. I can find Henri tomorrow when I've had a shower and prepared... I still need to consider what I'm going to say to him, other than the fact I've stalked him all the way to his home because my life is about to end, and this trip is my last hurrah.

Yeah, I need to work on that.

I don't feel like my life is going to end. Right now, it seems ridiculous that's even a possibility. I'm buzzing, fizzing like a shaken bottle of champagne.

Grabbing the key and knowing I'm going to have to give it back to the sour puss at the desk, I slip back out of the room.

Desk woman isn't there, so I drop the key in the box and make my way outside, the sunshine sinking into my skin, kissing the tip of my nose and turning my hair warm.

Turning right, I walk along the river with its brasseries and restaurants, all of them offering a plat du jour. I stop at a couple, perusing their menu, grateful for the Anglais page, of fresh caught fish or varying cuts of steak. My stomach growls again but I don't want to sit in a full restaurant, I want to explore. I'll seek out somewhere to buy a pastry and a coffee while I walk. There are narrow lanes leading away from the main drag, and I dive up one on instinct, thrusting forward into a warren of close shops, cobbled streets, and geranium-filled hanging baskets which splatter red, white and pink like they are waving a new national flag. The air in my lungs is sweet, tinged with the earthy scent of the flowers and leather goods being offered by the nearest shop which has handbags hanging on rails outside its windows. Automatically, I reach to touch the warm and supple leather, ducking my head when the owner blasts a string of French at me I have no hope of understanding, although I can get the gist he wants me to come inside and buy all his fine goods, not that he's accusing me of stealing any of them. He throws his hands to the side with a shrug as I walk away, and it makes my stomach lurch.

What am I doing? I came here to find Henri, not buy a handbag. This is typical Julianna, hiding not living.

Bollocks. With a newfound sense of determination, I go to head back down to the river. I can find something to eat eventually, but first I need to find Henri. I've got to face this full on. No more hiding, no more burying my head in the sand.

I manage a whole twenty seconds, until I'm heading back in the direction of the hotel and a familiar shape is walking towards me. I'd know the strong curve of the shoulders anywhere, the slim narrowing of his waist. I know them more than I know his favourite colour. What I don't know, or who I don't know rather is the tall blonde with his arm looped through his.

That's my elbow to hold I want to shout, but of course I don't. I stand there like a fish gasping for breath out of water and about to be gutted alive.

I can feel his eyes land on me, the familiar shiver running over my skin. I want to run, but my feet have cemented themselves to the pavement.

Too late, too slow, I spin and turn away, my cheeks so hot I think that they might melt off my face.

"Julianna?" His call is laced with total disbelief.

I keep walking. I can't run... because I nearly die, literally.

Although I'm pretty close to dying with total mortification anyway.

What the hell have I been thinking? We never made any promises to one another, we never even had anything set in stone to see one another again. The leggy blonde is his reason enough.

This whole insane love affair is all in my head. Of course, it's in my head.

I shudder as he grasps his fingers onto the bare skin of my elbow. My eyes are so hot with tears I can't see through the blur.

"Am I dreaming?" His nose skims my cheek, his sunshine and mint filling my senses.

I try to pull away, self-respect and all that, but he has me firmly by the arms. "Pretty sure I'm in a nightmare," I mutter.

His lips brush mine and my traitorous body liquifies at the touch. "Where are you running to, ma petite fleur?" And just like that he has me.

It's what I've been craving. What I've been living for, forcing myself on for; one more petite fleur.

I've heard it now. I can leave.

Or I can let his tongue steal into my mouth, seeking me out as I gasp into his embrace, hot tears stinging down my cheeks.

"Why are you crying?" Henri shifts back, thumbs brushing away my overwhelm.

"I thought... I thought... I'm sorry I came. I just... just wanted to see you."

Lowering his forehead, he rests it on mine. "I'm so sorry, Julianna, I hoped to come back by now. Things have been difficult."

I'm loosely holding onto the fact that difficult might not mean a blonde. But then he just had his tongue in my mouth. Unless that's a French thing I haven't been made aware of. No, they definitely do the two-kiss thing, three if they really like you. I think tongue rates above that.

Those midnight eyes shine in the sun. "I can't believe you are here." He's stepping back now, cool air scented with flowers rushing between us as he shakes his head. "This is crazy."

I wince and pull a face. "Do I get a stalker award?"

"You get the best gift known to man award." His face, which seemed shadowed with lines as I saw him walking towards me brightens, a luminosity directed straight at me like I'm the moon to his sun.

"Bonjour?" The blonde woman: immaculate cut shift dress; hair running like honey hanging down her shoulders, steps between us. "Henri, tu as les manières d'un porc." Her accent is lyrical like his. "You must be Julianna?" she adds in English. Sexy English too.

"Uh, yes." I have nothing else. I can't hazard a guess who she is, apart from maybe my arch nemesis.

Henri chuckles. "She just said I have the manners of a hog. She could have said it in English, but I guess she didn't want to scare you off."

"Oh," I smile up at her and instantly hate her on the spot. She has cheekbones you could ski off-piste off, long thick eyelashes, and that natural golden glow that looks like she jogs down the beachfront every day dressed only in a thong bikini.

"Odile is a family friend."

She links her arm through mine, leading me away from Henri. "We were just going for lunch to discuss his dear maman." Her English is faultless. I hate her even more.

"Oh, no." He grabs me back. He's so tanned and bloody gorgeous. How have I been missing this? His hair is longer, just a fraction, enough for it to curl around his ears and wave across his forehead. The suit, cut to fit his skin, is missing. Instead, he's wearing Henri a la Casual, a delectable and almost dreamy combination of pale-blue cotton shirt and navy chinos. On his feet are... are... leather sliders.

Who is this man? Where's the man mountain in the suit?

"Sorry, Odile, but it's been weeks since I've seen Julia. We will catch up with you later."

"What will we do?" I breathlessly whisper.

His eyebrow arches and it stabs me down deep in my stomach how much I've missed it. "What we do best."

"Henri!" My cheeks scorch, while Odile looks on with a wide and gleeful smile and holds her hands up.

"Well, I am not getting in the way of that," she laughs. "I'll head back, Henri. See you this afternoon?" She clicks her tongue and gives a small shake of her head, turning and waving over her shoulder. "If you can manage it."

His eyes are on me. "Honestly, I don't know what you two think I mean. I was proposing lunch, that's all."

"That's good. We can't go back to my hotel. The woman on reception is a dragon."

"You're here?" He grabs me again and I fall against him, breathing properly in what feels like the first time in weeks.

"Yes, I'm here."

"I'm never going to let you leave."

"Well, now that makes you the stalking weirdo." I don't get to say anymore because his mouth is on mine, weeks' worth of kisses raining down on me with the power of a fire storm.

19

CHOCOLATE

Our hands are merged like lovers, fingers sliding into grooves, palms pressed tight. "So, tell me about this hotel with the dragon?"

He doesn't ask me why I've come, what I've been doing. Days and weeks have disintegrated into dust as we've stepped in to being side by side. We could still be walking the path from Liv's house after Paige's birthday. Admittedly the weather is a damn sight better.

An inbuilt intuition can sense his perceptive gaze as it subtly reads me, and I know he can see the changes even if he's not mentioning them yet. I smile widely to try to make the dark shadows of exhaustion disappear from my face. Wishful thinking maybe, but worth a keen shot. "Henri, I can't believe you live in a place as beautiful as this." I'm still looking at the crowded buildings, the cramped streets with blasts of sunshine that hit you right in the face as you walk, turning from shade to heat in one step of footfall. Walking down these paths, Henri's hand in mine seems on the verge of familiarity, like possibly I've done this before, in a different life. I can only hope that life wasn't as tragic as this one.

"It's more beautiful now than it's ever been."

A grin stretches my face, chasing off more of those shadows. "Oh, my goodness, look at that." I point at the window of a patisserie. Macarons are stacked high around perfectly glazed cakes with surfaces like mirrors. My stomach gives a pitiful growl.

"You'd like cake for lunch?"

God, yes. I think I would. I nod eagerly and bite on my lower lip. "Would that make me an uncultured heathen, no salad first?"

"Ma douce, Julianna. There is nothing heathen about you." He leans in closer, breath brushing my earlobe. "Apart from maybe what you make me want to do to you in bed."

My body lights with the whoosh of a rocket launching for space, and he chuckles, running the tip of his finger across my cheekbone with a delicate touch and a small shake of his head. "You're really here," he says, his lips lowering to mine, body pressing flush into my curves causing me to tingle all over.

"I am. I hope that's okay."

Pulling back slightly, stealing the kiss away, he holds my face still. "You have no idea. No idea how much I've wanted to see you. Teasing telephone calls only made me more despondent."

"But you didn't come though?" There's a pathetic edge to my question. "The last time we saw one another, we..."

"Took a step?" His eyes dance and I want to fall into their rhythm and get carried away like those girls in fairy books who follow the tune and never come back to mortal life again.

"Yes."

"We did, but Maman, she's been…" His expression darkens. "There is so much on my shoulders, Julia." I lay my hand on his chest, willing to take the burden he carries despite not being strong enough to carry my own.

"It's okay, you don't owe me any explanation. We didn't make any promises."

With a small step he clears space between us. "Julianna, you've stolen my heart and you don't even realise it."

My chest rises and falls with a ragged unevenness: part the act of dying, part emotional splintering.

I've stolen his heart too late to enjoy it.

But I came here to live and live I will. One week of high octane, full sensory living.

"Henri, I…" I'm going to tell him, going to be honest, but he's looking at me like a goddess, like I shine brighter than anything else in existence, and I can't stand for him to see me as broken instead.

My stomach gurgles and he laughs, tucking me into his side and pressing a kiss on my forehead.

"You need cake, ma petite, and cake you shall have, just like Marie Antionette."

"Didn't she lose her head because of the cake?" I giggle, snuggling deeper, rightfully home in this strange land with flowers and sunshine and *him*.

"Maybe you'll lose your heart." He shrugs and my eyes meet his. Yep, it's way too late for that. It's been signed, sealed and effectively delivered by easyJet.

"Close your eyes," he demands.

"You can't keep doing this every time we eat. It's embarrassing." It's not embarrassing, it's sexy as hell, but a girl has to keep some pretence up to hide the fact that she needs to go back to the hotel ASAP.

"We're in France, this is practically pre-approved date behaviour."

"And we're on a date."

"Belle, Juliette, every moment between us is a date of perfection."

Well, when he says it like that. Acquiescing, I close my eyes, popping open my mouth gently. Henri has ordered the most decadent chocolate cake and dutifully I wait for him to plant a small taste in my mouth. Obviously, I can feed myself, being a grown woman and all, but hell if this isn't some sort of foreplay that should be passed down in folklore, from one man to another. Forget the bases, go for food porn.

A blast of bitter chocolate hits my tongue first and I start backwards, my tastebuds almost fighting against the bitterness that I thought would be sweet. The sugar comes second from the sponge; moist and sweet, it counterbalances the dark cocoa creating a perfect marriage in my mouth.

"Oh my god," I mumble around the mouthful of heaven.

"Now swallow and sip your coffee." I crank an eye at the word swallow only to find him smirking. God, I've missed that slightly lopsided smirk, love that lopsided smirk.

I swallow the cake and lift the small espresso cup to my lips, waiting for the bitter hit of the strong beans, but it doesn't come, the sweet sponge still lingering on my tastebuds swipes it clean away.

Lowering the cup, I meet his gaze. "That's heaven."

"And watching you is sheer torture. You're the most sensual creature I know."

I snort a laugh, which is not sensual in the slightest. "That's a lovely thought but not true."

"You really think that?"

"There is nothing sensual about me at all."

He reaches for the curve of my neck and gently brushes along the skin making me shiver. "The curve of your neck." The fingers drift higher to my lips which he gently pops open. "The plump edge to your mouth that begs to be kissed." Uncaring of other people sitting on the bistro style chairs at tables around us he sweeps his finger inside my mouth. "Your tongue that I've been fantasising about on my skin the whole time we've been apart."

"You have?" I ask as a gust of air squeezes from my lungs.

"You, ma Julianna, are in my head, my senses, under my skin."

Stupid tears sting my eyes. "I thought it might just be me who felt like that."

Lowering his hand, he tangles his fingers with mine, making me hot and needy for tangled limbs and kisses.

"Want to come and meet the dragon at the hotel?" I cock an eyebrow.

"Ah, but ma petite, I don't want you to think I just want you for your body." God, I love that smirk.

Picking up my fork, I shove the chocolate cake in my mouth as quickly as I can. I might want Henri, but I'm not leaving this behind under any circumstances.

He snorts when he sees the hotel I've chosen, kissing me on the cheek as his arm tightly winds around my back. "What?" I exclaim, holding back my giggle. "It looked pretty in the pictures."

He glances at the signboard swinging from a wrought iron arm in the gentle breeze and silently arches a sardonic eyebrow, while I pull my best *whatever* face in response.

The dragon watches us walk in hand in hand, lips in a tight line. I'm about to open my mouth to ask for my key when Henri launches into a volley of French which makes her argue back, shaking her head, and pointing her finger at the computer on the desk. He speaks again, words faster this time, his free hand gesticulating in circles and talking too.

Eventually, and when I've started studying the patterns in the marble floor, she hands over my key and he fires off a few remaining words. Silently, we walk for the stairs. As soon as we're out of sight, I turn. "What on earth was that about?"

"I told her you were checking out," he tells me with a classic Henri shrug.

"What?" I stare at him aghast. "No wonder she's annoyed. I've booked for a week."

Another shrug. "You don't need to stay here when you can be with me."

"But your mother?"

He shoots me a heart blistering smile. "Don't worry about that. Anyway, I live half an hour away from the city. It will be too far to have you away from me."

"Henri, I don't want to put you out." We are outside the door to room fifteen. "I'm just on holiday, but you are working. I'll just fit in around you, do tourist things if you're busy."

"Non. Now I'm on holiday too." With a wicked grin he opens the door to the room. "Starting right about now."

"Henri! Haven't we got to get my stuff and check out?"

He kicks the door shut. "You must have a lot of stuff to pack, no, ma petite?"

We both glance at my sprawled suitcase on the bed. The double balcony doors are still open, the curtains fluttering softly. From outside, the shouts and chatter of provincial French life continue, but within the room a weave of magic courses around me. His breath on my skin, the power of his body stood so close to mine, humming its energy in time with mine.

"I've never wanted anyone as much as I want you," he whispers against my neck. "You're all I think about, dream about. You must be a witch because the way you make me behave knows no bounds."

I turn, circling my arms around his neck. "The way I make you behave?"

"I've been fighting my conscience. My desire to be with you at war with the responsibility I know I have."

"Shh." I press my mouth to his, the bliss of surrendering to a kiss turning me soft and pliable. *He really wants to be with me?* The reality of that, the huge source of intensity that hits me knowing that fact, it thunders through my body.

"I'm here now," I whisper. "And I'm yours."

His lips seek mine, gentle at first but then gnawing with a hunger. His fingers wind into my ponytail pulling at the elastic and freeing my hair down my shoulders. I gasp a breath though when he pulls away.

"Non." His eyes are dark, drawing me in. "No more hotels. Now you'll come home with me."

"I have no problem with hotels." I start working on the buttons of his shirt. There's nothing more I want to do than to be lost in his arms with this new version of the sun streaming through voile, and the shouts of the world below. Heaven would exist in the moment like a perfect snowflake or grain of sand, and I'd get lost in the moment too, forever scoring it into my memory for the dark days ahead.

"Non, ma petite. I want to take you home. Show you who I am." He grasps my fingers, pulling them away from his shirt, and I angle my best pouty lips up to his face.

"I know who you are, Henri Carré, man of secret cheese exploits."

His broad laugh sparks through my veins. "It seems I need to show you more than I thought."

"You don't have to," I mutter, always seeking a get out of jail card for either of us to use when we need.

He chuckles against my lips: warm breath, lingering notes of coffee, chocolate, and my kisses. "I want to. I want this."

My kiss seals my lie. I want this too even though it's not really mine to have, so I do what any woman would who found themselves in an embrace as perfect as this would do. I block the negative and focus on living. It's all I can do.

20

CHEESE DYNASTIES

The wind blows my hair, streaming it like a scarf behind me. Henri's hand is on my knee as he weaves his vintage convertible around sun-drenched roads. The fresh scents assaulting my nostrils hit me over and over: sweet flowers, evergreens, deeper more earthy scents like farms, and then a blast of salt brine from the sea, mixing with aged leather of Henri's car. Closing my eyes, I inhale deeply, as deep as my chest will allow. Over and over, I scorch the smells into my brain. My stupid lungs won't open enough though, my breath not deep enough.

Damn you body.

"What on earth are you doing?"

"Remembering the smell." I don't bother to open my eyes.

There's a low chuckle mixed with the whip of the wind. "I can understand it smells slightly better than Fleet Street."

My heart sinks at the mention of work and my conversation with Rebecca. She'd been so pleased to grant my emergency request for holiday leave. Had sat through my futile attempts at training on the print run. But in my heart I knew my request for my more permanent leave would be coming.

"What are you thinking of? Please not work, no?"

"No." Reopening my eyes, I find him half-watching me, half-watching the road. My fingers find his on the bare skin of my knee and I give a squeeze.

"No, not in the way you think. I'm glad for the holiday. I need it."

Ah, wrong thing to say. His expression clouds. "You look tired."

"Being here will help."

Another sweeping gaze runs across my pale skin. "I'm going to feed you up, tan you at the beach, and make you so tired every night you'll sleep like a princess."

A laugh blasts from my chest. "You make me sound like a project."

He's not laughing. "I can see the changes in you, Julia." The way he says my name makes me warm and gooey. *Shuulia*. "I know it's been weeks, but it's not that long since I was last with you."

"I'm here now. You can feed me up like a Christmas turkey."

"Goose," he corrects and we both pull faces at one another's choice of festive meal. Maybe it's a good job that I won't make it until then. The thought catches me unawares, simply, sneaking in—if I wasn't dying then I can't think of any future Christmases without him at my side.

It's earth-shattering, blasting from nowhere.

This is the stupidest thing I've ever done in my life. To fall in love just in time to break my own heart. That's going to hurt.

To my surprise, Henri pulls the car over onto a small

and uneven layby at the side of the road. "What are you doing?"

Twisting towards me, he catches my face in his hands. "What are you thinking of?"

With a smile, I lean forward and kiss his mouth. "Nothing, just that I'm pleased I'm here. I don't do things like this, it's not who I am. Getting on that plane, it took all my guts." *And determination, and obsessive need to see you one last time.*

"You look so sad, Julia, and it breaks my heart."

"I'm not sad, I promise. Right now, I'm filled with joy, the utter joy of being here in this beautiful place, in the moment with you. I've missed you more than I can say, Henri. It felt so stupid because we were only ever a one-night stand that became two, that became..."

His hands cradle my face. "Became everything? Unexpected but true, no?"

"Yes, but I hardly know you. All I know is the bits I've seen. We've spent more time kissing than we have talking. It makes all of it seem like a fairy tale."

"Aren't fairy tales the best? Aren't you pleased that we haven't met in the mundane and boring way that will make for a dull tale to retell? Fate played a hand in this. Whether you believe in fairy tales that's a mighty thing."

"You really believe that? About fate?"

He nods, face solemn and so beautiful it makes the landscape dull in comparison. "You want to know things about me, and believe me, I want to spend all our time getting to know you. But you can't keep blocking what this is. Oui, we met by chance, but every man's destiny is his own."

My head drops as I try to force the sadness out of my heart. Live, Julia. Just damn well *live.* Though I know it's unfair for me to not tell Henri the truth, I just want to experience that *living* a little while. Because while he will recover from my not being honest from the beginning with time, I only have now.

With his fingertip he forces my gaze to meet his. "And the first thing to know about me is that," slowly, he turns my head, "is my home."

I blink in surprise, exhaling, "What the fuck?" with my breath. Holy shit balls.

"You live in a castle?" I breathe out my words, making Henri snigger and kiss the top of my head like I'm an adorable child.

"It's a chateau. We don't have castles in France, and we don't live in the whole thing anymore. Come, you will see."

Grinning, he fires the engine again, the vibrations running beneath my thighs.

"I thought you lived on a farm. You said you make cheese."

"I do make cheese, ma petite. The very best cheese."

Eventually, we turn off the winding road down a sunbaked driveway. The air is fresh with pine needles, tall trees standing sentry and dappling the road into splotches of light and shade. The drive curves into a circle in front of the grand fascia of the building, complete with fountain to drive around. I'm drawn away on a dream of balmy nights, carriages circling sparkling water as guests walk up the wide stone steps to the entrance in their finest ball gowns. "Henri," I whisper so low I'm not sure if I'm talking out loud. "It's so beautiful. I've never seen anything like it."

A couple walk down the front steps, arms linked around one another, skin sun kissed. Everyone here is beautiful; it makes me feel drab and grey like London. "Who are they?"

I turn to see his shrug. "Guests." His smile turns cheeky.

"We don't live in the whole building anymore. Maman converted it into a holiday destination thirty years ago, when she decided that being married to a cheese man wasn't going to provide the life stimuli she required."

"People come here on holiday?" I look up at the grand old building, beautifully preserved. His gaze must follow mine because he adds.

"She saved the building really. We would never have been able to keep it going without the foresight she had." Opening his door, he comes around to my side and opens mine. Awkwardly, I step out, but then breathe a sigh as he takes my hand and relinks our fingers. "Come, I'll show you."

I swallow, his mother sounds formidable and frankly terrifying if she runs this single-handedly.

"Don't look so nervous. No one bites here. Well, apart from me." He winks and my stomach give a little dive straight down to my toes.

Under the scorching heat we follow a golden pathway around the side of the building. When we've turned the corner my feet grind to a halt. "Jesus, Mary, and Joseph,' I gasp.

In front of what once must have been a large patio for holding parties on, overlooking immaculate lawns and fancy shaped bushes—seriously is that a swan?—is now a fine dining area. Silver cutlery shines, almost blinding as it reflects the sun, laid on crisp white tablecloths. The dining area is set under a large rustic wooden structure and as I peer up, holding my hand against the glare of the sun, I can see where canopies must stretch over the whole space.

"What is this place?" I turn, trying to take it all in.

"A," he swirls his hand while he thinks of the word.

"Gastronomique, you know, gourmet holiday destination. People come here to stay and eat well."

"A food holiday?" I quirk a brow. "Normally when people have a food holiday it means they are starting a diet."

He drops his head to one side, flashing me a white smile. "Mmm, not so much here."

"So, gourmet food?" There are immaculate waiting staff putting out glassware.

He answers with a typical shrug.

"Exactly how gourmet are we talking?"

"Dominique!" he hollers at a young chap sweating under a white shirt and black tie before firing off some quick instructions.

It really is too late for me to learn French properly. It seems almost a shame.

"You will find out tonight," he turns back and slips his hand into mine again. "I don't normally eat out here, but tonight for my guest I will. Maman will be pleased. She always wants me to show my face more."

"Your face should be seen everywhere," I blurt, earning me a warm press of his mouth on mine.

"With you by my side I will willingly oblige."

"I didn't bring anything posh to wear. This is as smart as it gets." I motion to my now creased sundress.

He shrugs. "Not to worry. We will find you something."

Okay... in a closet full of ex-lovers' clothes? *Stop it, Julianna.*

"So, if you don't like the dining bit, which is your domain?"

His eyes linger on my mouth for a moment, and I find myself holding my breath. "Come, I'll show you, and then I will introduce you to Maman. She'll curse my manners, but I'll take the wrath."

He really isn't helping—at all.

"Excellent. It sounds like I'm going to be served for dinner."

He roars a laugh startling some doves in one of the sculptured trees. "You're so adorable it's almost addictive."

I sneer a smile and wait to be led to his side of the family business, foolishly and totally unprepared for anything I might find there.

"So, three years ago I convinced Papa to turn organic."

I try not to laugh at hearing the brooding man mountain call his deceased father Papa. Try but fail, letting a small smirk escape my lips, which I then wipe away as quickly as I can. *Have some respect, Julianna, for God's sake.*

We are standing in the middle of an enormous kitchen garden where it seems every vegetable known to man is growing. Purple things I don't even know the names of shoot from the ground, different brassicas that would make Charlie die on the spot.

"Charlie would love this. You should invite her to see it, when..." I trail off because I almost say, *when I'm gone.*

His gaze searches my face, lips pursed.

"She owns a failing organic vegan restaurant in Notting Hill."

He nods, face brightening. "I know. I spoke to her about it at Paige's birthday. I've had some ideas for it while I've been back here in fact."

"You have?"

"Sure." His hand catches mine. "It's kind of what we do." Pointing to the vegetables and then back to the main house he adds, "Everything that gets cooked in there, comes from this land."

"Everything?"

"Oui."

"Even the meat?"

"Even the meat. We keep our own organic herds, ethically farm them, using them for different things. We make sure they eat the very best, so their lives are the happiest. It makes them taste so much better."

My stomach turns and I get a bit hot and sweaty. "Vegetarian, ma petite?"

"I've never been a declared veggie, but I like to mentally distance what's on the plate from its origin." I grimace trying not to think of the cows batting their long eyelashes. "This really isn't cheese is it?" I clarify.

"Ah, the cheese is my domain. Call it a passion, just like my fathers. But now we do things my way."

"Your way, what's that?"

"I'll show you." With a tug on my hand, he's dragging me off again, this time in the direction of a cluster of large sheds. We pass a herd of cows, all bellowing as they are urged along by a farmer in wellingtons. Henri speaks to him while I do the *Julianna tune out.*

"They've just been milked."

"So, they aren't eating cows?" I breathe a sigh of relief. Jeez, I couldn't meet their wide, brown-eyed stare there for a moment.

With a grin he presses his lips to my hair. "No, ma petite, they are worth much more for cheese."

"How so?"

"They are very rare, almost extinct. We feed them well, play the lullabies to make them relax, and in return they give us the best cheese in the south of France."

"You play them lullabies?" I ask as I squint up at his towering shape.

Clearly, I'm funny because he rolls his eyes. "You British are so pragmatic."

"What makes the cheese so special?"

"Every herd is fed in a different field. It means the grass is different. They only eat natural fauna, so the milk they produce is unique."

Wow. Who knew cheese could be so complicated? "So not the mafia then?"

Henri's mouth falls open and then he roars a laugh, bending at the waist. "The mafia?" Yep, there he goes again. It might be his heart close to giving out not mine. "Julia, you are truly unique." He sobers enough to wipe his eyes and straighten. "What convinced you I was mafia?"

"Well, you're very cagey about your cheese."

"Cagey, ma petite?" He wipes his eyes. I've made him cry laughing. "I just didn't want to bore you with cows. Cheese isn't the best chat-up line?"

"Chat up line, huh? Do you use them a lot?" I mean, I'm sure he probably does, but it doesn't mean I can stop my face from dropping.

Laughing again, he pulls me closer. "No. You think I have time for chat-up lines? Look at all these cows I have to sing lullabies too."

I snort a laugh and he catches it with his mouth, reeling me in close to his body, pressing me into what has become my favourite place. "Mon dieu, Julia, you're a breath of fresh air in this life I've found myself in."

I glance up and try to read his expression, but with his back to the sun all I see is shadow. Reaching onto tiptoes I seek out his lips again. Kissing really is a superior way to communicate. It's taken me nearly thirty years to find this out.

The kiss aches with hunger. I can't taste enough of him.

His hands slide down my back, strong and firm, pushing me into the blatant evidence that he's missed me too. "I need you," I say into his mouth. My body is burning with the intensity of a bonfire on a crisp November night.

"Let's get back to the house."

"Too far." I wind my fingers into his shirt, pushing my lips into the small triangle of skin exposed at his throat where his pulse beats, strong and even. My own pulse is doing something that's making my head spin, but that might not be failing heart syndrome and more a Henri one.

"The barn?" he doesn't sound convinced.

"How many steps?"

"None." He lifts me easily in his arms and I wrap my legs around him, mouth firmly fixed on his, tongue dancing into his mouth as he stalks us for the large green shed. He breaks his mouth from mine to demand something rapidly in his native tongue and there's the scatter of feet followed by the clang of the door.

"This will give the hands something to talk about for a while." He backs me onto a workbench and I peek a glimpse over his wide shoulder. No cows, not that it probably would have stopped me anyway. "This isn't what I wanted for us, Julia. I wanted to do this right for once."

"Henri. Every time is right." I can say this hand on heart and hope not to die. "Now fuck me quickly before I have to meet your mother."

Who the hell is this woman and what's she done with Julia Brown? Who cares? I don't.

To live I need to feel. To feel I need to have Henri inside of me, right damn now.

Impatiently, I slip my hand under my skirt, exposing my thighs, making his eyes burn as I lift up and pull my knickers down. His hands palm my skin, pushing my legs apart as he stares at my exposed core, the lick of fresh air foreign against the apex of my thighs. "I don't know who you are, or what I've done to bring you into my life, but fuck, Julianna—" I cut him off, grabbing his face roughly and bringing it to mine while his fingers skim high, brushing my thighs, seeking out my wetness and slipping inside, arching me backwards as long fingers hook and curve. Closing my eyes, I moan deeply and the sound rumbles from my chest as his free hand slides down the front of my dress and roughly palms my tit through the material, squeezing and making me cry out.

"Henri," I gasp. There's a burning need inside, unquenchable and so low it's on the point of pain. "I swear you can take your damn sweet time later, but right now I need you inside me."

His hand slips out of me and he steps back, eyes on the prize. "Don't move an inch." It's a guttural demand I have no plans on breaking. Unfastening the waistband of his chino's and then swiftly pulling out his trusty wallet and condom supply, he pushes his trousers down just enough for that beautiful big cock of his to spring free, standing to attention between us. I lick my lips but don't move as directed while he puts on a condom. He hauls me forward and lifts me into his arms and then gently drops me down, one long hand reaching around and down to connect us together. I gasp as he fills me, stretching me wide. It's been weeks and the sensation is enough for me to throw my head back. Sure, we are connected, he paces a few steps from the bench to the wall, pining me between him and it, like I'm stuck between the very best of a literal rock and a hard place. His hips drive, while his hands push down on my shoulders, ensuring that every thrust is so deep it makes me whimper. My shoulders scrape the wall, a mild sting overridden by the sensation of him inside me. The fire stokes quick, burning bright and making me push down harder, so every stroke is hitting the place I need it most.

"Oh God,' I cry as a wild and fast climax begins its journey from the tip of my toes. In response, his hips buck faster, his mouth falling to my neck, sucking the skin on my collarbone. Inflicting another perfect pain that has me shouting out. "Henri!" I scream his name.

"Julia!" He chases fast behind me, thrusting deep inside as he collapses us against the wall, whooshing the air out of my lungs. "Jesus, Julia."

We both still, breathing fast, in and out, in and out, and then I kiss his cheek and clutch him tight, my faulty heart bursting at the seams, while silent tears, a lethal cocktail of disappointment and joy, slip down the back of his shirt.

21

FÉROCE MAMA BEAR

"Stop fidgeting." Henri squeezes my hand as we walk down the hallway of the inner house. The family apartment is on the west wing. Yep—they have a wing.

And no wonder he'd looked at my small grey box of a flat with such horror.

"I can't help it."

With a tug of his fingers, he wheels me around and puts his hands on my shoulders. "It's just a meal."

"In a two Michelin starred restaurant in a hotel that you own." Ah, the secrets have unravelled while we've been locked in his private quarters. I wish we still were there, naked preferably. Instead, I'm wearing a midnight-blue silk dress that belongs to his sister and a pair of heeled sandals that his friend Odile has loaned me.

Getting dressed up for dinner is a new experience. I suppose I did say I wanted to live. Another thing to tick off my half-arsed bucket list.

"Would you prefer the mafia?" His smile widens, which is total cheating because it steals thoughts and words directly from my brain.

"Yes, I'd rather be stuck in the middle of a mafia turf war."

"That's ridiculous."

"Oh really?"

"What are you actually scared of ma petite?"

"What if she doesn't like me?" *What if she can see straight through me? Can see I'm broken. Knows that in a few days I'm going to walk away from this place and maybe never see you again? What if she knows you might love me, for some crazy reason I don't yet understand, and she knows I'm going to break your heart the way I'm breaking my own?*

"She's not going to hate you." His face falls. "Listen, Julianna, I need to tell you something."

My stomach lurches. "What?"

We are interrupted by the peering of dark-blue eyes around the door frame at the end of the hallway. Eyes exactly the same colour as Henri's.

I face him, open mouthed. "Please don't..."

Laughing, he clutches my face in his hands and pecks a kiss on my mouth. "Simone," he beckons the slender child forward once he's pulled away. "This is Julia, my friend." The girl, maybe ten I reckon, nods her dark-haired head. "And this is Simone, my niece."

She talks in rapid French.

"Anglais, Simone." He stops her.

"Pardonne, Uncle." She swaps to spotless English. "Grand-mère wants to know when you are ready."

Henri clicks his tongue; those lips I want to kiss all day long pressing into a firm line briefly before he smiles. "Right now. On time, as she likes."

Oh crap. She's going to know instantly the reason we are short on time is because we've been screwing like bunnies all afternoon.

His fingers clutch mine again and give a gentle squeeze and we turn, now a party of three, towards the main dining area.

I gasp as we walk outside, feeling Henri's gaze landing on me. I don't have any words, or any reaction at all, because I've never seen anything like this. Millions of tiny, warm-hued lights are wrapped around the wooden structure of the terrace's frame. Crisscrossing above our heads, they create a canopy of twinkling stars below those already lighting the sky. "Oh, my goodness, Henri, this is magical."

"Odile designed it." Simone turns. "She's very clever at things like this."

"She is." I smile at them both. "I've never seen anything so beautiful."

"Come, let me introduce you."

He leads me, not letting go of my fingers no matter how hard I'm trying to slide them from his grip, towards a circular table in the middle of the restaurant. It's a power position. From this spot you can see everything, and everyone can see you.

I don't know what I'm expecting, but maybe given the size of Henri, the last thing is a sparrow-sized woman, her features sharp and quick, dark-slate gaze flitting straight to where our hands touch.

"Henri, tu es en retard. Trop occupé dans la grange j'entends."

I have no idea what she says, but Henri drops his face down and smirks a little.

"Apologies," she switches to English. "I said, you are late, but I hear you've been busy in the barn."

Oh. My. God.

"My apologies. We had trouble locating shoes suitable for your beautiful restaurant. Your home is beautiful." Jesus,

I nearly curtsey. Henri holds me up straight and squeezes my hand one last time before dropping it and striding for his mother's side.

"Maman, you shouldn't believe all the rumours the staff spread around."

Her quick gaze flicks back over to me. "Usually when they involve you, Henri, they are true."

He narrows his gaze but keeps his smile firmly in place. "Maman, I would like to introduce you to Julianna Brown. Julia, this is Aline Carré, my mother. Ignore her tongue, she has too much time on her hands." He gives her an affectionate shoulder squeeze.

"It is because I'm a widow that I have far too much time on my hands. I only have my Henri here to care for me in my old age."

From across the table, I see their friend Odile, shoe saviour, roll her eyes slightly. Ah. I see.

"I'm sorry for the loss of your husband."

"Merci bien," she starts, but Henri tuts and she switches once again, a look of deploring disregard etched into her smooth skin. If Henri is forty-two she must be nearing seventy, but she looks mid-fifties at most. That's some face cream and sunblock she uses. "One can only hope to survive such heartbreak. Poor, Henri, my boy. Recovering from his father's death has been hard, especially considering the extra responsibility he also holds."

I shoot him a puzzled gaze while he motions for me to sit in the guest of honour seat at his mother's right side, pushing the chair in at my knees.

"Extra responsibility?" I ask.

"Oui, of course. His guardianship of Simone."

I fall onto the chair the last three inches. "Wow." I hold back my 'what the fuck', because I'm sensing a test here from the Mothership and I don't want to fail. Not that it matters. I'll never see her again. But I do like the chances of an odds-against challenge. "That is a lot of responsibility."

And really, you'd think he'd have mentioned it.

Especially after the barn this afternoon. I'm pretty sure that was a profound moment. We might not have made statements, but I sure as hell felt them.

"It's better for Simone to be in a settled environment." He quirks his brows together in an almost frown. He's reading from a script. I can hear it in his voice, so I play along.

"Oh definitely." But really what I'm thinking is what on earth is his sister doing in Paris when her daughter lives here.

"You look tired, ma petite," he murmurs, leaning close to my ear.

I nod. "I am a little. It must have been the early flight," I lie, because truly I'm exhausted, not just tired. My body is heavy, like lead sinking to the bottom of the ocean. It's a hot mess combination of flying, excitedly walking around Perpignan, and then an afternoon of Henri sex.

His gaze narrows. "Of course. That's why I take the Eurostar. It gives me longer to relax."

"I see," his mother, not to be excluded, speaks, "you're the reason for the extra trips to London."

Henri reaches for my hand and gives a squeeze. "I told you, Maman, it's all about fate."

Her small mouth tightens, reminding me for some reason of Barney's ass. I wonder how he is, and if Liv remembered to give him his allocated number of treats. Or has Paige thrown the whole packet of Dreamies around the place and Liv's vacuumed them up off her cream carpet?

"I'm not one for fate or such whimsy," she clips on in

modulated English. "Relationships are things you work at." She drives a hard stare at Henri.

My cheeks flame. "Well, we live in different countries."

"Exactly." She waves a dismissive hand in our direction and then adds something in French that makes Henri straighten up while her eyes glitter with fire.

The fight I'd had climbing onto the plane this morning, surviving the cab death ride, and the drive I'd had since sitting in Dr Francis' consulting room and deciding that I needed to see Henri one more time, begins to ebb out of me.

My head weighs heavy, but it's nothing to do with sensation in my chest.

"Henri.' I clutch his hand as my vision darts with black spots.

"Julia?" He fires off rapid words. "What's wrong, ma petite fleur?"

"I don't feel so good. I'm so sorry." I whisper through the crowding darkness swimming across my eyesight.

"Maman, I'm taking Julia to bed."

"In a guest room I hope."

He explodes from his chair, scraping it back across the floor. I don't understand a word he says but can put a tenner on the fact he's just told her to go and do one.

"Odile, Simone, our apologies." Gently he cups my elbow, helping me from my chair. "Don't worry, mon coeur, just follow me."

We walk in echoing silence down the enormous and ornate hallways, my vision slowly coming back. My legs are so heavy though, the heels on the sandals keep scraping the floor. "I'm so sorry."

"Don't be. The last thing I want is to eat a meal with her when she's in one of her moods."

"For someone so small, she's fierce."

"Lethal." His smile grows, but then falters. "What's wrong with you, Julia? And please don't brush this, uh, under the carpet." I love it when he has to search for words.

I open my mouth and then jam it shut again. At the door to his suite he pauses, cocking his head, arching a brow.

"It's just from when I was ill. I told you about it. I've never quite been the same since." This is the damn truth. Not the whole truth, but a version of it I can articulate to this beautiful man.

"You should have said if you didn't feel good, I would never have taken you to dinner."

"I didn't want to let you down. I hate considering myself as weak."

"Weak? Says the woman who flew to France in a bid to find a miserable bastard of a man who'd been too grumpy to call her the last two weeks."

"Well, when you put it like that..." I tease a smile. "So, a guardian, hey?"

He drops his head, fingers looping in mine. "Are you cross?"

"Cross? No. Surprised maybe."

"It was Maman's idea."

Hmmmm... I'm sure it was.

"You know she doesn't seem as heart-broken as perhaps I expected her to."

"She's up and down. Grief is a funny thing, no?"

"I guess."

"Come, let's get you asleep. I've got lots planned for tomorrow."

Chewing on the side of my mouth, I know I've got to say something. "Henri, sorry. I know it sounds weak, but I think I need to take things easy."

He watches me carefully in response. "I can see a

change in you, Julia." Plucking up my hand, he presses it against his chest above his heart. "It makes me get this tight feeling here that I don't know how to explain."

I close my eyes to the truth, to his ability to read me. That this man I've known a matter of months and seen only a handful of times knows me better than anyone. There's a bitter tang on my tongue that maybe I wish I'd met him sooner.

"You are shrouded in grey, when you should be every colour under the sun." He presses a soft kiss to my mouth.

"You can make me shine like a rainbow." Tears sting my eyes. Life, you cruel bitch, you've done a number on me. "How many steps to bed?" I smile with my question, already knowing the answer.

Silently, he lifts me up. Not our usual hold of my legs clamped around his waist, mouths hot and needy. This time he lifts me like a bride and carries me with reverence over the threshold and into his domain.

The room is beautiful. Everything an old-fashioned, green-hued white: the woodwork, the ceiling, the walls. Simple oak furniture blends in with the setting, while thick brocade curtains block the stars and moon. He places me gently on my feet and I walk for the golden material, sweeping it to one side to fill the room with pale silver. His fingers sweep my hair from my neck, lips brushing my skin with butterfly light kisses.

"It doesn't feel real being here." I say it to the moon.

"It's perfect you being here." His fingers tug on the zip of the dress, slowly lowering it down and then pushing it off my shoulders. "I wish you could stay forever."

A sharp stab harpoons my heart, a reminder of all the reasons why I can't stay. "I wish I could too."

He guides me to the bed and lays me down. "Don't

move," he murmurs, slipping down my body and beginning to kiss every inch of my skin. I don't move a muscle until his delicate tongue seeks out my core, slipping inside me, making me arch off the bed as I shiver and tremble in a way that etches a profound truth into my skin. When I'm still panting and settling my heart, he gathers me into his arms and holds me tight.

"If I asked you to stay, would you?" He yawns and kisses my ear.

"With all my heart," I say, because I'm pretty sure when I go home I'll be leaving what little is left of it here with him. I can't fight the tears, and I know he knows I'm crying, but he doesn't say anything, just holding me tight as the lie I've created between us takes its hold.

Truth is, I just don't have a heart to give.

22

WARDS IN THE MORNING

SUNLIGHT STREAMS through the open gap in the thick curtains, lasering my face with eye-murdering brightness. I stretch, toes and ankles stiff, as I acclimatise to the sound of my phone ringing. While one hand goes to the bedside table, my other reaches for Henri, only to come up empty. Hmm, that's disappointing.

"He said to tell you he will be back shortly. He's gone to check the herd."

With my feet scrambling uselessly against the bedsheets I try to sit up, pulling them with me to cover my nakedness.

Was the cover up or down before?

Oh God.

"Hey?" I say and push my hair out of my face as I try to find a surprised smile that doesn't look like a shocked grimace and paint it on my face.

"Hi." Simone is cross-legged at the end of the bed.

So, this is strange.

"I got bored waiting for you to wake up."

"And you often come into Uncle Henri's room?"

Jeez, what have I walked into here?

Simone laughs. "No. He'll tell me off."

I wait, wondering if she'll click she shouldn't be in here now, but the penny isn't dropping. Thankfully, my phone rings again. "I should get this." I pick it up and wait again.

Nope, she's not going anywhere. She pulls forward a lock of dark hair and starts weaving a fast plait with deft fingers.

Shaking my head and rubbing at my eyes, I answer Liv's video call. "Hey, you."

"You are so shit at staying in contact."

"Sorry—"

"I'll call when I land, I promise."

"Liv—"

"I promise if I do this then I will call three times a day to keep you updated."

"Shh." I warn, squinting my eyes. "There's a child sitting on the end of the bed."

"Huh?" She's brushing her hair, long blonde tangles seamlessly dropping into glossy locks. My fingers automatically drift to my mass of knotted curls. Ugh.

"I don't know?" I mime before swiftly turning the phone. "Simone, say hello to my sister Olivia." Averting her attention from her plait she looks up and gives a small wave. "Hi."

"Uh, hi…"

With a grin, I swizzle the phone back around. "Simone is Henri's ward, I think."

"Only until Mama comes back."

Simone drops her bottom lip and chews on it as she refocuses on another strand of hair to plait.

"Sure," I say, optimistically.

Liv's mouth is hanging wide open. "Ward?" she mouths to which I nod.

"Niece really..." I trail off, not really understanding the dynamics of it all. I really should spend more time talking to Henri and less having sex. I ponder this for a moment... nah, who am I kidding?

"Anyway, how are you?" Liv directs us back to the purpose of her call, mainly to over parent me.

"I'm okay. Sorry I didn't call yesterday. I got carried away when I got here. It's so beautiful, Liv. I've never seen anything like it."

She makes a snorting noise and shakes her head. "That's because you've never seen anything other than London."

"Oh, I'm sorry, Mrs World Seasoned Traveller."

We both giggle, Marbella at the ex's family holiday home isn't world travelling.

"Actually, it's going to be Miss soon."

"Huh?" I rub the sleep out of my eyes. "What are you talking about?"

"I went to see a divorce lawyer at work yesterday."

"And you wait for me to leave the country because..." I shoot her my best glare via Apple FaceTime.

"Because I didn't want you getting stressed, you've got enough on."

"Liv, I haven't got anything on." Let this be known as the Gospel truth.

"You know what I mean."

"So, what did they say?"

"That I've got good grounds."

"Of course, you have!" I burst out. "He left you pregnant without a damn backwards glance."

Liv shakes her head. "Anyway, this is exactly why I didn't tell you. But enough about me, how are you feeling?"

I shoot a quick glance at Simone. "Fine. Fine. I got really tired last night and couldn't make family dinner."

"Tired how?"

"Just tired, Liv."

I don't know what she wants me to say. Am I supposed to report to her every time I get breathless, or my hands lose all sensation, or my heart races so much it makes me think I might be sick or just pass out flat on the floor? "Remember I came here to live." I frown a glance at Simone who shows no signs of moving at all.

This is weird right? Why is she sitting on the end of a stranger's bed?

"Okay, well don't forget you've got Dr Francis next week. He's going to want you to keep note of any changes."

"Sure, sure," I say knowing full well that the time for keeping notes is up.

"And don't forget to keep your phone on you at all times in case the trans—"

"Okay, got it," I cut her off quickly and her face drops.

"You still haven't told him, have you?"

"Ooooh, really bad signal, you're breaking up." I cut her off, but then guilt stabs me deep in the gut and I shoot her a quick text: **Love you.** She sends back the eyeroll emoji and all is right in the world.

Which leaves me and Simone, two strangers sitting on a bed, one naked, one playing with her hair.

Sounds like a highly inappropriate kid's rhyme.

"I'll just get dressed." I say.

"D'accord. Sorry, I mean okay. Oncle Henri will be back soon."

"You don't have school?" I tuck my legs up. Clearly, I'm not getting out of bed anytime soon.

"No, I did some lessons this morning."

"Lessons?"

"Grand-mere thought it best for me to be tutored at home."

"Do you live in Paris with your mum some of the time?"

Looping my arms around my legs, I rest my head on my knees. I could really do with a coffee. Tea. Anything caffeinated.

"Sometimes I do, but she's very busy. She spends a lot of time..." Simone rolls her hands. "Creating."

"Creating what?"

"A mess, Grand-mere calls it."

Well, that's a bit rude.

"She's an artist though, right?"

Simone frowns at me and I try to make my question a little clearer. "Your mother, she paints?"

"Oui. I can show you?"

"I'd love that. But I have to get out of bed first." I point at the cover and my naked form underneath and Simone's cheeks pink.

"I'm so sorry. Don't tell Oncle Henri will you? He said I had to let you sleep."

"Of course not. Why don't you wait outside? I'll get dressed and then you can show me around? I didn't get much chance to see things yesterday."

"Okay." She nods, face brightening with a beautiful smile that has a glimmer of Henri but must be more of her parents. Where on earth is her dad?

"So, if you want to wait, you know, outside..." I trail off.

"Oh," she nods and scrambles from the bed. "I'll call William and Harold."

My skin prickles with alarmed sweat that has nothing to do with the morning sun now heating the room like a sauna. Please God, tell me there aren't two more 'wards' hanging around.

"William and Harold?"

"Oui, Oncle Henri's dogs."

I laugh, but it's got a nervous lilt, off-key, shaken and definitely stirred.

I really know nothing about Henri, and while I know he knows nothing about me, it still hits like a thunderbolt to the chest.

Once she's gone to round up the mysterious dogs, I scramble from the bed grabbing a thick white robe to pull over my shoulders. It's hotel thick, knuckle deep. With more effort than it probably deserves—damn useless body—I flop my suitcase onto the bed and rifle through for an outfit, settling on a pair of pale shorts and a ditsy strappy vest. My legs are far from sunshine ready, but a quick peek at the burning inferno the other side of the thick curtains assures me I will be a tasty bacon pink by the end of the day.

On a whim I pull out the peacock diary. I have no idea why I packed it, probably because it was the closest thing to a book to hand, and everyone knows you need a book on holiday. Automatically, I flick to my Henri inspired list at the front, a wide grin stretching my face until the corners of my lips sting. Near the windows is a desk. I'm sure it's got a fancy name I don't know, but regardless, I stalk for it and shamelessly rifle through the drawers looking for a biro. No biro, but I do find a Montblanc... farmer, my arse.

Chewing on my bottom lip I add: **Have sex in a barn** as a new entry and then put my obligatory line through it.

A tingle ripples down my spine as I think of what today might bring. Anything Henri shaped has got to be a plus. I need as much of him as I can get in this short amount of time I've got. I can't think about how I'll leave, what I will say, how I'll tell him I probably won't see him again. Today isn't for those thoughts, possibly not tomorrow either. Tucking the book back away in my case, I grab up my chosen outfit and slip into the bathroom before Simone comes back with the dogs.

Locked in the safety of the bathroom, I stare in the mirror, heart sinking at the changes that stare right back at me: cheekbones sharper, skin a little sallow. The pulse at the base of my throat thrums fast.

I haven't been truthful with myself, I know that much to be fact. Definitely haven't been truthful with Dr Francis or Liv. Lies are weaving me into a tight knot and I know one day soon the knot will snuff the air out of me.

Pinching my cheeks, I peer at myself closer. "Times up, girl." I breathe my words against the glass, misting my breath. "So just damn live."

In truth it doesn't matter if he has a ward, or a whole village of them.

A life to share with Henri isn't mine to have.

I breathe in deep, as far as my lungs will allow, which isn't far at all; like a rubber band has lost its elasticity and won't stretch anymore. The buzzing in my head is hard to ignore, but hey I've come this far, why stop now?

Turning my attention away from the depressing view in the mirror, I switch on the shower and jump in once the hot water is steaming and swirling in the air, wondering just what a holiday with Henri might involve.

"Oh, sweet Jesus." I step out into the ornate hallway, my gaze drawn firmly to Simone who is rolling with two wolves on the floor. Okay, maybe not wolves, but definitely the biggest dogs I have ever laid eyes on. They don't get walked, they pull sleighs, or buses, I'm sure.

"Wow. These are some dogs."

He's a dog person. I'm not sure how I feel about that. My thoughts wander to Barney and whether Liv has shaved his fur off yet. Poor Barney, I bet she's chasing him with the Dyson.

I hope Paige hasn't opened a window and he's escaped into an unknown neighbourhood. A cat as clueless as Barney could easily get lost in Notting Hill.

One of the dogs with mix matched eyes, giving him a loose-cannon expression, stands up, coming almost to my hips and gives me a long lick up the arm.

"He likes you," Simone says as she clambers from the floor.

"Where on earth were they yesterday?"

"Oh, Grand-mere won't let them in the house."

"You're brave bringing them in then." I give the girl a nod. She's got balls. I wouldn't cross *Grand-mere.*

Simone's slender face cracks with a wide smile. "She's, uh." She points at her head as she tries to find the right word and swirls her finger.

"Crazy?" I offer.

Simone's smile flickers. "Non, uh, getting her hair, uh, set." She pushes her hands with splayed fingers against her scalp.

Of course, you don't look that perfect and regal without a daily set.

"So, you wanted to show me your mum's work?"

Simone's expression clouds with confusion. I've got too used to Henri's perfect command of the English language. I'll need to revert to some basic English for this.

"Paintings. Mother." I motion a paintbrush, although why I do I have no idea. I can't even paint a wall without cocking it up.

"Yes! Come, I'll show you." She skips ahead down the long corridor while I trail behind looking at the paintings on the wall, the sculptures on tall pillars. This place is on the verge of blowing my mind. I can't imagine a life where waking up in a châteaux filled with priceless belongings is a reality. Although to be fair I'm still adapting to the thought of not waking up at all.

23

PANCAKES

UNDERFOOT IS A THICK, red carpet which covers cool marble tiles sliced with grey veins. Henri said cheese and in my head I had this vision of a simple life, maybe a country farm, some rambling buildings, farm animals braying at dawn. I definitely wasn't thinking a castle with round towers topped with conical spires like upturned ice cream cones.

We end up in a parlour I guess it would have been. It looks like it's a family-only room and not part of the hotel or whatever they call this huge place. There's an array of sofas, small side tables, and even a piano positioned, overlooked by the light of a set of French doors that lead outside.

I wonder what the French call French doors? I make a mental note to ask Henri when he comes back.

"These." Simone stabs her finger at an enormous oil painting on the furthest wall, its colours a vibrant combination of shocking pinks and turquoise. "Wow," I breathe. I can't quite make out the subject, it's abstract and no amount of squinting at it will make it become clearer. It's arresting though, tormented maybe.

I know nothing about art, but even I can feel the emotion running off its surface.

"It's beautiful, Simone. She's very talented."

"Merci."

I stand a while attempting to make sense of the brush strokes, occasionally distracted by one of the genetically engineered dogs who is licking its butt on the sofa. I'm pretty sure that's not allowed. My stomach gives a loud gurgle and Simone laughs. "You're hungry."

"I can't remember when I last ate." I think it might have been the cake. If Liv knew, she'd be straight on a plane over here to tell me off.

"I can take you to the kitchen."

"I'm not sure I should be allowed in a Michelin starred kitchen."

"Non." Simone shakes her head, reading the grimace in my face. "It's our private kitchen, no staff."

"Oh phew, something normal. Lead the way."

She winds us down corridors away from the over-stylised guest areas until eventually we must be in the private wing—a wing which is the same length as Liv's whole street—and pushes on a simple heavy and ancient oak door. It gives a satisfying groan as it releases the aroma of rich coffee beans while my stomach gives another distressed gurgle.

Odile is sat at a large wooden table that looks like it's been in situ for at least four hundred years. Six inches thick, it has a score of grooves and cuts that could cast it as a prop in a battle scene of a film.

"Bonjour, comment te sens-tu?"

Ahhhh, wait I know this! *Good morning, how do you feel?* "Je...vais bien, merci."

I'm good, thank you. Thank God for the limited school

conversational French I have remembered so I can at least try to make an effort. I vow if I do get a donor heart, I will learn the language.

Odile scrapes back her chair across terracotta tiles. "Here, sit. We were worried about you last night."

"No need." All the damn need, but let's not discuss it. "Not enough food that's all."

"Coffee?" She pushes a cafetière towards me and I'm almost salivating at the smell. It would be uncouth to ask for biscuits to dunk, so I pour the thick tar-like mixture and then doctor it with even thicker milk from a metal jug.

"Is this Henri's milk?" I ask, glancing up to find her watching me, lips twitching.

"It's from the herd, yes." She nods, biting down a smile.

What have I said?

Oh.

"I meant Henri's cows, not him." Whoosh, it's hot in this kitchen. Laughing, I pull forward the jug and peer inside. "That would be an impressive feat by any man's standards."

Odile peals a laugh and drops her head to her arm on the table, bronzed and exposed shoulders shaking.

"What's so funny?" Simone asks, but I just shake my head as I struggle to breathe. Laughter, embarrassment, dying. It all does something nasty to the chest area.

The door groans and Odile lifts her head as Henri walks in, banging her hands on the table as she peals off another laugh.

"What's so funny in here?"

Don't you dare tell him. She fires off some French and points to the jug while Henri's dark eyebrow curves and he looks directly at me. I could almost forget the embarrassment just by staring at his beautiful face. Almost... not quite.

"It was lost in translation." My lips quirk into a grimace at the edges.

With a long stride that almost leaves me breathless he's across the kitchen and crushing me to his chest. "You're awake early. I thought you'd sleep more." His kisses drop like gentle rain on my hair, and I lift my face to absorb some more.

Gentle hands cradle my cheeks and as he inspects my face, reading me as he always has, there's a frown between his midnight eyes, so I'm not sure what prose he's finding there on the landscape of my skin.

"What's on the agenda today? Are the cows all happy?" I ask to fill the gap his inspection has left hanging in the kitchen.

"Fuck the cows, Julianna." His lips lower to mine while I can sense the burning glance of our audience.

"Well, if that's what you like to do, I'm not one to judge."

God, that smile. It curves, luscious pillows of pink temptation. "You're a wicked temptress, ma petite."

And he thinks I'm the tempting one—I'll never get my head around that, will probably spend the rest of my days trying to work it out.

"Exactly, so just kiss me already and make this day start again." Delicately brushing my mouth over his, I make an erstwhile wish that every day could start with a Henri kiss. I'd happily slip into Groundhog Day if it began with a single kiss from him.

It's chaste and sweet, even so I sense the avid attention of our audience. "How do you feel?" His words brush my mouth, his eyes still closed.

"Better," I lie.

Midnight shines over me, hotter than the scorching sun through the open patio doors. The tilt of his head confirms my fib has been caught.

"A day at the beach," Henri gives a confirming nod, "that's what you need."

I break out into a panicked sweat.

"The beach? I didn't bring any swimwear."

"You came to the South of France without swimwear?"

Admittedly I feel a little stupid, but I wasn't anticipating lounging on the beach if I didn't find him or found that he no longer wanted to see me.

"I wanted to go back into town. It's so beautiful there and I hardly got a chance to see it." This is the truth. I want to crawl back over those small, winding streets, absorbing the geranium in the air, the tang of 'different' I've never really known.

"Oui, and you shall, but today you rest."

It's like he knows without knowing and I don't really know what to do with that. I could just bombshell the truth right now... but then if he doesn't know, and this is just a caring side of his personality that runs the show, I'd ruin this slice of heaven before it really got going.

Luckily my stomach fills in the gap by growling loudly. The midnight gaze settles on my face. "I haven't fed you." That beautiful face clouds with dismay.

"I'm a grown woman. I can fend for myself."

Sometimes.

That achingly beautiful smile spreads as he lifts his arm from where he's holding me close and broadly swipes it in the direction of an old range cooker and cream painted cupboards. "Then please don't let me stand in your way." His gaze glints. "I haven't eaten yet either."

Ah, a challenge. I push up my imaginary sleeves and worm my way out of his grasp. Challenge accepted.

Right. What do I know how to cook?

Henri, with the serene face of a saint in marble, sits down at the big oak table and stretches before reaching for a newspaper sat folded in the middle of the table. Momentarily mesmerised, I wait for him to open it with his newspaper loving ways, but first he shoots off undecipherable French at Odile who looks at me sharply and then gets up from her chair squeezing his shoulder as she passes him by, collecting Simone on the way out of the kitchen door.

"Where are they going?" I narrow my gaze.

He shrugs, bloody Frenchman.

Knowing that's the best answer I'm likely to get, I turn for the cupboards and rifle through. Hmm... limited skill set... unlimited resources.

Henri's lips teasing a smile are almost tangible through the air. Eventually I settle on some flour, eggs, and milk. Yes, pancakes. I've got distant memories of my mother making them for us on Shrove Tuesday and she's always just shook the ingredients in. Seems easy enough.

First go is rather cement-like, so while I try to loosen the whisk I've got stuck in the mixture, I splurge in more of Henri's milk which makes the whisk plop free and splash grainy liquid onto my face. There's a snort from behind me followed by a press of warm lips onto my neck.

"Julianna." Reaching long arms around me he takes the whisk and the milk from my hands and lays them down on the side before turning me in his caged embrace. His smile when he sees the mess I'm in brightens my entire universe.

"I have never in my life met anyone like you." His statement is sealed with a kiss that tingles right down in my toes. Hungrily, I kiss him back, all thoughts of batter, pancakes, eating forgotten within the tight intensity of how much I want him. I want him more than anything.

"Forget the food," I mumble into his mouth, words tangled with hot kisses.

"Non." Leaving me aching in truly painful ways, he pulls away. "Step to the side."

"I'm cooking."

"Non, you're making a mess."

"And who are you, the clean police?"

He glances at my hair. "I shall help you wash that out, just as soon as I've fed you."

Oooh, now we are talking. Henri in a shower is almost certainly a sight I need to see. I make a mental note to add shower sex to my peacock book. Satisfied that I'll get what I need shortly, I step over as instructed and watch Henri whisk up a light and thin batter. "The trick with crepes is to keep the batter thin so it spreads around the skillet quickly."

"Thank you for clarifying, Master Chef," I say, trying and failing to hold in a snort of a laugh.

"Well, they wanted to film the finals here."

That kills the laughter in my mouth. "What?"

"Truth." He crosses his heart with the whisk splattering us with more mix. Who cares? We are going in the shower just as soon as I've scarfed some hot food in my mouth to keep him satisfied. "But then Papa died, and it just didn't seem right. Maybe next year."

"Wow."

His gaze becomes serious. "Maybe you could be here when they do it?"

My stomach lurches—no, Henri, I won't be here. God, the thought makes me feel a little ill and I clutch onto the counter.

"Or maybe not." He shrugs at my visible, but silent response.

"No, it's not that..." I don't have anything to say apart from the truth, which I don't want to ruin this perfect sunlit moment with. "Come on, I'm starving, and I definitely need some help in the shower." I wink, trying to lighten the dark cloud hovering between us.

With a shrug, he pulls out a shallow cast iron skillet and cranks the knob on the ancient range.

I can't stand the silence. With his back turned he feels like the man mountain again I once sat next to in a bar. "Henri," I wrap my arms around his back, hugging him until he's wearing me as a backpack, "That's not what I meant." Lies, they keep falling from my mouth.

That's exactly what I meant—my silence said words I can't.

Space hangs around us as he tips a ladle of mixture into the pan and then swirls it around. The whole time I cling to his back moving with the curve of his muscles. "Henri," I say and tug him around, pulling his face down to mine, slanting my mouth against his until a shiver of unquenchable desire runs over my skin. Finally, he relents, wrapping me tight, folding me in and tucking me into the curves and grooves I still need to memorise. My heart beats wildly against my ribcage, my breath tighter and shallower until I'm breathless.

Strong fingers wind into my hair, holding me firm as his tongue probes, seeking me out. I let him in, no games to play in the moment, just an endless kiss to end all kisses. Soft, sweet, hard and intense, he switches the assault so I don't know what's coming one breath to the next. All I know is that I need his next move like a chess champion needs to protect his queen. I'd be Henri's queen, forever his, and in the moment I am. Until he pulls away and shouts abruptly in his native tongue.

"What did you say?" I gasp, still reeling from the air he's stolen straight from my lungs.

"I said the fucking pancakes." With that he lurches around me and pulls the smoking pan from the heat, shouting more as his skin connects with the handle.

Then his eyes meet mine and I meet his and he reels me back in, laughing against my mouth despite the fact his hand must be agony and I'm pretty sure I'm in heaven. The thought makes tears slip into our kiss tanging our mouths with salt water that I know he can taste but doesn't mention.

24

HOW LONG DOES IT TAKE TO START THE DAY?

What heaven tastes like is Henri's skin slicking against mine, pushing me against water splattered tiles, warm water beating down on our heads, mixing with our kiss the way the London rain once did.

"Julia," he breathes against my throat, kissing his way across my skin. One hand lifts, cupping a tit and giving a gentle squeeze that makes me moan, water flooding my mouth as I tilt my head with my gasp. Kissing down between my cleavage, he lowers to his knees as I lean against the shower wall for support, his hands splaying my ribcage down to my hips, holding all the womanly parts of me with a true reverence. It shines in his eyes, makes me burn with a burst of life that ripples under my skin, kick-starts my pulse, and makes me want to fight for every damn breath. Tilting my hips, his fingers slip around me and knead my ass; his fingers are someplace between heaven and hell: hard, dexterous, working man's hands that I'm willing to allow to take me apart. I whimper, closing my eyes, and they dip between my legs, pushing my thighs open from behind. Glancing down, I meet his gaze, his devilish grin as he leans closer and plants a kiss lightly on my heat.

God, this man. On his knees worshiping me. A dark need flickers in my belly. Hot and intense it tells me to take it all, everything this man has to give. Leaning back, I surrender to him and run my fingers through his hair as he makes me forget everything apart from this very moment.

Wrapped in a towel I hesitate at the en suite door. He frowns, a towel draped from his narrow hips like a masterpiece, water dripping from his shaggy waves down his golden skin. "What's wrong?"

"Is Simone going to be sitting on the bed again, 'cause I have to say, I'd find that weird after the noise you've just made me make."

His smile wolfs into a smirk. "Why would she be on the bed?"

My face contorts and I watch it in the mirror, but then I'm also staring at his back muscles, which truly I don't think I've studied enough yet. With a shake of his head, he sighs. "She's lonely."

"But she doesn't go to school?"

I don't know how we've gone from shower sex to talking about his niece in the space of moments, but clearly the Simone situation is odd and needs to be dealt with, and the truth is, I want to help him. I know I'm not staying, can't stay; this life isn't for me, but I want to play a role in Henri's life no matter how small.

"She should go to school. All children need interaction with others their age."

"Maman doesn't want to confuse her, because sometimes she goes to Paris too."

"Well, I don't want to sound too stern, but it has to be one or the other. Either she is here settled and in school, or in Paris. She can't just wait around without a clear routine."

I sound like my father, I can hear him echoing in my ears, *all children should have a routine, be taught to achieve, to have a role to play*.

Blah blah blah.

"Okay, ignore me. I don't think I actually mean that."

Henri's frown deepens. "You're repeating someone else's words?"

"Yeah, just ignore me."

"Non, you are right. Maman, she doesn't cope well with upheaval right now."

"I hate to be rude, Henri, but your father died eight months ago. And I know it was a shock, and it's horrible to lose a loved one..."

"But you think she's using it as an excuse?"

I shrug, *tout français,* "Who am I to say? I just got the impression last night at dinner that she wasn't very approving of your trips to London, and I can't help but wonder if that's why you haven't come back the last six weeks."

"She needs me."

"Of course, she does. But I think you need to think of yourself and your sister too, not just what your mother thinks."

And that's why I can't allow myself to need him too. Not now. Not at this point of desperate complication.

"So," I paint a bright smile on my face, chasing away the shadows of gloom that want to steal away these last few sunshine moments from my life, "Are we going to the beach or standing in the bathroom all day?"

"Beach." That frown deepens. "If you're well enough."

"Well enough to lay on the beach all day and soak up vitamin D? I think I can handle it." Handle it, crave it, need it like I need oxygen and a new heart.

"But if you want another shower...?" The frown finally lifts, and he gifts me with a beautiful smile. I'm taking that smile with me to the dark side.

"Sure, there's enough hot water for how long I'd do that in the shower with you?"

With a broad laugh he pulls me in, playfully wrestling me against his firm body. Heat ripples over me again, an endless dry scorch that exists when I'm with him.

"Okay, we really need to get out of this bathroom."

His own desire tents the towel, and he glances down chuckling. "Oui, we do."

On the bed are two small fancy looking bags, shiny with chic writing. "What's this?"

He drops the towel and I'm momentarily distracted from the shopping bags. That man is built and let there be no forgetting it. It's porno heaven where I'm standing right now. All I need is some cheesy music and I'd be right in the zone.

"Things, for you."

"Me?" Gah, now I'm torn between 'things for me' and porno heaven. "Did they magic their way here?" With a reluctant sigh, I step towards the bags leaving his beautifully carved body behind me. Let's be sensible here, we do need to leave this room eventually. Otherwise, his mother will have more to say, and I would like to make it through the evening meal tonight.

"Non, I asked Odile to pick up some things for you."

I can feel the blood drain from my face. "She came in, while we were in there," I point to the bathroom, "And I was making that noise."

Shooting me with a devilish grin he nods to the bags. "Look inside."

"But wait. We need to talk about this. Is your room always a free for all?"

He laughs and drills me with a *really* glance. So maybe this is how they do things in France? Deciding it's not worth wasting precious moments on, I pounce on the small shopping bags. Mmm, they even feel expensive, a delicate scent of rose coming from inside. "For me?" I confirm.

"Yes." I earn the cutest eye roll I've ever seen. "Are you not used to receiving gifts, ma petite?"

A lead weight drops in my stomach. "No, not really," I answer honestly.

"Hmm, that will have to change." Stepping closer, he lifts the remaining bag still on the bed. "Although I think this has become a bigger thing than the contents deserve. Next time I'll make it spectacular."

My familiar ice-cream scoop hollows me out, leaving me with that empty Henri-flavoured emptiness. "Next time, you'll have to go to the shop yourself, non?" I mimic the lilt and melody of his speech earning a kiss under my ear.

"I'm ageing here, Julianna."

Dipping my fingers inside, I scrunch them onto tissue paper, soft and crinkly. With a pout I pull it free of the small bag. It's a masterpiece of wrapping and I'm reluctant to tear the careful folds, sighing in dismay as Henri grasps the pale pink folded package in his large hand and tears where a small heart-shaped sticker is keeping it all together. "Brute," I grumble under my breath but sweeten it with a smile.

A gold bikini tumbles out, shining like a disco ball in the sunlight.

At least I think it's a bikini. Not one like I've ever worn. "What is this?" I breathe out.

"Swimwear. You told me you didn't pack any."

It dangles in my fingers, four triangles and some elastic.

"So, I organised."

"Organised some dental floss?" I lift it closer to my face.

"Dental floss?" His face clouds with confusion as he thinks this over for a moment. Finally, the clouds lift leaving a smile of pure sunshine behind. Leaning over, he snatches it out of my hands and inspects the triangle meant to cover a *derrière*.

"Well, ma petite, I do not know what you floss with." He gives the elastic an approving ping. "You will look sensational in this; not that I plan on anyone else seeing you."

I can't help but assess the bikini with scrutiny. "This is as foreign to me as the language you speak." I state, which he must find amusing because he pulls me in and kisses the top of my head. "Now hurry, Julianna, otherwise it will be dark before we get there!"

He has a point. We've spent so long doing absolutely nothing that surely the day must be over. "Aren't we too late for the beach now?" I ask, practically breathing a sigh of relief at not having to slink myself into bronzed triangles.

"Only if you're British and need to lay your towel down on the sand to secure your space." He winks.

Ha bloody ha!

"For the record it's the German's that started that trend."

"Sure, ma petite, now get changed."

"But what about the other bag?" I ask. With a deafening sigh he tips the contents out onto the bed.

"Oh." I give a little sigh of my own as I pick up the slither of blue silk that's pooled into a puddle on the bed.

"For dinner. I asked Odile to pick something up, I hope you don't mind. I could sense you were uncomfortable in borrowed clothes."

Honestly the dress was the least of my problems, but I've already put my foot in it enough for one day. Still, I can't help but say, "Are we dining with your mother tonight?" Why is it impossible to say these words without an inflection of dread?

A quirked smile greets my question. "Non, tonight I am taking you to town."

My heart soars and sinks at the same time.

"Henri..." with a gentle finger he lifts my chin.

"I know, you have to take it easy."

"Sorry." I wince.

"No need."

Turning, I pick up the dress. It's the same deep blue of his eyes. There's also a cream kaftan in the bag, I assume to go with my bikini. "She likes to shop, I guess?" I motion to the boutique bags.

"More than you like to get dressed. Now please, as gorgeous as you are in just a towel, the bikini is better for the beach."

I salute and then gather up my new belongings ready to turn for the bathroom. Henri catches my arm. "No. Get dressed here."

With resolute purpose he drops to the mattress of the bed and watches me with smoky eyes and a teasing smirk.

Yep, the chances of us getting to the beach at all are very, very, slim.

Very slim indeed.

. . .

It's only an hour later when we are on a blanket hidden in sand dunes, the sound of the sea lulling me to sleep. The warmth of the sun on my skin is almost magic, all my limbs becoming soft, loose at the limbs. Tiny balls of sandy glass rub my skin with the lazy trail of his fingers.

Henri is hot as hell in swim shorts—I'd breathed a sigh of relief at the lack of budgie smugglers. As much as I know he's packing down there, it's still no excuse for wearing speedos.

In a bid to protect my pale beauty—his words not mine —he's anointed me in factor fifty, but really, I think he just wanted to give me an orgasm in public as he pretended to apply sun cream to my back while his other hand slipped between my legs proving just how skimpy this bikini is.

One to add to the bucket list.

I must have fallen asleep because I wake to the low murmur of his voice speaking English. "I promise she is fine."

There's a pause as he listens to the other side of the phone.

"Just tired last night. More so than the travelling accounted for. Don't worry, I'm looking after her."

Liv. She must have called again.

He clears his throat and through my lashes I can see that serious expression on his face that looks like he's been carved from the finest marble. "What am I missing here, Olivia?"

Please don't tell him.

Please don't tell him.

I don't know how I'm going to say goodbye yet but somehow, I have to be the one to do it, I know that much.

"Okay, fine, I understand."

There's another pause.

"I promise you she's in the best of hands. She means a lot to me, Olivia. Perhaps you can relax, no, knowing that someone else cares as much as you?"

My heart beats wildly in my chest. A lump the size of a mountain in my throat.

All the thoughts of end-of-life care slip away as I consider living in the moment with him at my side.

How can this possibly be the end when all I want is it to be our beginning?

He hangs up, sitting on the sand, tan legs bent, my phone gently cradled in his grasp. I get up, ignoring the rush of blood to my head, the black spots that tell me I should lay down a little longer, and press myself against his broad back.

"How many steps to the sea?" I whisper in his ear, lips brushing his sun-warmed skin.

"Climb on."

25

TRUTHS BY CANDLELIGHT

Despite only travelling in Henri's car with the hood down to the beach, then lying on the sand, when we get back at five I fall face first on the bed, feeling Henri staring at me. "I'll cancel dinner," he murmurs as he tugs the thick curtains shut.

"No, I'll be fine." It's a lie right now, but I'll make it happen.

From his spot at the curtains, he turns and analyses me. "Julia, just sleep. I'll get the kitchen to make us something light for supper and we can eat on the patio here."

"No!" I'm talking into the darkness of my now closed eyelids. I can't keep them open. In the back of my mind, I've got a vague thought that there is no way I'd be able to feel like this at work. It would be me fucking up the print run, not Rebecca, and I would literally rather die than let that be the case. Along with this thought is another, far darker, that I will need to tell Rebecca I won't be coming back.

I can feel it now.

Henri explodes forward and I strain to look at him. "For fuck's sake, what is happening here?" Falling to the mattress, he clutches my hand and lifts it to his mouth, brushing his lips across the surface.

"I'm just tired."

Satirical Weekly, I wish you a fond farewell, but I think our love affair is over.

A gentle tug at my sandals brings me back from my scattered thoughts and I dig deep to sit up a little, finding Henri pulling off my sandals. "Too... tired... for that." I shoot him a sleepy wink. Mainly because I've been orgasmed out at the beach. Hell, if this is living, I've been doing it bloody wrong. Let that fact be written as a lesson for other women the world over.

"I'm chivalrous, remember, Julianna, not an animal."

To my surprise he kicks off his sliders and brushes the sand from his glorious calves—which reminds me I must remember to ask him how he keeps his body like that before I leave—and climbs into bed beside me, spooning me tight in his arms like a precious silver teaspoon from the fanciest of cutlery canteens.

"Don't you have to... check the herd?" I'm pretty sure he mentioned that on the way home. The cocoon of his embrace pulls me under, makes my exhausted body leech what little juice I have left.

His silence meets my questions, his arms tight, fingers brushing the hair from my face. "Shh."

I can see the end. It's a bright warmth that is tugging me along, one chink at the time. If I was to go now, would I be happy? Satisfied with the life I've now lived? Five months of startling existence to counter a world of grey.

Yeah, I'd be happy.

Despite the lack of space in my chest, the shallow breath I fight to hide, my heart is glowing with the heat of the sun.

"I'm so glad I met you," I whisper into the shadowy haze.

His arms tighten a notch. "I'm never letting you go. You're magic, ma petite. Magic that makes my heart sing."

Tears sting my eyes. "Henri, can you get my phone?"

He groans into my neck. "For you, anything." Despite his reticence he peels himself away from me and pads over barefoot to my straw holiday bag, fishing out my phone and then pacing back, slipping back under the covers still dressed like me. I take my offered phone, quickly clicking on messages and shooting one to Liv.

I love you. Kiss Paige and Lenny for me.

I almost don't wait to see what her dancing dots are going to say.

Don't you dare. Don't you bloody dare.

I grin, my face muscles the only ones still working.

Chill sis, just want you to know. I haven't told you enough.

Has he drugged you? Do I need to send a rescue party?

Laughing, I show Henri and he presses on the voice message button. "Non, not drugged, next time you can come along and feel the magic for yourself."

My chest hollows. Liv and I both know there won't be a next time.

There might not be a next week.

I slide my phone under the pillow and turn to face him. "Henri, I need to tell you something."

He just watches me.

The damn words. They just don't want to form, don't want to break this spell.

"Tomorrow." I nod. "Tomorrow."

"Go to sleep, mon coeur. I'll wake you for some food shortly."

"But what about the beautiful dress?"

"I don't care about dresses, Julianna." He leaves his words dangling. He only cares about me, and I'm lying to him, another night of secrets.

"Julianna?" A gentle kiss on the edge of my jaw brings me back around. I blink, confusion muddling my thoughts when the room is lit with sunlight—damn it, he let me sleep too long. When I can make sense of the room, I understand it's candlelight not sunlight illuminating the walls and surfaces with a golden haze.

"Did you do this?" I struggle to sit up, breath still too shallow. How the hell did this happen so fast? Bastard Sod's law that's what.

The room is lit by an uncountable number of candles. Big ones, church ones, small tea lights.

"It's nothing." He shrugs. Do I love his shrugs or hate them? Sometimes it's hard to decide.

At the foot of the bed is a room service trolley complete with gleaming silver-domed lid. "Would you hate me if I said I wasn't hungry?"

Dark eyes meet mine. "Would you hate me if I said you had to eat anyway?"

"Touché."

I shuffle forward, automatically keeping my movements small so as to not overexert my breathing.

Bastard bloody lungs.

Bastard bloody heart.

Why the fuck is this happening now? Yesterday I was shagging in a barn... *actually, now I think about it...*

Henri's expression is torn and pained. "Stay there."

Stretching up off the mattress, he walks for the trolley and lifts the lid before shooting me a grin. "It's only cheese and biscuits anyway."

"Good, I love a bit of cheddar."

Stalking back, plate in hand, he fixes his lips to mine. "Heathen."

"Cheese snob."

I submit to his mouth, falling into the kiss with everything I have left. When he pulls away those damn stabbing tears prickle my eyes again.

"Snuggle up." He motions me to get back into bed, while my gaze is drawn to the beautiful dress I should be wearing, draped over the back of a chair against the far wall.

"I'll get crumbs in the bed."

"Really?" His eyebrow does some major talking. "I've seen your flat. Crumbs aren't an issue for you I think."

"Ah, I've been meaning to talk to you about this."

"What?" With a knife he wedges some pale crumbly cheese onto a plate, scattering some small tomatoes, grapes, and what look like small pickles. My stomach growls.

"Well, Barney. He's going to be very cross when finds out you have a thing for dogs. It's a betrayal of the highest order. I think he'll break up with you."

"William and Harold?" He passes me a plate and then brings his to his side of the bed and scoots under the sheets. "They'd adore him."

"For breakfast."

"Not all at once, they watch their weight."

"Oh, well now you're just being rude."

Like the French sunshine he chases away the shadows lingering in my soul. "What do you think of the cheese?"

Thankfully I can breathe a little better, though I still

feel exhausted. At least I feel like I can speak longer sentences now. "I haven't got that far yet. Grapes come first."

If anyone has ever looked more disappointed in me, I don't remember. "Non, grapes with, not first." He rattles off some disgruntled French I'm glad I can't translate while I try to hold in my giggle.

"I know, I'm not a complete cheese novice. I just like to hear you talk French under your breath at me. It's incredibly sexy."

"Eat. Now." His frown pulls at his eyebrows. "And then I'll show you sexy."

Ah. Oh my god. I've forgotten what I packed back in London. Well, if ever there was a time for stepping out of my comfort zone, tonight is the night, because tomorrow if I stick to my plan everything will change.

I wolf down some biscuits despite the fact my appetite is coming in at just about zero. Henri shakes his head in true dismay as I shovel in some cheese, nodding my appreciation.

"I need the loo," I announce and manage to move slowly from the bed, taking a moment to grab a nondescript black bag from my suitcase.

Odile isn't the only one who can hit the boutiques. Before I travelled I visited a Notting Hill lingerie shop. I'm still sandy and wearing the bikini—which I'm pretty sure you aren't supposed to wear as long as I have been without it doing some damage to private areas. With a quick nip back to the bedroom with a, "Just forgot something," in Henri's direction, I pull my peacock diary and pen out of my suitcase before slipping back into the bathroom.

On a whim, I tug open the shower door and switch it on. While I wait for it to warm, I flick to my list at the beginning. It seems so stupid now to be keeping a record of all of these things, but it feels almost like I'm keeping a record of us, one for history. I write: **Have sex in the sea**, and then cross it out. Snapping the book shut, I jump in the shower, lathering myself in the lemon-scented gel he has on the shelf.

"Julianna?" There's a shout through the door.

"I'm fine, give me five."

He doesn't answer, so I lift my face to the powerful jets. The hot water is soothing, restorative. I should probably be thinking of the words I'll need to say tomorrow. I never thought I'd have to tell him, never knew that we'd get to this point. It was only ever meant to be a night of fun. But I guess that's life. It steals up and surprises you when you least expect it, squirming into all the tight spaces that you thought you kept carefully locked. I'd spent so long forgetting to live, keeping below the radar, that I'd long forgotten there could be a spark in the veins that pushed you from one moment to the next with only a heartbeat between.

Life was simply a heartbeat. Love the silence between.

Out of the shower, I dry off and rub the rose-scented oil Liv's gifted me over my skin until I glow like a brand-new penny. Then I slip on the black lace set I bought one rainy London afternoon. The bralette does something miraculous to my cleavage, the sheer shorts giving me curves I've never owned before. The woman in the shop had suggested a G-string, but hell, I was dying, I hadn't lost my mind yet. The sun today has tinted my pale skin with a hint of gold, and thankfully no bacon streaks.

With my hand on the bathroom door my heartbeat races. Good race I think.

Come on, Julia. This is what this thing called life is all about.

Dragging in a breath, straightening my shoulder and

swinging my hair out behind me, I yank open the door. Probably with more force than I need because it bounces off the bathroom wall making Henri jump as it slams tiles. "Sorry, I'll fix the wall tomorrow if I've broken it."

"And you'll be wearing that when you do?" One of his brows quirks and he throws back the sheet revealing his naked perfection underneath.

"Only if you wear that." I stalk for the bed, tossing my diary back in my suitcase as I pass.

Our lips fuse, his hands skimming my exposed skin. "Never has black lace looked so perfect."

"Never has naked looked so perfect," I counter.

I shiver as his broad hands rise from my waist, cupping my tits, pushing them together into rounded globes that make his eyes widen. Dipping his dark head, he presses butterfly soft kisses onto the swells and curves.

"This stays on," he growls, lowering himself, one hand still firmly cupping my laced goods, brushing circles with his thumb, making me arch my back. Kisses trail my body, tongue dancing a path downwards. My fingers find his hair, slipping through the long, dark waves, dancing around where they end at his neck.

When his free hand palms my thigh, sliding over my oiled skin, roughing over the delicate lace, I give a little tremble.

This is profound.

Every time with him has been out of this world bliss, but now there's this intensity burning. It's a dark need to feel him at the very root of me, a clawing desperation for us to be fused and connected in a way that words will never truly describe. For us to be a single entity with one breath.

"Henri," I murmur, drawing him back up towards me. "I really need you."

"But the lace."

"I don't care."

His eyes meet mine and I know he gets it too. He gets me. This unexpected soul mate of mine. A wild coursing sensation, foreign and unknown sweeps through my body, making my stiff heart swell. This is the same way I felt in the rain in Notting Hill weeks and weeks ago, but now I know what it is. I'm brave enough to know what it is.

He reaches for the cupboard by the bed.

"No." I pull him back. "Just you."

"Julianna," he breathes my name like a prayer.

"Just you." Hooking my fingers in the expensive black lace I push the knickers down, exposing myself to his hungry gaze, stretching to his sweeping touch as his fingers dip between my thighs. "No. I want my first touch to be you."

"But—"

With a smile, I spread my legs. "Believe me, I'm ready."

His head dips in acknowledgement and he settles between my thighs, pushing at my entrance with nothing between us. I slip my hands down his back, lowering him so we are connected across every inch of our skin, our lips slanted, fast and firm as he pushes inside, filling me, fulfilling me, further and further until I gasp his name, my eyes screwed shut.

This is where I need him.

Warm, soft but hard, firmly centred within me. It's electric, ripples flood my skin, everything heightened.

"You are the most beautiful thing, Julianna."

My eyes fly open to find him watching me. A dark heat licks inside me and he hasn't even moved yet. He closes his eyes, groaning softly as he rocks back and forth, gentle at first, the feel of him bare inside me almost I think bringing us both to an unexpected ending.

I clutch in a gasp of air, holding it in my lungs, not wanting to come already, but it does nothing. Every stroke of his hips teeters me on an edge of the unknown and my orgasm blasts hard and I dig my nails into his back, arching against his weight. "Shit," I gasp.

That is not what I wanted to happen at all.

Henri though is grinning, no, smirking, that boyish dimple teasing me. He rolls us, keeping us connected. "Ride me, ma petite."

I'm gonna ride him like a bareback pony. I circle my hips grinding him deeper. His hands settle at my sides, keeping my rhythm as my orgasm creates a sensitivity that's almost on the point of pain. Our gazes lock. Holy shit, another tingle builds.

"Oh, dear god," I groan. The angle is everything. Electric pulses shoot me down deep, all the while his hands keep me steady, his hips rising slightly to meet my dance.

"Julia," he sighs my name, hand reaching for my tit, squeezing, somehow freeing it from the lacy confines and spilling me over the top.

I glance down at how we are connected, how I'm exposed, and it's the most wanton thing I've ever seen. It's another log onto the fire of my pleasure.

"Henri, I'm going to come again." I pant my words, each one exhaling on a puff of air.

Flipping us over, he drives home so fast and so deep. I scream his name as I come apart. He shouts his release, clutching me tight as an unexpected warmth fills me with an almost territorial power.

Me Julia.

Henri mine.

His lips land on mine, planting kisses, soaking up tears I didn't know were there until I taste them on his mouth. Roughly, his hands clasp my face, holding me still, making me look deep into his storm ridden eyes. "I love you, Julia Brown."

A stupid sobbed whimper leaves my lips, and he kisses it away while I clutch onto him like a lifeboat drifting in the Mediterranean. "And I love you."

26

IRRESISTIBLE

"Tell me about Paris." We've been snuggled, curved in warmth, one last flickering candle our only light with the shine of the moon.

"Ugh."

"Ugh, is not the right response when talking of the capital of lurrve."

"Ugh." He drops his hand to cover his eyes and shakes his head. A small smile curves his lips. I want to kiss that smile forever.

"Okay, tell me about the Eiffel Tower. I've never been."

I'm watching him with stalking closeness that I can see his skin blanch in the half light. "Scared of heights, my lover?"

He peeks through his fingers at my use of the label he'd once given himself. "Not heights. Tourists."

"Well, you know, I'm a tourist, so maybe I should just go and put my clothes on if you don't like us so much." I go to get off the bed, but he pulls me back with a firm tug and fits me back against his chest, his arm a barrier so I don't dare move again.

"I should remind you; we are in a hotel your family owns full of tourists."

Ha. I've stumped him into silence, although I've shot below the belt. It's more than obvious that this venture is led by his maman and not him. He's happier with his cows.

"I suppose it's an engineering feat," he grumbles, and I chuckle against his warm skin.

"Would you think me a foolish romantic if I said I always wanted someone to propose to me at the top of the Eiffel Tower? That they were willing to get down on one knee and submit to the ridiculousness that is the cliché of romance, just for me?"

With gentle fingers he turns my chin. "I really am very scared of heights."

Snorting a laugh, I shake my head. "Don't worry, Henri, I'll let you off."

"You still love me though?"

"Until my dying day." Turning, I crane my neck to kiss his cheek, not letting him see the rogue tear that escapes my eye.

"Now the Louvre is worth a visit. Sometimes when Gabriella is at her most frustrating, I just walk the corridors, taking some time."

"Why is she frustrating?" I squidge myself over so I can see his face properly, the expressions that dance in the candlelight.

"Because she doesn't take anything seriously."

Pursing my lips, I contemplate this. "Should life be serious?" I can tell him right now that it shouldn't. I've got my membership pin badge for that group.

"No."

"So why is she frustrating?"

He scowls at the ceiling.

"So, it's really the situation your mother has created that's frustrating? Let me guess, she thinks Gabriella should come back here too?"

"It's not that straightforward. She's still in mourning, she wants us close."

"I'd say it's pretty easy."

He shakes his head, lips pressed.

"You know my parents, they suffocated me, always expected me to do everything right. I was the eldest, I had to set an example. I never even really did anything wrong, yet they still blamed me when Liv followed her wild path. They blamed me for something I didn't do. Everything I've done since has been cast in the light of that time. Months ago, you told me I lived a life in grey. Well, you, my lover, live a life of repression, here at the will of your maman. Is this even where you want to be? In a hotel that isn't your dream, when really you're a farmer at heart?"

There's a lengthy pause, and I think I've overstepped the mark. Finally, he kisses under my ear, his arms closing me in tighter until my already empty lungs are depleted of all air.

"In January, I was in London because I was meeting a farmer who has managed to rebuild a herd of truly rare cattle. I was talking of taking over some land and starting what we do here over there. It would be different. A different type of cheese process to here. I wanted the challenge."

"But?"

He doesn't answer for a long time.

"Then the following month I went back to tell him it was a no go, I couldn't do it. But then I saw you again, and right then in that moment I knew I wanted to move to London. Not for cows, not for the challenge of what I could achieve, but because I knew that I'd found something in you I never thought I would."

It hurts. All of this hurts because... "But you didn't."

"No, I didn't." His eyes meet mine. "And if I did now? If I packed a bag and left with you now?"

I can't answer. *It's too late.*

And even though he doesn't *know* yet, he can hear the words in my silence.

"Let's get some sleep." I nestle down so he can't see my face. I'm pretty sure it's a picture of pure heartbreak.

I wake to warm fingers of sunlight reaching around the curtains. I pat the bed, expecting him to have gone to check his herds, but I tap tight arse cheeks instead. Nice. Automatically, I crank an eye to check Simone hasn't come for a morning chat, breathing a sigh of relief when it's just us in the room.

Gosh what a miserable mess he's in here. Part of me wants to go and seek out his mama bear and tell her to let her grown ass son live his own life, live her grief herself and not destroy him with it. But I won't. Because she's damn scary.

I'm exhausted and not just physically. Although yes, my energy if it were flickering on a battery light would be coming in at about two, but mentally too. All night my sleep was disturbed by his words. That he wanted to come to London just for me but didn't.

I can hardly complain, can I? For five months I've been keeping the mother of all secrets from him. But then I never expected it to come to this. It was only meant to be one night.

Maybe I can say that over and over again to myself until

I end, but I know the truth deep in my heart. Even that first night this was something else.

He felt it too.

This last few months of mine feel like a tragic waste of time. More of a waste than the barren years of my life all put together.

Regret. It's a bitter tasting pill.

Could I stay here?

Is that a possibility? If I tell him the truth, could I stay here and see out these final stages with him? Would he even want that?

Fuck. I should have told him the truth right at the start. We could have been anything together by now. Instead, we still teetered on the cusp of something that could only be nothing.

One thing I do know is that I don't want to go home. Turning, I look at his stretched-out form, golden skin, messy waves of dark hair. The stubble on his face a dark shadow I could lick like a lolly.

No, I don't want to go home.

But do I want him to see me the way I know I'm soon going to be? I don't think I want that either. It's bad enough he's already witnessing this spectral ghost I'm becoming.

I don't want anything that's going to hurt, yet still I know it will anyway.

Picking up my phone, I slip on some underwear and shorts and one of Henri's t-shirts with the stealth of a ninja and sneak out of the room. I try to remember the way to the family kitchen and after a few wrong turns I find the heavy wooden door. Pushing it open, I tuck my head in. I could do without his maman right now. I'm not sure I could keep myself civil.

Thankfully it's open and I walk straight for the patio

doors and push them open, letting fresh and fragrant air wash over my face. Gah, it's heaven.

And I'm going to ruin it.

I eye roll myself, which I think is a new low.

Flicking on the kettle and searching out some mugs, I prep some coffee before heading out onto the patio. For a moment I hold my phone in my hand, staring at the screen.

Then pulling up my big girl pants I dial Liv.

She doesn't speak... must be waiting to see if it's me or Henri calling.

"It's me."

There's a loud exhalation. "Please tell me you aren't dead."

"Yes, I'm calling from the other side."

"Fucking hell, Jules. I haven't slept a wink. You freaked me the hell out last night. I shit myself it was going to be Henri speaking from your phone."

Tears sting my eyes, bloody things, it's like blinking glass. "Sorry."

"What's wrong? Why are you calling so early? You're struggling aren't you? Sooner you get home the better. I'm going to have serious words with Dr Francis about this."

"Liv. Stop."

"What?"

"What if I didn't come home?"

"What the hell do you mean?"

My throat is so tight I can barely squeeze words out. "I love him, Liv. I don't think I can leave."

"You haven't even told him yet, have you?" She's exasperated with me. It's in her voice, and I'm not surprised. It's crazy and yet it's what I want.

"I'm going to today."

"And then what he's going to say, 'sure, hang around and I'll watch you slowly die'."

"Liv!"

"Sorry." There's a wrenching sob. "Jules, I can't stand this. You can't be for real?"

"How about if I stay for another week, assuming he doesn't throw me to the curb for being faulty?"

Liv sighs. "He's not going to do that, he loves you. I could hear it, see it even, and that was months ago."

"I just, I just..."

"Want to enjoy it now that you've found it."

"Is that so wrong?"

"It's not wrong. I just can't stand you being so far away. And..." She heaves a deep breath. "Maybe I'm a bit jealous."

"Because I've finally got a boyfriend?" I snort a laugh.

"Because you don't need me anymore." There's a sniffle from the other end of the line.

"I'll always need you. You're my sister. I've just got to live for a little while longer."

A silence stretches between us. We both know that Dr Francis will have nothing to say that can help.

"Is it really bad?"

"What?"

"How you feel?"

"I'm just tired. Really, really tired. Like I'm stretching myself too far and can't spring back into shape. Like baggy knicker elastic."

"Enjoy it, Jules. If anyone deserves a happy ending it's you."

"I'll see you soon. I promise I'm going to see you."

"So, what happens now?"

I look up at the sun until it dries the trails of my tears.

"Now I'm going to make him a coffee and tell him the truth."

"Good luck," she whispers. "And answer your goddamn phone."

We hang up and I take a moment, breathing in the air, trying to stretch my lungs a little with the flower scents swirling around me. There's a freshness preceding what looks like another storming hot day.

I'm making coffee when there is a clatter behind me. I pray it's Henri and hope to fuck it's not his mother, breathing out a relieved sigh when I see it's Odile.

"Morning." I smile. "Would you like a coffee?"

"Perfect. It was a late one, the guests didn't want to go to bed."

"Sorry if I'm distracting Henri from helping, although I get the impression he's happier with his cows."

She laughs and I wish it didn't tinkle like fairies chiming together. "Henri is always happy with his cows."

"Thank you so much for shopping for me yesterday." I reach up into the cupboard and grab her out a cup. "It was very kind of you to go out of your way."

"No problem, I knew the colour would suit your colouring."

I watch as she takes her banana clip out of her hair and steps towards me. "Here, turn around."

I do as she asks, pulling a 'what the fuck' face.

"You should wear your hair up like this." She twists it and fixes it in place with the clip, leaving her own blonde mass falling around her shoulders. "Henri loves necks on show. He finds it *irresistible*."

"Oh right, thanks for the tip."

Okay, this is weird. Kind, I guess, but weird as hell.

My stomach drops as a little spark of truth flickers to life in my head. "How do you know?" I try to laugh it off, my exposed neck strangely uncomfortable.

"Of course, I know, I'm his wife."

I turn slowly to face her.

"Well ex-wife I suppose." She shrugs like she's not quite sure but then sees my face, her own mouth popping open.

"Oh god. He hasn't told you, has he?"

I'm almost entirely sure the earth has disintegrated beneath my feet.

"You're his wife?"

"Ex." She holds her hands up, but it's too late, my happily-not-for-much-longer-ever-after has just splintered in two.

Henri is married to Odile. Something he's failed to mention. And I'm pretty damn sure that's worse than my secret.

Married trumps dying and that's a fact.

27

THIS IS REALLY GOING TO HURT

"You're married?" I screech back into his bedroom. My blood is pumping fast. I need to catch my breath but can't. Fingers in tiny fists, there's a buzzing in my digits like they are expanding into cartoon hands.

Calm it down.

Mr Married is still sprawled in all his now flawed perfection.

"You're married and you let her buy me a bikini!"

I have the perfect view of his eyes flying wide open, midnight storms and stars falling.

"Julia?" He scrambles up. For some ridiculous reason I'm staring at his dick, probably because I know it's the last time I'm going to see it. "It's not like that."

"How long have you been married?"

His face falls. It doesn't stop me from wanting to karate kick it—if I knew karate.

"Tell me." I step closer, chest too tight. "And don't you dare fucking shrug."

He freezes. "How will knowing how long make it any better?" Oh my god. That's practically a verbal shrug.

"How long?"

"Ten years."

My legs fold. Breath coming in small gasps. *Ten years? Ten. Years.*

No. Just no. Stumbling forward, I pitch for the patio doors, pushing them open and falling through. Outside the sun has been eclipsed by the moon, or maybe I just can't see it.

"Julia, please." Henri struggles to chase after me, pulling jeans up, no underwear.

"Ten years," I repeat to myself.

"Julia, I'm not married anymore, it's over."

I wheel around. "That's funny, because Odile is confused about whether you are exes or not." This isn't strictly true. "Oh my god. You still live with your wife. You let me wear her shoes."

I'm not sure if it's the bikini or walking in his wife's shoes that hurts the most.

"Julianna, will you please just stop? It's not like that. Odile is a very old family friend. We've been separated for months. There is no love between us."

"How long?" I know the answer before he says it and I drop my head. "Let me guess. Just before your dad died."

Stalking forward, I poke his chest. "You know when I met you and realised you were so much older than me, I thought you were a grown up. You aren't a grown man, you're a fucking mummy's boy."

I whirl away, shaking my head. "I can't believe I just told Liv I was going to stay. I'm such a fool. I can't believe I've wasted this precious time, here, with you, a lying bastard."

"I've never lied."

"You never told me you had a wife. I specifically asked

if you had a girlfriend. What? Did I not use the right label so then you didn't have to tell the truth? I've been here under the same roof as her for days now."

"I know. I'm sorry. It's just the more time that passed, the harder it became." Catching my hand, he reels me back in. "I love you, Julianna. I've never felt anything close to the way I feel about you. I told you, you're magic in my life."

"Married, Henri?" The fight starts to seep out of me, that numb exhaustion rushing back in making my limbs heavy, legs hard to move. A pain stabs in my chest, an ache that makes me rub my left ribs. "Living with her all this time that I've been falling in love with you." I can't breathe. There's a sob that wants to let go, but it's vacuumed in my chest like a hard lump of coal.

"Julia, you are everything to me. You make me want to fight this situation I'm in."

"But you haven't. Your *maman* thinks you're getting back together, doesn't she? That's why she treated me so dismissively. She thinks I'm a fling."

It all makes sense now. That flick of dismissive fingers, her open hostility even on our first meeting... her real daughter-in-law of choice was already sat at the goddam family table.

It's too much.

I pull away.

"I'm going home."

Absently I rub at my arm. It's heavy, odd, weighed down so I'm uneven.

"Julia, ma petite, you said you wanted to stay. We can fix this."

"No, Henri. It's too late for me to fix anything. I should never have come. Should have stayed with Liv which was always our plan." I march back for his room; pretty sure his mother is leaning out of a window somewhere in her castle punching the air with glee at my sudden end. Right, I can book a taxi to the airport. I can be home by the time Paige is out of pre-school.

I want to run, but know I can't, so I power march for the bedroom. I'm at the door when I stop.

"Julianna!"

His face flickers, mouth opening, but the heaviness in my arm explodes into fire. My chest contracts, but not the way I've got used to. No, this is an elephant reverse parking onto my heart.

"My tablets," I hiss, bending, holding my arm. It's so sudden, so quick, I almost laugh in surprise.

"What bloody tablets?"

"In. My."

Nothing else comes out. The burn from my arm spreads like a fire through an old, gutted tenement block. It burns everything in its wake, extinguishing my breath. I can't stand under the force of it.

The last thing I see is Henri reaching forward to catch me, his face a mask of shock, as my heart explodes in my chest.

Finally, I reach my end.

Dr Francis lied. It's the last thought I have. This hasn't been twelve months at all. Nowhere even close. What a lying bastard.

28

DIFFERENT SHADES OF WHITE

Death is such a funny thing. From the moment you are born you are conditioned to never think about it. Loved ones go, grandparents, family, and we know to wear black and sit on a pew, shed tears that don't help, tears that feel helpless in the great scheme of life. What do tears achieve?

It is salt water I'm first aware of.

One droplet. Two. Three. Splashing on my hand like rain in a puddle.

Death is such a funny thing. Tears feel real even when the end has been reached.

"Jules?"

There isn't a single will inside of me to open my eyes. I like the dark. It's nice here, numb. The sound of a whooshing noise fills my ears. Rhythmic and soothing, a bit like breathing.

"Jules, sweetie, I'm here."

Who is that? Don't they know I'm listening to the ocean on the sand. Not the Perpignan sea. No, not the sea with *him,* breaker of hearts, sandy orgasm giver.

No, this sea is the Atlantic, angry against rocks,

punishing the earth for something it will probably never understand.

"When will she wake up?" The voice buzzes in again. There's a flurry of words I don't understand and then the blissful note of a voice I think I'd know anywhere, calling my name, Waterloo Station, Oxford Street, hell.

Oh fuck. I'm in hell, aren't I?

"They said, they don't know."

"Don't know what? If she will wake up at all, or just when?"

There's a breeze near what I think was once my face. A low murmur that pulls me to the surface of the ocean. "Ma petite, I want to have a word with you. You'd better be ready."

I try to blink. Nothing happens, just a never-ending void and the whoosh of the sea.

"She's waking."

It's Liv, sat by the bed, her face a white and pink splodgy mess as though someone has tripped over while carrying an Eton mess.

"I thought I'd lost you." Her hand squeezes mine. Putting her head down next to my waist she sobs, shoulders shaking. "I thought I'd lost you."

Trying to lift my hand to comfort her I fail, because it's weighed down with tubes and wires. *Do not look at the tubes, Julia, do not.* Too late. Ugh. I think I'm going to hurl.

Liv, almost on instinct, reaches for the sick bowl, although I'm distracted by the movement of a hulking shadow lurking in the corner of the room. It moves, slipping through the door before I can react.

I was so angry with him.

So angry.

Now, now... it seems so silly. As far-fetched as it all seemed, it also now seems entirely plausible. I already knew his mum was a half-cooked control freak... I should have listened. Should have not nearly bloody died.

Liv helps me up as I retch into the bowl, but nothing comes up. "What happened?"

She starts to cry, which never bodes well. "You had a massive heart attack, Jules. I don't know how they restarted your heart."

The tears run faster down her face, but strangely I'm detached like the words we are speaking aren't about me at all. I can only think of one thing, one person; like my entire existence has zeroed down to the size of a pinhead.

"He's cross with me, isn't he?"

"Jules, he kept your heart pumping while the ambulance came. You'd be dead if it wasn't for him."

"No. But I mean he's cross, annoyed that I overreacted."

She shrugs... far too long in a French hospital. "He hasn't spoken. Hardly at all, apart from to say he'll go to get your stuff."

Oh God.

I really am going home.

"How long have I been out?"

"A day."

"What?!"

"Jules, I need to try to find a way to get you home."

"No, Liv, wait. I need to speak to Henri."

"Julia! What about Paige, Lenny? Don't you want to see them?"

"Yes, yes of course I do, but... I was really mean, stupid really."

Death it seems paints life in different shades of white. You realise that nothing is pure, nothing is untainted. I realise now my stupidity to believe otherwise.

I was wrong. Dying trumps marriage.

"Can you try to get Henri back for me?" Streaks of tears slip down my face.

Liv bites her lower lip and then clutches my hand. "Jules." She gives my fingers a tight squeeze. "This is it; you do know that? I've spoken to Dr Francis. He's making arrangements for you to go straight onto his ward when we get back, but he says we should have looked at hospices."

Turning my face, I stare at the wall. "Please get Henri."

She waits a beat, but I don't turn back, and eventually she pats my hand again and leaves. I cry, staring at cream walls.

The end seemed so very far away, funny that it's so quickly here.

I wake again to the shift of air next to the bed. Please let it be him. Please let it be him.

Turning, I open my eyes, only to find anger and betrayal staring right back at me. "Henri," I sigh his name, a wish on my lips.

My fingers stretch automatically waiting for a connection with him. It doesn't come, so instead I pull the oxygen tube from under my nose, attempting to make myself half normal. "I'm so sorry I got angry. It came as a massive shock, but I shouldn't have overreacted. I guess I was jealous. She's so beautiful. When I arrived and saw you together in town, I figured you'd upgraded. It made perfect sense to me, you looked like you fitted together." My words are running into one another, exhaustion, sleep, and dying making them string with breathless little pauses.

"A massive shock, Julianna?" His words are moderated, even. The depths of his eyes hold shadows I don't want to fall into. "Imagine watching the woman you love with all your soul crumple to the ground with no warning, almost, almost…"

I shake my head, but the tears start. "It was so hard to tell you. I planned to, today." Oh, that's not right. "Yesterday," I amend. "I wanted to tell you, because I wanted to stay with you. I knew there was only one thing that would take me away from you." I don't say it.

"I never told you, but my father dropped down dead in front of me. Just like that." Henri snaps his fingers, and a little bit of hope leaves my body with a gasp of air. "We were out on the fields, just the two of us, where we most liked to be, and he fell. I had to carry him all the way home knowing it was too late to save him, that he was already dead in my arms."

"Henri, I'm sorry." I hitch my breath as it combines with a sob. "You saved me though, Henri, Liv told me. I'd be gone now if it wasn't for you."

Slowly he shakes his head, dropping his stormy gaze.

"Henri, please."

When he raises them to meet my face there's a sea of defeat staring right back at me.

"I should have told you I was married. It was a silly secret to keep. Silly, because I haven't been in love with Odile for years, a fact we both knew. Our relationship had become one of business and ease."

"I'm sorry, I get that."

He holds up his hand.

"But dying? Julianna," he whispers my name.

"I'm so sorry. Just the faster I fell for you, the more I never wanted it to end. I met you the day I found out, and you gave me this little spark of life right when I thought it was over."

"And you realised you still had things you needed to do." His face pinches, skin tightening around his eyes.

"What do you mean?" I ask. A tightening band grips my chest as he pulls my peacock book from behind his back.

"Oh, Henri," I whisper, shrinking back against the pillow.

He flicks to the page with dreams and aspiration.

"It seems you planned to have a busy few remaining months." He skims my stupid words. "It also seems you found someone to help you with your plans."

"It's not what it looks like." I lift my hand from the bed and hold it out for him to give it back.

"You were never going to tell me about your illness, were you? I was just a means to an end. You planned to leave at the end of your week here and not even tell me. I would have come to London, knocked on your door only to find someone else living in your grey cube. Or even worse, you would have left it for Olivia to tell me."

He watches me with splintering brutality. "No?"

"No!" But my lie stains my cheeks pink. "I so wanted to see you one more time, but I didn't know how to tell you. When the doctor told me this was it, all I could think of was you. That you hadn't been back, that I might never..." I run out of steam, my heart is giving warning pulses in my chest, sharp shooting pains run down my arms.

"Ah yes." His gaze drops to the open pages. "You needed sex in the sea, correct?"

"No. That's not true. Everything on that list I've written since we've done it. In hindsight, not as a wish."

He stares at me and it's like we are planets operating from different sides of the universe.

"Come back to London with me, Henri. It's not going to be long. Please. For me. That diary." I stab my finger at it, but it's a pathetic effort. I'm pathetic. Broken, useless. "Everything in there is the highlight of my life." I can't say anything more, my throat tightens, eyesight flickering with my familiar black spots.

"I can't watch you die, Julianna." I can only just hear him around the whooshing in my ears. With all my effort, I lift my hand and reposition the oxygen under my nostrils, inhaling greedily at the cold shoot of air. "I just can't."

I nod, no effort left. "I understand."

On fluid and strong legs, he gets up and slides my book under my hand before bending and kissing my forehead. "Goodbye, Julianna Brown."

I can't say goodbye. Just won't.

I watch him leave and just hope to hell the end comes quick, because life now really doesn't seem worth existing in at all.

29

LONDON CALLING

THE TRIP BACK IS NUMB. Empty. A private ambulance speeding the superior French roads, taking the Eurostar. There's been much discussion about what was the quickest and safest way. Discussion I'd tried to doze through, torn between no longer caring, but also petrified of what might happen if I did fall asleep.

What if the black and endless depth of sleep never ended?

Liv squeezes my hand. Face pale and drawn. I'm hurting people left, right, and centre without even trying. "Not long now."

I shrug. *Tout français.*

This was for the best. What was I thinking? Did I really want Henri to see me like this? No, I didn't. I must have been high on that hospital bed to even consider it.

I need to find a way to get Liv to leave my side when the end comes. I don't want her to forever see that either. If she's a pain, I'll have to send her for a bag of Maltesers or something.

Just like that I'm making an evil master plan for dying. Keeps a girl busy, I guess.

"I'm assuming Dickweed Darren has the kids?" I murmur, rousing myself from my drowsy fog.

"He says he can have them as long as I need."

"No need at all. You can tell him you'll have them back today."

"Jules!"

"No, really, you won't be able to stay at the hospital anyway."

Through the pained fog I see her bite her lip. "I've been looking at hospices. I hope you don't mind."

"Whatever," I grumble.

"Julia." Liv squeezes my hand. "Henri loves you. I think he loves you so much he can't bear to watch you go through this. You should have seen him when I got to the hospital. He was destroyed. He looked like a madman, hair all wild, face savaged with worry."

A little sigh escapes my lips. "Can we not talk about him again?"

The squeeze turns into a pat. "Sure."

"I mean, if he really loved me, he would have been brave enough to face this with me. He's probably with Odile right now, making his mother happy."

"Jules, I don't think—"

"Let's not mention him again. He doesn't exist anymore, okay?"

"Sure."

"I mean, it's not like I'm planning on dropping down dead to the floor like his dad did. I'm planning for this to be a civilised affair. I'll just eek out like a ghost in the night."

"Julia, you did drop down on the floor in front of him.

How the hell did you keep your tablets a secret while living in the same room as him?"

"Let's not..."

"I know. Let's not talk about him anymore."

I'm aware of Liv turning and speaking to the faceless nurse who's riding with us. I've no idea who they are, apart from the odd blur of white. A true professional. A cool rush spreads up my arm from the cannula at my elbow.

'Jules, you have to sleep."

"No. I don't want to sleep."

It's too late though, darkness is edging in, walking spindly fingers into my consciousness. No. Please don't make it dark. I clutch her hand, fighting against it.

"Liv, how did you pay for the ambulance?" It's the last thought I can round up before a void of black steals me away. She's going to kill me for not having travel insurance.

I know we are in London before I've opened my eyes. The air is different, cool on my face. May in London is worlds apart from May in the South of France.

Bollocks. I block thoughts of honeysuckle and marigolds.

"Julianna Brown. What have you been doing?"

I groan at Dr Francis.

"Just catching some sun." I try to smile but my mouth won't move.

"I said a relaxed break, not having major heart attacks. I don't know how you survived."

Henri.

His name whispers through my brain like wisteria in a breeze.

"Sorry," I grumble. I'm vaguely aware of some shifting

of the bed, a heave and a ho, and then I'm planted back down again, opening my eyes to the London hospital I spent so much time in two years ago.

"Right then, obs, rest, and I'll be back shortly to chat."

I roll my eyes. What are we chatting about? "We don't need to spin this out. You can just tell me how long right now."

Dr Francis wiggles his grey brows. "How can I do that without your obs? You're feisty this morning, Julianna."

It's childish but I pull a face.

"Jules!" Liv chides so I pull a face at her too.

"Good luck," he tells her before leaving the room, a nurse bustling in shortly to disturb the dark silence Liv and I are embroiled in. Her phone pings as I'm being hooked up to various beeping machines and she glances down at me, sighing out a deep breath before her eyes find mine.

"Don't kill me."

I give her a weak smile. "Well now I probably will."

"Mum's here," she blurts.

"What the actual fuck, Liv? You can't be for real." It clicks a switch inside my head. "That's how we got home isn't it? Mum and Dad paid for that private ambulance."

She doesn't get a chance to say anything more because the door reopens and a woman, who's vaguely familiar looking, walks through.

"Julia," the stranger in a floral skirt and home knitted jumper steps up for the bed and grasps my hand. "Oh, my goodness. Look at you. My baby."

I want to huff a breath but that would mean me having a breath to spare.

She leans in, Lily of the Valley sparking locked memories. "Is that sunburn on your nose?"

And that's my mother.

"Snow burn."

"Oh, Julia. When Liv called I didn't quite believe it. I never thought this would happen."

I shift on the plastic mattress. If I could gain an inch away from her this situation would feel a whole lot better.

I open my mouth, but I haven't got a word to say. Not one single word.

"I'm so very sorry, so sorry. I've been so foolish." It's okay. Apparently Mum is going to talk for both of us. "I tried so hard to protect you."

"Listen," Liv cuts in. "I'm going to go and get a coffee."

Mum nods while I send Liv a stink eye.

After she's left, Mum spends some time faffing, tucking in my blankets, fluffing the edges of the pillows, smoothing the ends of my tangled hair. I wonder if I've still got bed hair from my last night with... *Stop it, Julia.*

Sleep edges its way back in, crawling in with a stealth like steal.

Mum's waffling on, talking as she titivates around me, always busy. The woman never ever stopped. Always wringing her hands, always looking like the world might end at any moment now.

"Do you need a drink, baby?"

I try to laugh, lips dry though, cracking with the effort. *I'm her baby now?*

It's a long time since I've been this woman's baby.

"Mum, stop." I summon the words. "I don't need you here. I don't know why you're here."

"This is all my fault." More hand wringing. The woman is a master at saintly supplication.

"It's not." For fuck's sake why is talking so hard? "You didn't give me meningitis, and contrary to what you and dad once thought about me, I didn't catch it from anyone else either."

"We just wanted to keep you safe. That's all we ever wanted, for you and Liv to be nice sensible girls, safe, protected."

"You did that job real good, Mum. Two years ago, you didn't even come to see me. I didn't do things the way you wanted, and you cut me off. Disappointed in the failure I was."

"No. I didn't."

Okay, this is boring. I don't want to listen to this during my final moments. And it is. There is no avoiding it now.

"Can you get Liv back for me please?" I shudder in a breath. "And thanks for getting me home. One decent thing you've done for me in the last fifteen years."

"Jules, I need to speak."

"It's too late. The only thing you can do for me now is look after Liv. Please." My eyes burn. "Get out. Get out."

"Julia, please."

"No. Get out." I'm struggling to sit, pulling at wires. I'm in an all-out sweat, but I don't care. "I'll get Liv to pay you back for the ambulance. I don't want anything from you."

"What are you talking about, what ambulance? Jules, please, calm down." A machine starts to beep, and Mom's eyes fly to it. "Please calm down."

"Calm down." I nod, pulling at the wire under my nose. "Calm down, Julia. Don't be so aggressive, Julia. No, you aren't going to the park, Julia. Stay in your room, Julia. Stay safe, Julia. Don't trust anyone, Julia. You," I stab my finger at her, it's shaking, not quite on target, "failed at parenting. You failed both me and Liv and I hope this moment haunts you forever. You scared me out of living, and I can't ever get that back now."

The door flies open and Liv streams through. "Oh my god, what is happening?" A nurse is not far behind, pushing me back down on the bed despite my last power surge. Like an outage about to darken a city I flicker with strength once more, twice more, three, and then I'm spent.

Done.

"What have I done? Just go, Mum," Liv is whispering. At least I think she's whispering, but I'm no longer sure.

My room is rather like Waterloo with people coming and going. Nurses are fiddling with my machines, setting up drips. They should probably just take it all out now.

"Stop," my call is feeble. "Just stop."

A nurse pats my hand. "Just try to keep calm while we make you more comfortable."

"No. I want to see Dr Francis."

"I'm here." There's a gentle pat of my toes while Liv settles back up in the chair by my head.

"It's over, isn't it?" I heave in my words, sucking them in because pushing them out seems one feat too far.

"I don't think we can move you to a hospice now, Julia." His words are laced with kindness and I'm so grateful to him. So grateful, but also so damn gutted. This is it, and I have one thought in my head. Just. One.

Henri.

God, it's torture knowing I won't see his face again.

"We'll make you comfortable, Julianna, okay?"

"Call me Jules." I smile faintly. "It's probably about time."

After he's left, we lapse into silence other than a steady beeping and the sound of my oxygen machine.

"He showed me how it's happening," Liv whispers. "Do you want me to tell you?"

I shake my head. "I can live without the CliffsNotes."

She chuckles but then starts to cry, her tears splattering my skin.

"I'm sorry I ruined everything by going to France."

"You didn't. I'm glad you went."

"Liv. I want you to go home now."

"Not a chance."

"Please."

"No."

"Tell me how you paid for the ambulance?"

There's a stretch of silence and I find her fingers, giving a squeeze.

"Just please tell me it's not Dickweed."

She laughs a snotty sound. "No. Henri."

Her admission strikes a final blow. "God, he really didn't want me to stay in France, did he?"

I turn my face away and stare at nothing. "Liv, please go home. If I'm here tomorrow, I'll let you come back."

"Who put you in charge?"

"Me. I'm the eldest, I've always been in charge, I just like you to think otherwise."

"Let me stay?"

"No. Go get those kids and give them the biggest hug you possibly can for me. I'll be okay. I'm going to sleep."

I. Am. Not. Going. To. Sleep.

"Jules, please."

I turn my face away. "I'm scared, Liv."

"So am I. That's why I have to stay."

"That's why you have to go. Anyway." Breath. "Barney will be wanting his dinner." Breath. "You don't want to know what he'll do to your sofa." Breath. "If you don't feed him on time." Breath.

"That cat is a pain in the backside, Jules."

I almost turn. "Look after him." Breath.

"I will." There's silence filled with her sobs, but I refuse to turn around. I can't do a goodbye, don't want to.

"I s-uppose." Breath. "Y-you could s-swing by tomorrow and s-see if I'm still k-kicking." Talking is hard. Trying to keep breathing even harder.

A watery kiss lands on my forehead. "You stupid mare. Where else would I be? By—"

"Don't. Just don't."

It hurts. I know I'm hurting her by not turning to face her. This could be it, and for that exact reason I can't make myself do it. How do you say goodbye to your sister?

No. I'll face this alone. It's better that way.

What would it have been like to have Henri hold my hand, help me be brave?

Silly, Julianna.

Stupid, Julianna.

It was all just a one-night stand that went epically wrong.

30

FOR WHOM THE BELL TOLLS

I WAIT ALL NIGHT. All. Night.

At three I ask the nurse on the literal graveyard shift if she's got some matchsticks to keep my eyes open. She laughs and says no, but she can hold my hand instead. We pass an hour, her talking, filling the space in the room. I breathe less and less. There's a weird sensation in my feet.

"What's wrong with them?" I ask.

"Just some swelling. Want me to get a damp cloth to cool them down?"

"No, it's not too bad."

"Would you like some water?"

I can't remember when I last drank anything. Strangely, I don't feel empty. I shake my head and the nurse gets up to adjust the drips going into my arm, frowning as she looks under the bed. Without a word she resettles and picks my hand back up. This time though she doesn't talk.

We both wait.

At seven she pats my hand and says it's the end of her shift and I groan at the sunlight outside the window. I can't even die right. I can't slip away in the night to spare my sister the pain. No. Of course I can't. I've got to put her through another day of this. Another day of goodbye.

The tea lady comes in with her trolley, but I just shake my head. Tea can't do anything now, and even if I fancied one, I don't think I'd be able to keep it down. My stomach is twisted into tight knots.

As expected, Liv rushes in, straight to my face, clasping it in her hands. "I knew I'd see you again."

"J-just so d-damn lucky."

I see her frown as she looks at my face. "I spoke to Rebecca last night. She wanted to come and see you, but I told her no. I think she thinks you're just having a turn."

"Have they f-folded?"

Liv's lips flicker. "I knew you'd ask that. She said to tell you no, but yes."

Strange relief washes through me. At least she can't fuck up the print run now.

"I'm going to go and get some ice for you; you can suck on the chips."

"No." I grip her arm, my hold so feeble it's actually flickering on my embarrassment register.

"Please, Jules. Am I the only one still holding out hope that a heart is going to come?"

I give the most pathetic snorting laugh I have ever mustered. "Only you, sis."

"Well, I am," she states resolutely. "And I'm going to get ice." She's fiddling with her phone. "Don't go anywhere."

I huff a short puff of a laugh. God it feels good to almost smile. The machines don't like it though and one of them starts to beep a really annoying high-pitched wail.

Liv grabs my hand and a nurse rushes in checking me over and then the machines. "Just a loose wire." She peers at me closely and I catch the sympathetic smile she gives Liv. "You comfortable, Julia?"

"Jules, please, and yes." I think they are giving me something in the tubes. Whatever it is, it's got a nice fluffy edge to it.

"Okay. Ice." Liv turns just as the door bangs open, making her and the nurse both jump. My heart, well...

"Thank fuck." Henri storms in, like a whirlwind of navy, just like how I first met him. "I thought I'd be too late."

Liv sighs. "Bloody hell, Henri."

"Sorry," he barely glances at her. "The flight got delayed." He leans over me, sunshine and wildflowers. "Ma petite, I've seen you look better."

"Y-you came."

"Of course, I came. Because I'm pretty damn sure you're the love of my life, you bloody frustrating Englishwoman. I'm not letting you go anywhere."

"Henri." Tears prickle my eyes, slowly morphing into fast balls that torrent down my face. I don't have anything else to give, just tears. "I'm s-so glad." Breath. "Y-you're here."

"Me too, ma petite. Now where's this doctor? I want to discuss a new heart."

Liv's gaze meets mine and her lips quirk in the corner. "I'm going to grab some breakfast, you guys okay?"

I don't answer because I'm too busy staring at Henri's face, memorising every single speck of detail I can find. The crinkles around his eyes, the curve of his mouth, the dark lashes that pause on a blink just to prove how pretty they are.

The nurse bustles out after giving Henri a stern talk on disrupting the tubes. He nods solemnly all the while stroking the back of my hand with his thumb, skirting around the plaster at the wound site of my French hospital stay. Then we are alone, unsaid words electrifying the air.

"You came?" I wince as I try to move. With a gentle hand he pushes me back down.

"Rest, mon coeur."

"I didn't think. I'd see you again. Henri. I'm so sorry. Sorry about Odile. Sorry about. That stupid list. I promise."

"Julia." I melt at the way he says my name. "It's okay, it's okay. I'm sorry. I took my fears and regrets out on you, and I should have told you about Odile, you would have understood. Now you are here like this because of me." He drops his dark head like a grieving angel. "This is all on me."

"Henri." Breath. "I knew when I came to France that." Breath. "It could happen. Dr Francis, he told me. I went straight to Liv's and told her that I couldn't not see you again."

"She must hate me."

"I don't think so."

"What's happening to you now?"

I do my very best immobile French shrug. "Now everything shuts down, I think. It's started, I'm so, so..."

"Beautiful." He drops a kiss on my forehead. "So beautiful."

"I've been." Breath. "Trying to get rid of Liv. I don't want her to be here at the end, don't want her to remember me like that."

Henri's face drops. "I know what it's like, ma Julianna, but don't take away her chance to say goodbye." His face steels into something like a murderous mask of vengeance. "Not that you will need to, a heart will arrive. I have faith, it will."

Bless his little cotton socks.

"It won't. I've known for months. It won't. My blood." Breath. "'s unusual."

"So? So is mine? It shouldn't be a big deal."

"I'm B. Negative. A match takes. Longer. Or something. I forget what they said." My eyes are fluttering shut. Why, now that he's here, is sleep stealing in?

"Mine too."

Our eyes meet. His hand lifts mine pressing our palms flat together. I love the rough and smooth of his touch. Even our blood is the same, this unexpected soul mate of mine and me.

"Henri," I whisper, drawing in as much air as I can so I can try and say the important stuff clearly. "That day in the bar you changed my life. You kickstarted my living on the day I knew it was going to end."

"And you mine, my woman of mystery. Fate wanted you to be mine."

"Henri. I know how losing your dad." I don't think I can finish my words. I pause, mustering up the sounds that will articulate what I want to say. "Affected you. Please don't let me do that to you too. I'm so glad you're here, so glad I get to see that annoyingly handsome face one last time, but you need to leave with Liv."

I'm done. The words have taken what little I have left.

"Are you insane?" The rest of his words are very fast and very angry, totally incomprehensible. "Non."

"Please, promise me."

"I'll do no such thing. I will never leave you, not ever."

"Promise me," I demand with the force of a kitten whisked up in a hurricane.

He kisses me instead, lingering on my lips, and then sits and holds my hand.

. . .

Liv sits with us for a while, and I doze in and out. Henri is looking at his phone and I'm pretty sure he's on the dark web looking for an B negative heart.

My eyes meet Liv's and I give her an encouraging nod. She shakes her head and I answer with another silent nod. Standing, she leans over, running her cool fingers down my face. "Love you."

"Love you."

Pale, she turns for the door. "Henri, you coming?"

Startled, he stares between us. "Non."

She raises her arms at me. Was that her best effort, seriously? Jesus. The door opens as Dr Simmonds steps in, followed by Dr Francis.

"Jules, how are you?" He steps for my chart and gives it a brief flick through.

"Tickety boo."

He smiles and looks at Liv, while she looks at him with something like hope in her eyes. His lips press into firm line, eyes meeting hers, and her face falls, while that last little flicker of hope in my chest snuffs out.

"Olivia?" he asks her. I'm struggling to hear. There's some static in my ears I can't focus around.

I squeeze Henri's hand, hoping to telecommunicate that he should listen for the both of us.

"Liv," she says.

"The sister." There's a brief smile and that little kindle of hope flickers again… until he says, "Next of kin, I assume?"

Boom. And there it goes.

With a wave of his hand, he beckons her over and they talk in low voices with Dr Francis, gesturing at something on the chart; probably my newest and most pointless obs.

They head back out, both doctors giving me gentle smiles that communicate sympathy. It's not a new heart, but you know, the sentiment is there. Liv follows them outside, leaving just Henri and I. Me and my mystery man.

"What were they saying?" I whimper to Henri.

"Mon Coeur, I think they were saying that you should hang on."

I attempt a snort, but it sounds rather like blowing snot bubbles.

I am so fucking tired.

I reach shaky fingers for his. "I told you."

His fingers brush at my hair, delicately tracing down my cheek. "And I told you, ma petite fleur."

This is unfair. He's breaking all the promises, every damn one. Taking a pickaxe to them and splintering them to pieces.

Smash.

A tear rolls from the corner of my eye and he catches it, popping it, caught on the tip of his finger, into his mouth. Smiling, stormy night eyes shining. "Another taste of you."

Unfair.

Smash.

I want to cry harder, want to give it some, but my chest hurts, every breath is like running a marathon just from sitting on the creaky sheet of a hospital bed. I hike in another gasped breath, as a large palm smooths my hair and lips press into the top of my head, a lifeline I want to cling onto even though I know my time is up.

When I can breathe, I shift slightly, looking up to meet his gaze. "You promised me." I guilt him with a deploring stare. Please leave, my eyes say, although my tongue is having a problem expressing the words. Stupid tongue.

That look of beautiful solemnity comes over his face.

It's my favourite look, dark and brooding, all things that make my heart flutter. Stupid heart. Literally.

"Ma petite Julianna, I never promised." He leans a little closer, breath brushing my skin, making me ache for days full of sunshine, laughter, and tangled cotton sheets.

My heart races again, pounding loud in my ears. I clutch at my chest, touch weak, barely holding myself together. That beautiful solemnity darkens into heartbreak. It splinters what's left of me straight in two.

"Henri, please." I gasp his name, remembering another broken rule between us.

No names.

No strings.

Yet here we sit. Rather, I lie; he stands, looking like a man on fire.

Rules are there for a reason. I must remember that for my next life.

Oh God. My breath comes even faster.

The next life... it's almost here and I still don't know if I even believe. How can I go not knowing?

Stop everything. I want a do over.

This can't be it.

Strong fingers entwine with mine. "Ma petite fleur, look at me."

I do, unwillingly unable to keep my eyes from his. The shining pools staring back at me almost make me lose my mind. "I'll never leave. Be damned any promise I ever made."

A smile ghosts my mouth. "Cheater."

He shrugs, pure Gaelic charm. "Hey, I never said I wasn't." The brightening of his face calms my heart, exhaustion tugs me down.

I don't want to close my eyes.

What if I close them and nothing happens ever again?

What if that's it? Forever and ever.

"Don't be scared," he whispers.

Scared.

"I am," I whisper back.

Turning my face with gentle fingers, he gently pushes a kiss on my lips. Even at the end of my days it's still the most beautiful taste. Warm and succinct, just the perfect pressure, the perfect time, not too long, not too short.

"I'm so glad I got to kiss you."

"Well…" His lips curve. "That's not all we've done."

"Lay with me." My fingers feebly tap the bed.

"You know where that ends." He frowns at the size of the hospital bed. He's six four and built for rugby and doing things to me that turn me inside out and upside down.

"Squeeze on."

Henri glances at the door. For an awful moment I think he's going to leave me, that he's going to do as I asked, but then he toes his shoes and kicks them off. Loafers on a hospital floor next to my unused fluffy slippers.

He settles down, curving a protective embrace around my failing chest. "I'm sorry," he mutters.

"Don't be."

Dampness lands on my shoulder and I feel him sob gently, his large frame rocking me like a babe in arms.

Undo me.

But then I am undone.

There's nothing left to untangle.

"I wish I could be your Juliette again, wish we could go back, do it all over." I almost shout it. I don't want to go to the other side of never without him knowing just what it's meant, what he's meant. Being his Juliette was magical, made the last few months something more than I ever would have thought they could have been. Being his *Julianna*... has changed my life.

Henri turns, a tear still dangling on the edge of his dark lashes like the last droplet on a year of insanity.

"You'll always be my Juliette, my Julianna, my everything." He's humoured me so much, put up with my rules, the way I've needed things to be. I know he's left everything to be here with me right here at the end. God, it really must be a love thing after all.

I push my face into his chest, the cotton of his shirt, that spice that seems to cling to him. "I'm so glad I met you."

Using the tip of his finger he makes me look up. "Even though you fought me the whole way, ma petite fleur?" One of his dark brows arches. His teasing look. God, I love that look too.

I love all his looks.

Can't believe I won't get to see any of them again. Can't believe that my stupid heart is going to fail, and no replacement can be found. Right when I want to...

Want to...

"Tell me what you'll miss the most?" I ask the buttons on his shirt.

Henri tightens his arms, and I could just melt right now. Become a puddle of chocolate ice cream against his sugar spun wafer. "You in black lace."

Ah, the lace.

His hands on my thighs, riding silk and lace across skin that I didn't know could be adored the way he did it.

"Just the lace?"

"Burnt pancakes. Coffee at midnight. Eurostar. Always wanting to find you and never knowing where I would see you again. Sand. Candy floss. Amber perfume on your skin."

Right now, in this very moment at the end of everything I am adored.

"I love you," I say.

"And I love you."

I look up, blinking against everything that could have been. "Henri, you have to keep this promise."

"What promise?"

"The one you're going to make now."

His face slips back to that beautiful shadow where the storm in his eyes brings rain and sun.

"Hold me until I sleep and then leave."

Henri shakes his head, lips pressing into a firm line. "No."

"I want you to. Remember me with lace and amber. Candy floss and laughter. Not a corpse who lies in your arms."

"Ma pe—" another shake of his head, "Julianna, they still might find a match."

Aw, he's so damn cute. Stupid big hulk of a man.

"Hold me until I sleep." I snuggle down, ignoring the beep of the machine as it shouts in dismay at my moving the tubes in my arm and airways.

Tears roll from his lashes and absorb into my skin.

My time is nearly up.

Every breath.

Every stuttered beat of my heart takes me one moment closer to the end. I'm so tired now. So drained. Energy is like treacle, moving too slow through my veins. Slug. Slug. Slug.

God, if you are there...

Thank you for bringing me the greatest gift I ever could have hoped for.

I close my eyes. Henri's hand brushes through my hair and I focus on the sensation: soothing, reassuring.

He plants a kiss on my mouth. My last kiss.

The last kiss.

On the cusp of nothing, I hold everything as my lips whisper their last word, exhaustion tying me into a final bow I know I can't undo.

"Henri."

31

THE PRICE OF LIFE

I OFTEN WONDER *what it would have felt like to never have woken up. Would that dark abyss have just stretched forever? My search for a bright white light had only revealed more dark, more emptiness.*

I guess no one wants to know that's what greets them.

I would never have wanted to wake up if I'd known the chair next to the hospital bed was empty and would never be filled again.

That inside of me belonged a B negative heart that shouldn't have been mine.

I would never have sat on that bar stool, never would have said yes to dinner, never have succumbed to that first kiss if I'd known that our last would have been so bitter.

Six months of ground zero. Six months of walking into my grey cube of a flat, feeding my cat and then staring at the ceiling.

Six months of grief that is insurmountable.

No amount of Charlie's health juices will ever lift this doom.

Six months of listening to the whoosh in my ears like the

sea that just won't go away. Whispers chase me, his voice, over and over, telling me to wake, telling me to live, telling me I'm his everything.

The price of love is too high for me. The price of life is beyond comprehension.

The kicker comes in the form of those thoughts, voices that spring into my head, normally when I'm staring at a blank TV screen. Live, Julianna. Live, ma petite fleur.

The voices don't end.

The scar on my chest will never stop hurting. Every pill I take to keep this heart is a bitter pill to swallow.

"I'm coming in," Liv calls through the letterbox. "If you're naked you'd best get moving."

I don't bother to answer.

She comes in anyway, plopping herself down on the sofa, reaching for the remote. This is what we do now while Lenny is at nursery. We sit in silence, two sisters side-by-side.

Until today, because she throws the remote down. "Enough is enough. You need to wake up now."

"Please don't. Just don't."

"You are being a selfish, ungrateful pig. Wake up and stop dreaming!"

I stink eye her. "Why don't you say what's really on your mind?" I grind out my words. What does she mean? Is she on drugs? I peer closer, looking for tale tell signs I read about in a trashy magazine.

"Do you realise how much he loved you to do that? The thought of a life without you was so pitiful that he didn't want to face it. Wanted you to have life instead of him. The only person with a B negative heart to give."

"I know." I nod to the folded letter still sitting on the coffee table where I put it my first day out of hospital. The letter with his words, explanations. The guilt that will just

bury me six feet under in the end. It seems so ridiculous. Why would he do that? Why did he do that?

"Clearly, the man had no brains." My cheeks burn to talk about him this way, but it's easier somehow. If I can just shut off, then I don't have to feel.

"I'd say he loved you beyond all reason."

"Still didn't tell me he was married though, did he?"

"Oh my god. What is wrong with you?"

"What's wrong with me is the fact that I'm alive. Stupid alive, living a life I never even lived properly the first time, and he, he..."

"What?" Liv steps closer, right in my space, stealing my air.

I'm getting confused. My thoughts are muddled, a swirl of ice cream under the brutal force of a spoon and Paige's determined hand.

Paige. I miss her.

Lenny. I want to cuddle.

My arms tingle a new sensation that makes me stretch them. Fingertips wiggling against... what is that? Cotton?

"And what would he want from you now, Julia? Huh, what would he want?"

Liv is getting smaller, fading out. Black is sweeping a cloak of night around my shoulders. There's a loud beeping and it's pushing away my grey cube of a flat. The sofa disappears. I think I might be in an Oscar winning movie that no one wants to admit they don't understand.

I wait for his voice, knowing I will always hear it. It will never not be with me, singing in my heart and soul.

"He'd say, 'Live, ma petite fleur. Live'."

And if I could do it again... if...

It burns through me. Life. It tears me apart, running hot like lava at the centre of the earth ready to erupt.

I would sit on that bar stool. Would have said yes to dinner. Would have succumbed to that first kiss if I'd known that our last would have meant I'd learned to live.

The only thing I'd ever wanted was to live...

My fingers curl, grasping at warmth.

The whooshing of the sea fades out, leaving me for the first time in what's felt like months.

"Ma petite fleur, you took your sweet time."

"Hen—?" I croak his name, choking on an obstruction. There's something in my throat. He's here, next to me. My eyes burn. Dreams. Nightmares. That's what they were I realise as reality bursts through my consciousness before starting to fade again.

"I'm not going anywhere, mon coeur, not ever. You are mine."

Cool hands take the place of his. Brisk, industrious, the babble of voices that don't make my inside mellow the way his does. "Stats are good, BP settled."

"Henri," I call his name, trying to reach for him.

"I'm here," he says but he's too far away.

"Breathe in now please and then out in one long exhale." I do. There's a pulling which makes me gag and my windpipe clears of the obstruction.

The sweet tang of hospital air, bleach and disinfectant, scents that never smelled so good, blast my senses.

"Open your eyes." The warm hand is back, lacing through mine.

I do. It's not easy. They are stuck with cement, or sand. Hopefully, it's the golden grains of France and not builder's sand.

"Henri." Tears leak from my eyes as I see him. "You're alive. I had the worst dream."

His smile... so damn... everything. "You're alive too, mon amour, I can't ever lose you. Not ever."

He falls down to the seat, shoulders shaking, head in his hands, but for the first time in forever I don't want to cry.

No.

Now I want to live.

EPILOGUE

HENRI

I can't look down for the life of me. I'm clinging to the security barrier with the resolve of a free climber hanging from a rock face.

I know down below Simone and Gabriella are laughing. Their laughter is lost on the wind, too many damn tourists to make it heard. I know Gabriella will have her arms wrapped around Simone, daughter and mother happy together.

People come up here for fun? They all need their heads examining. I'd rather stick my hand up a birthing cow's rear end than do this.

But... a promise is a promise.

Even if they do involve standing three hundred metres above the earth. The wind blows and I'm sure the whole damn thing sways.

Best to just get this over and done with.

Until I turn and see her. Hair streaming in the wind,

wisps of tangled chestnut waves, her eyes wide as she takes in the view, dangerously close to the edge, and I know this moment can't be rushed.

Grinning, I step back into a safety zone, casting me in a shadow from the June sunlight.

She is everything. Every dream, every nightmare, every waking moment in between. I could watch her for days and never grow bored, never plan to get bored.

Who knew you could fall so irrevocably in love with someone? That meeting five times would change your whole existence.

Who knew I'd wait forty-two years to understand what living was?

She grins, turning to face me, her hair whipping across her face, which she pulls at with her fingers. "Are you scared, mon lion?" That twinkle in her eyes is devilish; the bud of her perfect rose mouth stretching into a wide smile.

"Not scared, just valuing the power of gravity with new understanding."

"Come here." She holds her hand out and I weave our fingers, reminded of the first time I held her hand and something in the action shifted the earth beneath me. "Look, you can see everything. I've never seen anything so beautiful."

I watch her, a smile growing.

"Oh don't, please." She rolls her eyes. "Don't you dare say, 'I have'."

"What? I have." Laughing, I step up close and wrap my arms around her. If we are going down, we are going together. To live without her would be unbearable. No, not even that; it would be impossible.

I don't often think back to that moment in the hospital when she slipped away, her body shutting down into a coma that naturally she couldn't pull out from. Eventually, she would have stopped existing within that deep sleep. I'd held her so damn tight in my arms, knowing I'd only made it with hours to spare. My stupid pride nearly stealing those vital moments away from me. Feet had pounded outside the door, bursting through as I continued to rock her. Liv's face, blotchy and pale staring at mine with a wild woman's eyes. A trolley followed after, doctors busy, not speaking as they lifted her away, putting tubes down her throat, traversing the body I loved so much.

"Here." Grinning, I pull the diary out of the backpack I've been hauling around tourist hell.

"What have you got that for?"

My little flower steps closer, holding out her hand for the battered book.

"We've got one thing to still cross off."

Julia's eyes widen as I pass her a biro and then drop to one knee.

"But..." she whispers, "it's not written on there."

"I know. You can add it and cross it out. That's the rules, right?"

She nods, her brown eyes shining with obsidian depths.

"Julianna Brown, love of my life."

People are stopping to stare, eyes on us rather than the view. But this is her dream, and I will give her everything she damn well wants, *everything*.

"I want to spend every moment of my life with you, as my wife, my heart, my soul."

"Henri," she sighs my name but then quirks a smile. Her shoulders drop, a look of serene bliss smooths across her face, lips turning up with a hint of a heart-stealing smile. It's a look that tells me that the two of us are meant to be. Fate. Serendipity.

Perfection.

With a growl of possessiveness, I pull her down to me, bringing her body against mine. Her heart, a gift from a stranger beating against my chest. "Is that a yes?"

"Everything is always a yes for you."

My fingers shake, something they've never done before, as I slip on a simple band with a square cut diamond–I am after all only a farmer. The happiest and luckiest farmer to ever have walked the earth.

In a kiss that makes my blood pulse in my ears we seal the deal. People clap around us. Laughing, she claps her own hands in glee. "This is the most sappy and romantic moment of my life."

"Good. Now write it on the damn list."

"Can I do it when we get down? It really is very touristy up here."

This. Woman. Seriously.

I stand and pull her up after me. Giving a small wave to our audience we slip back into the lift, the guard giving us a smirk. Yeah, buddy, I know you've seen it all before. But I bet you never saw a dying wish come true.

Down on the ground, Gabriella assaults us, inspecting the ring, demanding champagne. "I know the best bar. Come, let's go." I hold her back though. "Next time, Gabby, we've got a train to catch. In fact." I check my watch. "We should go and get our stuff from the hotel."

"We have? Are we going home already?" The kiss of the sun on Julia is vitality personified. It makes my own heart swell. I only realised just a few short months ago when she started to glow, just how ill she was when I met her. Would I have done things differently if I knew? Would I have talked to her more instead of kissing the life out of her and fucking her six ways to Sunday? Who knows the answer to that? We are just what we are. Our history will always stand the way it does. I will always know what it feels like to have her dying in my arms, not once, but twice, and I will always know I will live every moment of my life to the fullest in response to that.

"Not home. Other direction."

I wait for her to explode. Three. Two. One. "London?" Kisses rain on my skin. PG kisses, because you know, our niece is in attendance.

"I have a hotel booked."

She squeals again and jumps on the spot. "I'm calling Liv. Telling her the news." She wiggles her ring under my nose like I haven't seen it before.

"She knows."

"She does?"

"Whose permission do you think I asked?"

Julia stares at me and I stare back, then shaking her head she opens her bucket list and scribbles down the wish she'd told me when she'd been a goddess illuminated by candlelight in my room just over a year ago. Grinning, she crosses it through, but then pauses, tapping her teeth with her biro. With a furrowed brow she quickly adds something else and then snaps it shut.

"I thought it was finished?" I ask, reaching for the book, but she shakes her head and slips it into the bag she has crossed over her body.

"It was,' she replies archly. "Now what time is the train? Because I don't think champagne is a bad idea at all."

A week later we are on our way home. Her head is resting on my shoulder on the Eurostar, her breath gentle as she dozes against me. I'm fiddling with the diamond on her finger, watching it catch the light, reflecting the facets of life.

When she stirs she pecks a kiss on my cheek. "Sorry, I don't mean to keep falling asleep."

"It's fine, ma petite fleur."

My little flower. My English rose. She will always be that to me. Always.

"I can't wait to get home. I hope the dogs have behaved. If I find Barney in shreds...well..." She stretches, curving her newly bloomed and revitalised body right in front of my face. Talk about torturing a man in public.

"Don't worry, Odile has them all under control. I'm more worried about the shop still standing." I kiss the top of her head, attempting a peek down the front of her sundress.

"You leave my shop to me, and you worry about the cows."

"My cows are fine." I grin back at her.

With Julia's drive for perfection, we've created a cheese empire; our *cheese mafia* as she calls it. She runs an artisan shop in the town, and we ship all over France and further afield.

"It makes me so happy for you to think it's home. I know leaving London is never easy."

"It's easier than you know, Henri." She turns, eyes solemn. "The moment I first got out of that taxi last year, I knew it was meant to be my home. Something about the way it felt, the familiarity. And anyway, I've told you..."

"...Vitamin D is essential for your health." I chime in. For such a long time I thought she was using that as an excuse for letting me stay in France. Then one day I saw her breathing deep, pulling air into her lungs, face tilted up to the sun, and I knew that she'd stayed there because she needed it, loved it. Now our farmhouse is covered in honeysuckle, and hanging baskets swinging every colour under the sun.

"What did you write in the diary, Julianna?"

In the reflection of the Eurostar window, I see her bite her lip.

"Tell me."

"I wrote *baby*."

I stare down at her wide-eyed. "No way. It's too dangerous, and you know it." She might have a new heart, but that doesn't mean every day isn't a fight to keep it. "No." I state simply.

"Yes." She snuggles back down, wrapping her arms through mine. "You know I always get what I want."

I sigh, kissing her hair. "I know, ma petite fleur, I know."

The End.

COMING SOON

THE EX-APOCOLYPSE

Book two in the Notting Hill Sisterhood.

Number one life mistake: Marrying the wrong man.

Twenty-nine and a divorced mother of two. It's not quite what I had planned.

Life is funny though, it gives with one hand and takes with the other.

Now it's time to date again, so everyone says, but my ex has left apocalyptic devastation in the place where I once used to have trust and hope.

Enter Ryan Simmonds, cocky, infuriating, and downright irresistible.

He says he can show me how to find the perfect man. The caveat, though, is that I mustn't fall for him.

Which should be easy... right?

Available to pre-order here

SIGN UP FOR AN EXCLUSIVE JULIA AND HENRI CUT SCENE HERE

https://BookHip.com/PNKNZQJ

I would love to see you in my FB Reader Group Anna's Bloomers! Feel free to pop along and say hi!
Anna's Bloomers

Reviews are like gold dust to authors, any time you have to provide one is always gratefully received.

ACKNOWLEDGMENTS

It seems the more of books you write the harder this page becomes.

Therefore I shall keep this short and brief.

Thank you, Nikki A, Andrea Lynn, Sarah and Donna for being my champions with this book.

Thanks to all the girls at GMB for their endless chasing emails asking me where things are.

For my readers who I hope love this book as much as I do, thank you for your continued support.

And of course my long suffering family.

This book came about while I was in the midst of writer's block on a different project. I started Julia Cameron's The Artists Way, and within a couple of weeks Julia and Henri just burst into my mind.

So with this in mind, I'll be enterally grateful to Julia Cameron for unleashing my blocked inner voice and reminding me why I do this.

Anna

Surrey, 2021

Made in the USA
Columbia, SC
14 November 2022

71243997R00190